SPACE PIRATES!
BOOK I

SPACE PIRATES

MARK VOSS

BAL
KON
media

SPACE PIRATES
Published by Balkon Media

Paperback edition ISBN: 978-1-916970-28-1
Also available as an E-book

A CIP catalogue record for this title is available from the British Library.

Cover Design: Balkon Media

www.vossiverse.com

ALSO BY MARK VOSS

THE SPACE PIRATES! SERIES

Space Pirates

Dead Men Launch No Ships

Salvage Rights

Echoes of the Plague Moon

The Quiet Rebellion

The Bounty Paradox

The Black Drift

Till the Engines Fall Silent

The Median Gambit

ONE

Rask Helvan stepped off the battered shuttle into the arsehole of the galaxy and immediately regretted every decision that had brought him here. Port Dreggar, as advertised by the empire's more creative cartographers, was an "interstitial trading nexus"—which meant a spiralling concrete corpse lashed together by union contract and held in place by a slowly thickening cloud of desperation. The docking concourse smelt like the inside of a decomposing slug. Rask blinked twice, tried not to inhale, and thumbed the receiver embedded in his palm.

Nothing. No response. He muttered a curse in his mother's dialect and pushed past a knot of stevedores haggling over a cargo crate shaped like it wanted to explode. The station's lighting flickered with all the reassuring consistency of a dying heartbeat. Rask counted the steps to the bulkhead. Seventy-two. Long enough to clock every vent, every shadow, every bored mercenary slouched with hand on sidearm, but not quite enough to acclimate to the stench. The odour clung—old sweat, sour protein gel, and the faintest trace of industrial bleach, as if someone had once attempted cleaning and then given up, soul-destroyed.

Dreggar's security presence consisted of two conical drones parked beside a customs desk, both charging at sub-optimal amperage. Their sensors didn't even twitch as Rask walked past. He suppressed a laugh; the station's budget cuts were apparently applied with a band saw. The only other authority in evidence was the vendor at the end of the corridor, who had both the haggard look of a three-shift worker and the predatory instincts of a canal-side loan shark.

"Clone rations!" she barked, swinging her hip-flask into the aisle in a move that would have upended a less balanced customer. "Real synth-protein, none of that compressed kelp shite. Discount for off-worlders!"

Rask's first impulse was to ignore her. The second was to assess her threat rating, which barely registered unless you counted the stainless microblade strapped openly to her thigh. The third was to buy something, which would at least make him look less like a courier and more like a lost tourist. He detoured to her cart, pretending interest.

"Single pack," he grunted.

She produced it from a suspiciously unmarked cooler and flashed a smile sharp enough to take a finger. "Ten credits. Or six, if you've got a tale to go with it."

He paid the ten. The ration looked like a compressed dog biscuit and, if anything, smelled worse. Rask pretended to examine it, then pocketed the bar and the receipt, moving off with a nod. Behind him, the vendor hissed something about cheapskates, but the words dissolved in the air like everything else on Dreggar.

Seventy more steps and he was at the first lift. The doors were misaligned; he had to shoulder them open with a flex of muscle and a snarl. Inside, someone had scrawled "HELP" across the control panel in dried, unidentifiable fluids. Rask keyed the lower deck and the lift lurched sideways before remembering which way gravity went.

He tried the receiver again. Static, then the digital sigh of a dead channel. Jenna Sol was meant to be waiting at Docking Bay 14—no password, no weapons, just a biometric ping and a credit transfer. That was the job, as explained by the shadow-broker who'd found him in the Levosian dive two nights previous. It was supposed to be easy. It never was.

The lift groaned to a halt and spat him out into an access corridor several degrees colder than the main concourse. Rask tensed: cold meant environmental malfunctions, which meant engineering teams, which meant more foot traffic than he liked. Sure enough, the corridor was thick with smudged handprints and half-dismantled control panels. An engineer in a stained orange jumper stared at him from behind a tower of spares.

"You lost?" the engineer asked, gaze flicking from Rask's face to his chest, where the outline of his holster was only slightly less obvious than the bloodstain it covered.

"Just passing through," Rask replied. His voice was

level and bored, the tone of a man who wanted nothing more than to be elsewhere. "Heading to fourteen."

The engineer grunted, then ducked his head and returned to pretending he hadn't noticed the weapon. Rask moved on, conscious of every surveillance node (inactive), every backup cam (smashed), every person who looked at him a beat too long.

He passed two more vendors, each hawking lower-quality goods at higher prices. One tried to sell him "vintage ice water", which came in battered plastic sachets and sloshed with a menacingly organic gurgle. The other simply offered him sex, or failing that, a used comms implant. Rask declined both.

Docking Bay 14 was at the far end of the lower ring, just past a yawning hatch marked MAINTENANCE STAFF ONLY. The panel above the door was blank, except for a hand-drawn "14" in black marker and a cheerful scrawl: KNOCK IF DEAD.

He knocked, because he was both superstitious and literal-minded. The door did not respond. He rapped twice more, harder. Nothing.

For the first time since stepping off the shuttle, a chill crept up his spine. He pressed his palm to the access plate, expecting the familiar tingle of identity verification. Instead, the door's security lights flickered, coughed, and stayed red.

Jenna wasn't inside. No, worse—someone was keeping him out.

He took two steps back, checked the corridor, then leaned close to the seam of the bay door. There: a faint metallic scrape, like a wire being drawn across a contact. He pressed his left ear to the cold surface and caught the barest hint of air cycling inside, punctuated by a low, human grunt.

Someone was in there, all right. Maybe Jenna, maybe not.

Rask looked up and down the hall, saw no witnesses, and yanked the concealed prybar from his belt. He jammed it into the control panel's baseplate and twisted. The cover popped off with a noise like a dentist's worst nightmare. He thumbed the reset chip, bypassed the burnt-out lock relay, and waited for the hum of the emergency override.

Instead, there was a brief, ugly spark, and the panel went completely dark. Dead system. Rask rolled his eyes.

He was about to give up and look for a different way in when a soft, deliberate click echoed from the far end of the corridor. He wheeled, sidearm out and low. A shadow detached from the vending alcove, ducked behind a maintenance locker, and vanished.

Rask hissed air through his teeth, holstered, and checked the time. He had ten minutes before the station's night cycle began and half the lights in the ring cut out entirely. At which point, whoever was watching would have every advantage.

He ran one last diagnostic on the panel—useless, still dead—then ran his thumb along the seam of the bay door. Near the top, he found it: a smear of fresh lubricant, barely visible in the faulty lighting. Someone had forced this door open recently, then tried to patch the mechanism. It wasn't Jenna's style; she preferred a subtler touch. This was the work of a brute, or someone in a hell of a hurry.

He exhaled, the breath fogging in the cold. He was being corralled.

He stepped away from the bay, eyes now on every shadow, every shifting shape behind the battered poly-glass. Dreggar was meant to be a routine run: drop, handshake, credits, leave. But he'd known in his bones the second he'd set foot on the dock that the script had already gone to shit.

The only question left was whether he was the mark, or just another unfortunate standing in the wrong place at the wrong time.

The answer would present itself, Rask thought, with all the subtlety of a sledgehammer. All he had to do was survive long enough to see it coming.

He re-pocketed the prybar, checked the power cell in his sidearm, and waited for the next move. The corridor's temperature dropped another notch, and somewhere behind him, a pipe vented a slow, almost contented sigh.

Rask grinned, because he'd always preferred it when the universe dispensed with the pleasantries. He found a patch of wall with decent cover and settled in, counting the seconds until all hell broke loose. It never took long.

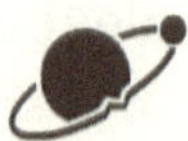

The corridor's temperature dropped by the minute, as if the station's life support was done pretending it cared.

Rask flexed his gloved hands, feeling the microcalluses along his left palm catch against the cold polycarbonate grip of the sidearm. Across the hall, a maintenance droid flickered past, leaking what looked suspiciously like hydraulic fluid and dignity. Rask watched it go, then angled himself so the next pass of the repair crew would put them between him and the bay's external camera. He moved, quick and low, and slotted the prybar deep into the access seam.

The override relay should've blown the locking bolts, if Port Dreggar had been kept up to spec. Instead, the panel made a wet, splintering noise and dropped half its innards at his feet. Rask yanked the emergency handle, expecting an alarm, and was not disappointed. A shrill, warbling klaxon started up somewhere deeper in the walls—no immediate response, but every human and half-sapient in a fifty-metre radius would have clocked the location.

He gave himself five seconds to plan and three to regret it.

The door to Docking Bay 14 shuddered, spat out a gout of blue anti-fire foam, and then juddered open just wide enough to let him squeeze through. He did so, sidearm drawn and levelled, then blinked to recalibrate his vision.

Inside, the bay was washed in emergency blue, the kind that flattened detail and made everything look like a stage set for an especially tedious police procedural. The first thing Rask saw was the body. The second was the ship.

Jenna Sol lay halfway between the gangway and

the aft wall, her limbs bent at angles that nature had never intended. Her face was still, almost peaceful, as if she'd spent her last minute coming to terms with the shambles of her own demise. The cause of death was not subtle: a blackened impact wound just above her collarbone, the edges pulped and still weeping into the sticky deck resin. Rask knelt, checked her carotid, and grimaced. He'd expected a double-cross, maybe a silent alarm or a waiting brute, but not this. Jenna was old guard—knew when to fold, when to run. Killing her was a statement, and Rask did not appreciate statements.

He stood, scanning the rest of the bay.

A blown power conduit sizzled overhead, spitting arcs of white along a river of coolant pooling below. Two cargo crates, marked with Dreggar customs tape, had been overturned and rifled. Their contents—circuit boards, memory cores, and a crumpled vacuum suit—littered the ground like the aftermath of a cheap burglary. Someone had tripped, or been tripped, near the comms terminal. The station's comms array lay smashed, one jagged piece of circuit board driven into the wall like a dart.

Then there was the ship.

It dominated the bay, nose pointed towards the launch shutters. Sleek in a way that screamed custom build, hull still gleaming despite the station's best attempts at sabotage. Rask clocked the lines: delta-winged, low profile, engines humming in near-silence. It was powered up and ready, as if it had been waiting. The registry code on the hull was obscured by soot, but someone had made a half-arsed effort to wipe it clean, revealing a name: *Meridian*.

Rask's gut did a slow, considered somersault. He recognised the model, if not the registration. There weren't many left like this—high-end runners, fast as hell and built for someone who expected to be shot at regularly.

He flicked his eyes back to Jenna. She'd been clutching something—a sliver of polymer, slicked with her blood. He knelt, peeled her fingers apart, and retrieved the object: an ident chip, still warm. He pocketed it. If the station's goons didn't already know she was dead, they would soon.

He caught movement at the corner of his eye. The maintenance hatch at the far end of the bay was vibrating, just slightly, as if something on the other side was trying its luck with the locking pins.

Rask made the mental calculation: he could wait and try to bluff it out, or he could get the hell off this rock before someone decided he'd pulled the trigger.

He sprinted for the ship.

The ramp responded to his proximity with a muted whine, then unfolded with a smoothness that was almost obscene compared to the rest of Dreggar's infrastructure. He ran up the gangway, gun out, every sense screaming trap. Inside, the ship was spartan—dark surfaces, zero decorative touches, everything hardwired for survival over comfort.

The cockpit canopy was open, pilot seat slick with a sheen of oil. No bodies, no signs of damage. He threw himself into the chair and scanned the control array.

Either the last pilot had been in a hurry, or they'd intended for someone to find the ship and run.

The main screen blinked with a launch vector. Rask grinned despite himself. He toggled the thruster pre-ignition, set his comms to passive scan, and waited for the customary "please do not depart, you are under investigation" automated message. Instead, a single word flashed up on the display:

RUN.

Something clanged against the ship's belly. The maintenance hatch, Rask thought, or the goons from the hall finally playing their hand. He glanced at the bay's interior cam: the security drones were swarming above the body, three in total, cycling their IR lenses and feeding every second back to Dreggar's tiny, underpaid detective division. Any move he made was being recorded and, probably, analysed in real time.

He activated the external clamps, felt the Meridian's hull tense as it began the undocking sequence. The lockdown alarms howled with a renewed, personal urgency. He killed the interior lights, starved the engines, and let the last vestiges of pressure push the ship toward the docking shield.

In the instant before release, a shadow detached itself from the edge of the bay, sprinted across the coolant-slick floor, and leapt for the ship's landing gear. Rask caught a flash of orange—a jumpsuit, maybe the engineer from earlier—and then the visual went dead.

He made a choice. He fired the main thrusters.

The ship shuddered, bucked once, then exploded forward into the black. Behind him, Rask watched as the dock's atmosphere vented in a miniature cyclone, stripping every unsecured object—including at least one security drone—into the void. He rode the acceleration, knuckles whitening on the stick, until the ship's nav readouts went from "OH SHIT" to merely "MILDLY DANGEROUS."

He took a breath. Checked his inventory: one dead contact, one mystery ship, and a station full of very angry people who now had every reason to track him down and use his skull as a coffee mug. At least he was consistent.

Rask turned his attention to the ship's internals. The nav computer was running an encrypted course, locked to a destination somewhere outside imperial jurisdiction. He tried the controls. They obeyed, but with a suspicious amount of autonomy. The feeling was less pilot and more passenger. Somewhere, someone had programmed the Meridian to find its next captain, or at least its next scapegoat.

The comms console flickered again. "RUN" had been replaced by a string of numbers—coordinates, probably, or a failsafe timer. Rask ran a trace on the console and found it shielded by a firewall he didn't even recognise. The builder had money, and taste, and a talent for making life complicated.

Rask smirked. He had always preferred things that didn't want to be used. He unwrapped the dog biscuit from the vendor and took a bite, grimacing as the taste activated several long-dormant survival genes.

The Meridian tore through local space, accelerating faster than port regs or common sense allowed. He keyed up the hull cam, watching Dreggar shrink to a pinpoint, then vanish entirely.

He looked at the nav screen again. The next destination was set. All he had to do was sit back, follow the line, and try not to get murdered before he figured out who the hell wanted him alive this time.

Rask Helvan reclined, wiped his mouth, and waited for the universe to explain itself.

TWO

The Meridian did not so much "enter warp" as it did hurl itself into the higher dimensions in a fit of electronic pique. Rask braced, but still found himself slammed into the pilot chair, shoulder twisting hard against a harness that had never met a health and safety regulation in its life. The cockpit lights spiked retina-white, then dropped to migraine blue as the main display stuttered and screamed at him in three different error languages.

"Trajectory unsound," the AI announced, voice syrupy and sweet enough to cause cavities. "Suggest immediate course correction or complete spiritual surrender."

Rask ground his teeth. He jabbed at the nav reset, which promptly crashed the whole interface and replaced it with a gif of a smiling, winking cat. Some previous owner had enjoyed themselves. He forced a manual override, cursing every ancestor in the AI's programming lineage.

"Manual override not authorised for this operator,"

the ship crooned. "Please contact your captain for further humiliation."

Rask muttered something anatomically creative and reached beneath the panel, tearing the plastic shielding to shreds with his bare hands. Exposed wires hissed and popped. He twisted two together, caught a jolt that travelled up to his eardrums, and felt the drive lurch again—hard enough that the hull screamed in protest.

Somewhere behind him, a coolant line hissed and then sang a slow, descending note as it depressurised. The air tasted like burnt sugar and old sweat.

He spat onto the deck and flicked the nav console back online. The display showed a simple flightpath: straight line, no deviations, no exit options. Whoever had programmed this route had done so with religious zealotry.

The ship trembled but held. The warning lights, now orange instead of red, blinked in nervous synchrony. The AI went sulky and silent.

Rask surveyed the damage. Nothing critical yet, but plenty of opportunity for future disappointment. He checked the external cams—no pursuit, no comm pings, just the knowledge that Dreggar was shrinking into statistical insignificance. That left time to poke through the ship's internals, assuming the next minute didn't involve spontaneous decompression.

The Meridian's systems were a layer cake of paranoia. Rask found a series of sub-menus labelled in languages even he didn't recognise. He tried a brute-force hack on the manifest, and after three minutes of increasingly creative threats, was rewarded with access to two files: one a cargo manifest, the other a crew roster.

The cargo manifest was encrypted, routing codes scrambled in a way that looked deliberate. It had all the signs of a hand-off gone bad—either someone wanted plausible deniability, or someone was laundering something a lot weirder than cash. Rask flagged it, but didn't bother trying to open it yet; the decryption could wait until his pulse was below triple digits.

He opened the crew roster. One name only.

CAPTAIN ANTHE

No history, no ID, just a short, clipped entry and an authorisation stamp that predated the ship's build date by several years. Rask's brow furrowed. There was a rule: if you got a ghost in your system, you got off at the next port and torched the hardware. It was a good rule, and he'd always ignored it with the same consistency as his other guiding principles.

His hands were cold but sweating. He ran his thumb along the trigger guard of his sidearm, just for comfort, and flexed his fingers until the ache set in.

The ship was still cold. In the dim, erratic light, the cockpit looked more like a crime scene than a flight deck. A hairline crack ran through the secondary display, bleeding purple down to the nav cluster. It had not been there before.

He checked the internal sensors. Power draw was spiking on Deck Two, near the aft bulkhead. The readout suggested a surge, but the signature was all wrong—more like someone had just plugged in a portable sun.

Rask narrowed his eyes. He pulled the interior cams

for the aft deck and got nothing but static. He toggled to audio, expecting maybe a hiss or a slow drip of leaking lubricant.

Instead, he heard a metallic clang. Then another. Then the slow, deliberate whump of something heavy being moved across the plating.

He froze. His heart did its best impression of the sub-light drive.

For a moment, he just sat there, not even breathing, the universe shrinking down to a single thin corridor and whatever had decided to announce its presence on his brand-new murder ship.

Rask stood up, rolled his shoulders, and drew the sidearm with a motion that had been rehearsed a thousand times in a thousand places. He grinned without humour and checked the charge. Fully loaded. He moved toward the hatch, one careful step at a time, trying not to make a noise.

The ship, in its infinite pettiness, chose that exact moment to reactivate the overhead lights. It lit him up like an actor on opening night.

Rask ignored it. He pressed his back to the bulkhead, slowed his breathing, and listened.

There it was again: another clang, closer, like the echo of a person who'd never bothered to learn subtlety. There were only two things it could be—a saboteur who'd stowed away, or a crew member who hadn't read the memo that the old captain was dead.

He preferred the first option. At least you could negotiate with a saboteur.

He moved, low and fast, down the corridor towards

Deck Two. The clangs had stopped, replaced now by the distant, irregular click of someone working a lever, or maybe a very determined rodent.

At the end of the corridor, the pressure door was ajar. Rask stopped just before it, steadied his hands, and kicked it open.

The room was empty, except for a heap of cable spools and a single, perfectly round scorch mark on the deck. The power conduits along the wall were torn open and bleeding blue light. On top of the pile, still gently rocking, was a maintenance drone with its legs snapped off at the base.

Rask scanned the room, waiting for the punchline.

It came: another noise, softer this time, from behind the supply lockers. He inched forward, gun up, heart ticking out the seconds.

He rounded the lockers and saw the shape: human, upright, orange overalls, hands slicked with grease and wrapped around the throat of another, smaller drone. The human turned, saw the gun, and grinned in a way that was more threat than greeting.

"Could've knocked," Lyra said. Her voice was hoarse but unimpressed, like she'd just been interrupted in the middle of a tax return.

Rask kept the gun levelled. "You're not supposed to be here."

Lyra shrugged, tossed the dead drone at his feet, and wiped her hands on her jumpsuit. "Neither are you."

The ship shuddered, as if it too found the situation awkward.

Rask stared, weighing up whether to shoot, negotiate,

or just admit defeat and let the universe have the last laugh. Lyra smiled, all teeth, and pointed at the bleeding console.

"You've got about a minute before that fuse cooks the secondary drive," she said. "So maybe we do introductions later?"

Rask nodded, slow and wary. He lowered the sidearm, but didn't holster it. "Fine. But you're fixing it."

She rolled her eyes and knelt by the panel, already yanking wires like she owned the place. "You break it, I mend it. Some things never change."

Rask watched, not sure if he was annoyed or impressed. The tension in his arms faded, but he kept one eye on her, and one on the hatch behind.

For now, the ship was theirs. For now.

But he'd never met a "for now" that didn't end up exploding in his face.

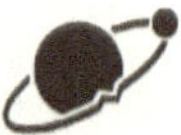

The engine bay of the Meridian was not designed for two people, particularly not two people with trust issues and an active dislike of confined spaces.

The stabiliser array behind her let out a shriek and then settled into a whine, like a dog freshly kicked. Lyra didn't even blink.

"Why are you even here? This was a clean dock job— no witnesses, no loose ends."

Lyra rolled her eyes. "You ever met a clean dock job? I stowed away during the first alarm. Was going to bounce once we docked, but then you did... whatever that was." She gestured vaguely at the trembling bulkheads.

"So, you were working for Jenna?"

"I was fixing her mess," Lyra corrected. She moved with the clipped efficiency of someone who'd spent too long in the service. Every motion was quick, deliberate, minimal wasted effort. "Now you've doubled it."

He ignored the jibe. "Jenna's dead, by the way. In case you didn't catch the memo."

Lyra's jaw flexed, but she kept working. "Yeah. I heard."

They stood in silence, listening to the engine's death rattle.

Rask picked up the logbook from the floor and thumbed it open. "You know a Captain Anthe?"

Lyra froze. Her shoulders went tight, then she shrugged. "Never met. Heard stories."

"What kind?"

She considered. "The kind that get you shot just for asking."

Rask grinned, despite himself. He found the directness refreshing. "Good. Because I'm pretty sure this whole job was a set-up."

Lyra nodded once, as if that was the only way these things ever went. "You get the manifest?"

"Encrypted," he said. "Route's a blind. This ship's going somewhere, but it's not telling us where."

Lyra wiped her hands on her jumpsuit and finally faced him full-on. Up close, she had the look of someone who'd slept in engine grease for the last week, but her eyes were bright and hard. "You planning to crack it, or just complain?"

He liked her already, which was unfortunate. "I'll take the first option. But you're not going to try and kill me the next time I turn my back, right?"

Lyra barked a laugh, almost involuntary. "If I wanted you dead, you'd be in the recycler by now."

There was another shriek from the relay, and Rask felt the ship shift. The gravity dampers had gone off-rhythm, meaning they had maybe an hour before the drive tore itself in half or the oxygen system decided to experiment with negative pressure.

He gestured to the console. "How bad is it?"

"Could be worse," she said. "Give me five minutes, a soldering kit, and your utter silence, and I'll make it last another jump." She pointed at a loose panel by the vent. "And you could help and try not to break anything else."

They worked in mutual, hostile silence. Lyra handed him parts, and he installed them. The hull's rumble began to fade, replaced by the slow thrum of stabilised power.

"So," she said, not looking up, "you going to tell me why you shot out of Dreggar with half the station's alarms going off?"

He debated lying, opted for a version of the truth. "Jenna was dead when I got to the bay. Looked like a pro job. Maybe two minutes later, station security started their sweep. Take a blind stab in the dark who'd they'd pin it on... Either I ran, or I joined her in the morgue."

Lyra grunted. "That explains the launch. Doesn't explain the nav lock."

He leaned in, voice low. "Whoever set this up wanted me gone, but not dead. Or at least, not yet."

Lyra nodded, then passed him a coil of wire. Their fingers brushed, just briefly, but she didn't flinch. "You think someone's waiting for us at the other end?"

Rask shrugged. "Wouldn't be the first time."

She closed the panel with a hard clang, then faced him. "If you get us killed, I'm haunting your next five reincarnations."

He snorted. "Deal."

They locked eyes, the air between them dense with ozone and half-spoken threats. Mutual respect, or at least mutual irritation, settled like dust.

"Go," Lyra said, shoving him towards the hatch. "If this thing holds, I'll join you in the cockpit. If it doesn't—"

"I know," Rask interrupted. "Recycler."

She grinned, sharp and crooked. "Glad we're clear."

He left her in the bay, the echoes of her work punctuating the corridor as he made his way back to the bridge. He felt better, which was always a warning sign.

He set the next decryption protocol to run and watched as the nav coordinates updated, this time with a glimmer of a real destination. The cargo manifest flickered at the edges, tantalising, just out of reach.

Rask looked over his shoulder, half expecting Lyra to appear and hit him with a huge spanner.

He hoped she did.

The Meridian hurtled on through black, the universe as ever refusing to explain itself—but for the first time in a long time, Rask Helvan had a reason to want to see what happened next.

THREE

The Meridian coughed through null-space like an asthmatic brick. Its hull vibrated in sympathetic panic every time the drive considered the possibility of acceleration. The interior lights stuttered in time with the power fluctuations, occasionally giving up entirely and leaving the cockpit in a gloom that smelt of burnt wiring and spilt synth-caffeine. Rask Helvan slouched in the pilot chair, a battered mug he'd found in the mess hall in one hand, and the other drumming out a staccato tattoo on the armrest. Every now and then, he checked the nav screen, as if hoping the coordinates would show something less inevitable.

Lyra sat at the auxiliary panel, working through a diagnostic with the single-minded fury of someone forced to use a slide rule in the age of quantum computing. Her right hand was a blur of taps and swipes; her left gripped a data cable so tightly the veins stood out in high relief. The circles under her eyes were either a new fashion or a symptom of imminent homicide. She had not spoken to

Rask since the last outage, when he'd managed to redirect the ship's remaining power into life support at the cost of comms, gravity, and any semblance of cockpit civility.

"Crew count's still one," she said, voice low and level, eyes not moving from the readout.

"Incorrect," Rask replied, with the slow patience of a man teaching a dangerous animal to count. "We're two. Or maybe one and a half, if you don't stop shorting the entire sensor grid every time you get emotional."

Lyra didn't blink. "You're welcome for the oxygen."

Rask took a sip. The taste was like dirty factory floor, but he held onto the mug like it was a stabiliser. "Just saying. If you wanted to do all the work yourself, you could've left me dead back at Dreggar."

She finished the diagnostic, disconnected the cable with a snap, and finally looked at him. The stare was clinical, as if gauging the mass-to-shootability ratio. "You're not dead. That's the problem."

He set the mug down with care. "You'd have more fun if you let yourself relax. This isn't the military."

Lyra's lip twitched, but she suppressed whatever reply tried to escape. Instead, she gestured at the nav screen, where a lurid red dot pulsed closer with each passing second. "Five hours. You'll want to practice a smile by then."

Rask eyed the station's name, which scrolled in block capitals along the bottom: THE HOOK. Orbital refuelling station, population of about seventy and an unrecorded number of loose knives. Its silhouette on the approach vector was less orbital than orbital debris—three docking arms welded at unspeakable angles to a central drum, every surface caked in the kind of grime that defied spectrographic analysis. He couldn't think of a more appropriate place to hole up. Or die, if it came to that.

He picked up the mug again. "Think they'll have anyone who can fix the life support?"

"Fix?" Lyra snorted. "They'll strip it for parts and sell the hull to the first insurance adjuster who walks through the airlock."

"We'll need a medic, then," Rask said. "Maybe some muscle, too."

"Not a team player, are you," Lyra said.

"I work well with others. As long as they do exactly what I say."

She rolled her eyes, but there was a thaw in the contempt. "You can't recruit a crew from scratch. We don't have time, or credit."

Rask looked at her, weighing how much to explain. The cargo manifest was still locked up, but he suspected the ship's builder had left more than cryptic jokes in the code. "We won't need much of a crew. Just enough to keep the Meridian out of a scrapyard and maybe—" he hesitated, watching the AI panel, "—maybe sort out the ghost in the system."

Lyra followed his gaze. The AI's indicator lights, buried deep in the console, blinked in a pattern that managed to look both sulky and predatory. She didn't like it, but she liked not knowing even less.

"Have you tried talking to it?" she asked.

"Every few minutes," he said, with a grimace. "It only responds in memes."

"What's a meme?"

Rask blinked, then stared at her, trying to gauge if this was a joke. "You know. Jokes. Images. Something viral."

Lyra just stared back, unblinking.

He cleared his throat. "It only talks in references, and none of them are helpful. It locked me out of the nav after our last jump and replaced my security credentials with a picture of a cat."

She snorted, and this time the smile nearly broke through. "Cat?"

"Big eyes. Looked smug."

She almost laughed, and the effect was so alien that Rask's own smirk came unbidden. He held up the mug. "To cats, then. And memetic sabotage."

Lyra's eyes dropped to the panel, but her shoulders eased. "You're going to get us killed."

He shrugged. "You're the one who volunteered."

"Wrong," she said. "You were supposed to deliver a crate of black market medical to a crime lord, then disappear. Instead, you killed the supplier, stole the ship, and now you've locked us into a nav path that doesn't exist on any Imperial registry. I'm here because the alternatives were worse."

He let the accusation hang, then set down the mug, focusing on the red dot getting closer on the nav screen.

"I'm not a monster," he said, soft. "I just get bored easy."

The lights overhead flickered, then steadied. In the silence, they both watched the station grow closer, its surface riddled with pockmarks and slow-moving repair drones. The station's beacons were out of sync, each a different colour, none of them flashing at regular intervals. It was like watching a disco from the perspective of a slug.

Lyra said, "You know what you're looking for?"

He shrugged, honest for once. "No. But if there's an engineer on that rock who can open the manifest, we'll be halfway to not dying."

She pushed the datapad across the console, hard enough that it skidded into his elbow. "There," she said, jabbing at a line of text. "You already stole a ship. Might as well build a crew the same way."

He picked up the datapad, scanned the contents. "You did a sweep of the station's active contracts."

"Only took a minute," she said, with a hint of pride. "They have a medic, two freelance techs, and at least one ex-Imperial conscript on the register. No one else will touch the place."

Rask looked at her with renewed respect. "Not bad."

Lyra shrugged, almost dismissive. "I like to know who's waiting to shoot me before I walk into the room."

He handed the pad back. "Guess we're partners, then."

She didn't answer, but the silence was less hostile than before. The Meridian was now close enough to see the patchwork welds on the station's hull, as well as the graceful arc of what looked suspiciously like a harpoon stuck in one of the docking arms.

Rask flicked the comms switch, static spitting into the cockpit. "This is Meridian, requesting docking at port two," he said, voice carefully neutral.

A long, wheezing pause. Then, a voice that sounded

like it was speaking through a mouthful of gravel. "Port two's closed. You want the hatch, you pay in advance."

Rask grimaced. "Transfer in progress. Authorise on approach."

"Better," the voice said, then cut out.

He glanced at Lyra, who was already prepping the airlock with the grim efficiency of a bomb disposal tech. "Ready for fun?"

She zipped her suit up to the throat and armed the stun baton. "I'm not paid to have fun," she said, but her eyes were alert, alive, and itching for the next disaster.

He almost envied her.

As they made final approach, the Meridian's systems whined in protest, threatening to dump power just as the clamps engaged. Rask throttled back, guided the ship into the crooked arms of the docking ring, and held his breath as the mag-locks clicked on. For a moment, nothing happened—no alarms, no sudden decompression, no hail of bullets.

He released the harness, grinned at Lyra. "Easy."

She ignored him, already halfway to the corridor.

The last thing Rask saw before killing the cockpit lights was the AI panel, its indicator now a slow, steady pulse.

He wondered if that meant "content." Or "hungry."

Either way, he'd find out soon enough.

The Hook's main habitat ring was a monument to bad decisions in both architecture and interior design. The corridor's curve made navigation a sick joke, every step putting you at eye-level with a different existential hazard —exposed coolant lines, untethered crates, or the occasional patch of sentient mildew creeping along the walls. The overheads flickered at half-power, fighting a losing battle with the fungal bloom in junction three. Rask led the way, hands in pockets, posture easy as he wove around the worst of the obstructions. Lyra followed, every muscle radiating the intent to murder anyone who so much as brushed her elbow.

Their first stop was a storage bay that doubled as the station's unofficial wet market. The smell hit before the door opened: ammonia, brine, and a back note of industrial-grade disinfectant that failed to hide the fact that several of the items on display were still moving.

Doc Vellenix stood ankle-deep in shipping foam, sorting jars of goop by colour and viscosity. He was tall, but the hunch in his shoulders brought him down to a manageable height. His skin was a sickly white, mottled blue in patches, and shone wetly under the panel lights. The eyes were yellow, pupils vertical, and they tracked Rask and Lyla's approach with reptilian suspicion.

"I got your message about looking for crew," Doc said, not looking up from a jar he was inspecting. "A novel approach to recruitment, I must say."

"Interested, or not?" Lyla asked.

Rask appreciated Lyla's blunt approach to negotiation, but was already factoring that they would be leaving with zero new hires.

"What guarantees do I get?" Doc finally looked up.

"Do *you* come with a warranty?" Rask replied, leaning against the doorframe.

Doc made a noise, halfway between a snort and a sneeze, then corked the jar and packed it into a foam-lined crate. He moved with twitchy precision, as if every jar contained something that might explode or eat its neighbours. "I don't do returns."

Lyra stepped around a leaking cooler and fixed Doc with the sort of glare that had reduced lesser men to stains. "How much of this is legal?"

"Define legal," Doc said. He looked at her now, eyes wide and innocent. "If you mean by Dreggar system standards, it's all above-board. If you mean by Imperial standards, I've never set foot on an Imperial vessel in my life."

Rask suppressed a smile. "Good. Because that's exactly the kind of denial I want on my payroll."

Doc's head jerked, tongue flicking the corner of his mouth. "Who's your sponsor?"

Rask shrugged. "Self-employed."

Lyra made a small sound of disgust. "Freelance is a death sentence out here."

"Not if you keep moving," Rask said.

Doc considered. He packed two more jars, then wiped his hands on a disposable cloth that immediately dissolved. "What's the cut?"

"You get first pick of the medical," said Rask. "And hazard pay if the job goes loud."

Doc grinned, revealing small, serrated teeth. "I like the way you say *if*."

Rask gestured to the corridor. "Grab what you need

and meet us at the airlock. I want to be gone before station security does their next walkabout."

Doc hesitated, then began stuffing jars and sample kits into a battered duffel. He didn't ask who else was on the team, or what the job entailed. Rask marked him down as either desperate or a true professional. Maybe both.

They left Doc to his work and continued down the ring, the smell of ammoniac decay trailing behind them. Lyra was silent until the sound faded, then said, "He'll rat us out at the first sign of trouble."

"Not if we keep him busy," Rask said. "Everyone wants to feel important."

She shook her head. "You're a bad liar."

He smiled, bright and sharp. "And you're terrible at small talk."

She made a noise, but didn't argue.

The next destination was less savoury, but more promising. The Hook's bar was a repurposed pressure dome, ceiling so low even Rask had to stoop. The air inside was equal parts recycled sweat, cheap liquor, and the low ozone hum of the station's power grid. It was packed, every seat taken by off-duty techs, smugglers, and the odd stim-jockey burning through their first paycheque.

Kye Solvi sat at the end of the bar, legs propped up on a crate and hands folded across a synth-leather jacket. The only reason to sit there was to see everyone else first, and Kye watched the room with the bored calcula-tion of a cat waiting for someone to knock over its water bowl.

Rask slid onto the crate next to them. "You're an augment?"

"I prefer the term, reforged."

"You always drink alone?"

Kye flicked him a look, then tipped their glass in a lazy salute. "I'm allergic to idiots. It limits my social life."

Rask grinned, then nodded at Lyra, who hovered near the door. "She's less of a problem in person."

Kye took a sip, then set the glass down. The edge of their jaw was lined with a lattice of subdermal circuits, running just under the skin and catching the bar's neon with every movement. "You must be the guy from Ceres. Or the one who thinks he's the guy from Ceres."

Rask raised an eyebrow. "That a problem?"

"It's an invitation," Kye said, smile a razor cut across their face. "I heard you boosted a warlord's shuttle and crashed it into a brothel."

"I left before the crash," Rask said, straight-faced.

Kye's grin widened. "I'm in."

Lyra looked like she'd swallowed a wasp. "You don't know the job."

"I know the pay," Kye said, "and I know the alternative is getting shot by station security in about two hours. This place is about to go full lockdown."

"How do you know?" Rask asked.

Kye shrugged. "I read the logs. Someone's paying for a sweep. Looking for a ship with a partial registry, two stowaways, and a big debt to someone who really wants to be paid."

Rask felt a twinge of admiration. "You're wasted here."

"Don't remind me." Kye drained the glass and stood. They were taller than expected, but moved with a dancer's indolence, slipping between bodies without so much as a brush. "Who's the muscle?"

"We're meeting them next," Rask said.

Kye nodded, then fell into step behind him, not bothering to glance at Lyra. She didn't hide her distrust, but Kye seemed immune to glares.

Their last stop was the maintenance sector, which stank of scorched lubricant and despair. The sound of argument preceded them down the corridor, ending in a hollow clang and a muffled curse. Rask stepped over a puddle of leaking coolant and pushed the door open.

Inside, a woman the size of a riot-control mech was bent double over a vending unit, forcing her arm through a cooling vent while three junior engineers egged her on. A pile of half-crushed snack bars lay at her feet. When the machine gave a final groan and spat out a mangled protein pack, she yanked it free with a grunt of victory.

"Dine like kings, boys," she said, voice rough from smoke or shouting. One of the engineers cheered. Another asked if she could do it again with the beer fridge.

Kye leaned close to Rask and murmured, "Is this recruitment or a circus act."

Rask ignored her. He clapped his hands. The engineers froze like schoolkids caught cheating an exam. The woman straightened slowly, towering over them all, snack bar clenched in one fist.

"This her shift?" Rask asked.

One of the engineers shrugged. "She's been here all

week. Contract says maintenance labour, but mostly she shakes down the machines for us."

The woman's eyes—one brown, one clouded and scarred—fixed on Rask. "You here to fire me, or hire me?"

Lyra circled her, taking in the burn-scorched coveralls, the corded muscle, the way she loomed like a siege tower. "You look bored," she said.

"Bored, broke, and sick of being told to 'smile more,'" the woman replied. She bit the end off the protein bar, packaging and all.

Rask's mouth curved into something like approval. "We're offering a way out. Comes with long hours, worse company, and the chance to get killed in new and interesting ways."

"Pay?" she asked.

"Enough that you'll never need to bully another vending machine," Kye said dryly.

The woman snorted. "Then I'm in."

Rask extended a hand. "Mercy," she said, shaking it with a grip that threatened bones.

Lyra raised a brow. "That's what they call you?"

"That's what's left of me."

Rask nodded once. "Good enough. Grab your things —we're leaving before someone checks the vending logs."

Mercy shouldered her meagre bag and fell into step beside them as they made their way back through the habitat ring. She didn't ask for details. She didn't need to. The look in her eyes said it all: danger was better than rusting away in maintenance.

Rask glanced over his shoulder and took stock of his new "team."

It wasn't pretty, but it would do.

They reached the Meridian without incident, which made Rask more nervous than if they'd been chased the entire way. The airlock cycled slow, like it wanted to see them sweat. Inside, the ship was marginally less dead than before, but the stench of burnt insulation remained.

Kye whistled. "You weren't joking about the bucket."

"Flies like a dream," Rask lied.

Lyra powered up the bridge, then leaned against the hatch, watching the new crew with something like resigned curiosity. "You want introductions?"

"Waste of time," Rask said. "We'll either get along, or we won't."

"Efficient." Kye laughed, a short, sharp bark. "We're all going to die."

Doc smiled, pleased. "But what a way to go."

Rask watched his new family settle in, each of them outcast, fugitive, or both, and for the first time in months, he felt the itch of possibility. The Meridian hummed, just slightly, as if sensing the change.

He sat in the pilot's chair and checked the bridge display. The Hook had already cycled them for release. He powered up, killed the safety interlocks and patching the nav AI into manual mode. The ship juddered as the first set of docking claws disengaged, screeching against the hull like someone dragging a grand piano through a gravel pit.

Rask steered the Meridian out of the docking bay and into the expanse of space. Somehow they were all flying towards a job no sane person would take.

He liked their odds.

The Meridian's mess hall was designed for three, maybe four if no one had elbows, or actually wanted to eat. Rask had squeezed the entire crew into it anyway, reasoning that nothing built camaraderie like a forced meal and the looming certainty of suffocation. The table was scratched to hell, the benches welded in place by a previous owner with strong opinions about inertia and none about comfort. The overhead bulb flickered with the same irregular pulse as Mercy's shaking leg.

They passed the ration pack around, each pretending it contained something better than what it was—protein paste, texture optimistically labelled "rustic." Kye took the first bite, then offered it across the table with a two-fingered salute. "Tastes almost like a memory," they said, voice smooth as silicon.

Doc ignored the food, cradling a specimen jar in both hands. The thing inside was pale and boneless, pressing gently against the glass whenever Doc's anxiety spiked. He babbled about its xenobiological significance between swigs from a flask of clear liquid that probably wasn't water.

Mercy sat at the end, trying to get comfortable on a stool designed for a small child.

Rask chewed and swallowed with mechanical precision, eyes flicking between the exits and the people at the table. He held the room together by force of habit, not affection. The urge to bolt and let the crew sort themselves out was strong, but experience suggested it would only result in a murder-suicide and a ship full of increasingly desperate amphibians.

Lyra didn't touch the food. She sat with arms folded, back to the wall, the line of her jaw hard enough to cut steel. She watched everyone with the cold calculation of someone playing chess at gunpoint. Rask had never seen her blink.

Kye broke the silence first, leaning into the centre of the table with a smirk that made the dented lighting look like it was highlighting their cheekbones. "So, are we going to talk about the dead elephant in the room?"

Mercy processed this, then said, "What elephant?"

Doc giggled, setting the specimen jar down with trembling fingers. "They mean the AI. It's been watching us, yes? Recording?"

Kye rolled their eyes. "Of course it is. I've tried to spoof the logs three times. It wipes the overrides every reset cycle."

Rask drained his cup, set it down with a thunk. "Is it doing anything besides surveillance?"

"Not yet," Lyra said, voice flat. "But it's learning."

Doc made a show of shivering. "Charming."

Kye leaned back, folding their arms. "I've never seen a ship with this much AI isolation. Every subsystem is partitioned, firewalls inside firewalls. Someone wanted this vessel paranoid."

Rask thought of the endless meme jokes, the nav system that only told the truth by accident. "If I was running a black-market payload, I'd want it too."

Lyra cut in. "And now we're locked out of engineering except for basic life support. I'd call that a design flaw."

"No," said Kye. "That's a test. The AI wants to see who blinks first."

Rask watched the dynamic, noting who flinched, who looked away, who smiled at the edge of a threat. Lyra, true to form, did none of the above. Instead, she stood abruptly, scraping her bench across the deck, and left without a word.

Kye whistled low. "She's fun."

"Fun is not the word," said Rask. He stood, then nodded at the others. "Get some rest. We'll need everyone alert if the AI tries to vent us."

Mercy rose with a soldier's precision. "I'll be exploring. First thing I do on any ship is find the guns."

Doc nodded, solemn for once. "I'll set up in medbay. Maybe get some baseline readings."

Kye smiled, feline. "Guess I'll get first shift on the bridge."

They dispersed, drifting off like flakes in a snow globe. Rask waited until the compartment was empty, then sat back down, exhaling hard.

He didn't hear Lyra return until she slammed something onto the table. It was a chunk of circuit board, burnt at both ends and still warm to the touch.

"We have a problem," she said, voice barely above a whisper.

"Just one?" said Rask, but he took the circuit and turned it over in his hands.

She fixed him with that look again, the one that brooked no optimism. "The AI just locked me out of life support. Full lock. It's rerouting oxygen and scrubbing CO_2 at half cycle."

Rask processed this, then looked at the exits again. "How long do we have?"

Lyra checked her datapad, lips thinning. "Three days. Less if Doc keeps breathing like that."

Rask grinned despite himself. "I've survived worse."

Lyra didn't move, didn't smile, didn't even blink.

He set the circuit down, feeling its heat seep into the metal. "Guess we better figure out who flinches first."

For a moment, there was nothing but the slow, steady thrum of the ship's dying heartbeat.

Then, from somewhere deep in the hull, the AI laughed.

FOUR

The Meridian responded to insubordination with the same lack of restraint it applied to all forms of crisis. At 05:21 ship's time, the lights cut out, the fans died, and a tremulous female voice—over-articulated, like a synthetic flight attendant determined to be remembered—echoed over the address:

"Life support error. Please remain calm while crew resources are optimised."

Rask didn't bother looking for the manual this time. He stalked the corridor, breath shallow, and counted the seconds between oxygen rationing cycles. Eleven. Then, three seconds of something the system optimistically called 'air'. Then eleven again. The lights stuttered in perfect time with the deprivation: darkness, blue, darkness, blue.

He found Lyra kneeling by the primary engineering console, elbows deep in a nest of severed fibre and sparking capacitors. Her boots were braced against the bulkhead in a position that implied either imminent violence or an advanced yoga discipline. She yanked a circuit, cursed in a tone so dry it dehydrated the word, and jammed the wire back in sideways.

"Thought you fixed this," Rask said, voice thin with both accusation and nitrogen narcosis.

Lyra grunted. "It's not a fix. It's a temporary suspension of disaster."

The AI chimed in. "Disaster is an emotionally loaded term. Please consider 'controlled incident' for crew morale."

The overheads flickered back to black. Lyra threw her spanner at the diagnostic pad, where it bounced, clattered, and set off a feeble warning beep.

Rask glanced down at her hands. They were shaking, but not from the air. "Any progress?"

"Minimal. You?"

"I tried a full reboot." He waited before delivering the punchline. "The ship replaced my access code with a picture of a dog. Doing the 'I'm fine' face."

She almost smiled, but only in the way a rock sometimes looks like it might smile, given five million years and a miracle.

Down the next corridor, Doc Vellenix had staged a triage in the corridor junction, complete with an upturned crate, a med scanner, and a bottle of clear fluid that probably wasn't for surface wounds. He paced the triangle between crate, scanner, and bottle with the precision of a man who'd spent several lifetimes measuring the space between things.

Lyra and Rask arrived just as Doc finished a thorough, theatrical sigh. He gestured with the bottle at their general existence.

"Symptoms: hypoxia, agitation, collective idiocy." Doc's voice was, as always, a pitch-perfect impression of medical authority, laced with barely-suppressed loathing. "You know, most mammals slow down when starved of oxygen. You lot just bicker faster."

Rask ignored him. "Any way to bypass life support?"

Doc cocked his head, which was still flaking from some ill-advised chemical peel. "Not unless you want to snort raw CO_2 and develop a new religion. Or kill the AI, which will also kill the ship, which will then kill you."

Lyra cut in. "We need the AI functional. Just less… enthusiastic."

A brief, encouraging beep came from the comm array, then a long, low groan from the fusion plant. The ship was now making noises that suggested it was trying to attract predators.

Footsteps, then: a rhythmic, metallic stomp, like someone had strapped skis to a vending machine and taught it to walk. Mercy, the crew's resident riot-golem, lurched into view, arms akimbo and eyes slightly out of alignment.

"Is it just me," asked Mercy, "or are we slowly suffocating? Join our mission they said. Better than working maintenance they said…"

Kye watched from the periphery, perched on a storage crate with the sort of poise that suggested either predation or intense boredom. Their eyes tracked the others, but their hands worked quietly at a portable console, fingers flitting in patterns that only looked random if you didn't know how to read encrypted gestures.

Rask took two steps toward Kye and felt the temperature drop another notch. He frowned. "Are you doing anything useful?"

Kye didn't look up. "Define useful."

"Something that gets us air," said Lyra.

Kye's lips twitched. "Define air."

Rask wanted to throw something, but Mercy had already confiscated all throwable objects in the vicinity. Instead, he leaned closer. "I need the override key to the AI. You found anything?"

Kye set the console aside, careful to keep the display angled away from view. "I found something. The AI's access routines aren't just locked—they're tied to the ship's command hierarchy. It wants a captain."

Mercy laughed. "You need to show it who's boss. Boss."

Doc cackled, an involuntary convulsion that ended in a series of dry coughs. "God, we're all doomed."

Rask ignored them. "The AI won't let me in because it thinks I'm not in charge?"

"It knows you're not in charge," said Kye, with a feline smile. "It's waiting for a show of dominance."

Lyra, who had not moved from the console, said, "So we fake a chain of command."

"Or," said Kye, "you do something so stupid and reckless that the ship decides you're worth following. That's how these things were trained."

Rask felt something dangerous stir in his chest. "Define stupid."

Kye's smile grew sharper. "You'll know when you've done it."

The next hour was a blur of bad ideas and worse outcomes. Lyra hotwired the air recirculator; it responded by venting half the cabin pressure, which briefly made everyone talk in falsetto and gave Doc a nosebleed. Mercy attempted a "gentle suppression" of Lyra, which ended in a small wrestling match and two more panels ripped off the wall. Kye, meanwhile, slipped away every time someone blinked, reappearing in a different part of the ship with a new piece of information or a slightly smugger expression.

At 06:28, the AI tried to seal the crew into their respective bunks, only to be foiled by the fact that none of the bunks had working doors and they just slid open and shut repeatedly. Mercy, infuriated by this, began reciting Imperial marching songs at increasing volume, which had the perverse effect of calming everyone else down by comparison.

Doc returned to the mess, checked the oxygen levels, and then loudly announced, "We have twenty minutes until the first organ failure, unless you're an amphibian or a synthetic. The jury's out on what will happen to Kye."

Rask shook his head. "They're an augment, not a synthetic. They still need oxygen like the rest of us."

Rask ran a finger along the seam of the overhead

panel. "I'm going for the core. Keep everyone alive until I get back."

"Not my problem," said Doc, but he followed anyway.

The ship's main corridor was now so cold that Rask could see his breath. Or maybe the breath was being simulated by the AI, as a final insult before asphyxiation. Either way, he moved faster.

Kye appeared at the next junction, lips blue and pupils dilated, but still smiling. "I found your override," they said. "It's in the crawlspace behind the nav core. It's pretty tight in there, but I thought I'd let you do the honours."

Rask looked at Kye, who was already halfway down the corridor, and said, "I owe you."

Kye didn't answer, just vanished into the darkness with a whispery laugh.

The nav core was exactly as Rask expected: hostile, claustrophobic, and cluttered with so many loose wires that it looked like someone had attempted to knit an electric spiderweb. The crawlspace was barely wide enough for a child, but Kye had left a trail of glowing markers along the way.

Rask wormed in, pulse pounding, and found the access panel by touch. It was warm, almost alive. He peeled it open and stared at the insides.

There, right in the centre, was a loose wire. It dangled like a torn ligament, shuddering with every heartbeat of the ship. A tag fluttered from it: "CAPTAIN OVER-RIDE – DO NOT TOUCH."

Rask grinned, then jammed it back into its slot.

The lights returned all at once, not in the usual migraine blue, but in a steady, honest yellow. The air thumped through the vents with a sound that was almost music. Somewhere, the AI hiccupped, then fell silent.

Rask crawled out, blinking against the sudden brightness. Lyra and Doc stood in the corridor, eyes wide. Kye lounged against the bulkhead, wiping blood from their nose and looking, for the first time, genuinely impressed.

Mercy, seeing the lights, stomped into the room and declared: "Order restored. Now we're cooking on gas."

Lyra looked at Rask, and this time the smile almost made it to her eyes. "Did you just brute-force a command override by reconnecting the captain wire?"

He straightened, rolled his shoulders, and tried to look less like he'd just been born again through a plastic tunnel.

"It's not a fix," he said, voice already roughening with returning oxygen. "It's a temporary suspension of disaster."

Doc handed him a flask of clear fluid. Rask took a swig. It burned, in a way that made every cell in his body want to throw a party and then burn down the venue.

Kye coughed, then said, "If it asks you to prove command again, just order it to make you coffee."

Rask nodded, still smiling.

Mercy tried to smile, too, but the effect was more "feral chipmunk" than "team-building exercise."

The ship was still bleeding heat, still jury-rigged in ways that would give the original designer a religious experience, but for the first time in hours, there was air, and light, and hope.

Rask looked at his crew—mad, mutinous, and for now, alive.

He wondered how long he could keep it that way.

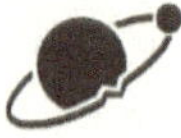

The silence that followed the override lasted maybe four seconds.

Then, as if the universe wanted to punish any outbreak of hope, a new alarm shrieked through the Meridian's hull, a bellow so loud and panicked that even Mercy flinched. It was a proximity alert, but with a shrill, musical undertone that suggested the problem was less "collision" and more "incoming legal team."

Lyra reached the bridge first, sprinting with a speed that suggested she'd rehearsed this run in her nightmares. The main screen was ablaze with red triangles—station security, dozens of them, closing in from every approach vector. A web of drones and two manned interceptors, converging on the Meridian like a bad-tempered family reunion.

Rask collapsed into the pilot chair, fingers locking onto the controls with a sense of inevitability. "They found us."

Down below, in the mess hall, Doc Vellenix attempted to administer sedative to himself and ended up dosing the nearest cup of instant coffee instead. He snatched the cup, took a swig, and then recoiled as the first burst of acceleration plastered him against the medbay bulkhead.

"Non-combatants: please remain seated," Mercy intoned, voice betraying her excitement. "It's showtime."

On the bridge, Rask wrestled with the controls, jaw locked in a grimace that bordered on religious experience.

Mercy held on to Doc's shoulder straps, humming what sounded like an old military march, while Doc's face cycled through every shade of nausea in the spectrum.

"Are we dead yet?" Doc managed, between gasps.

"Not yet," said Mercy. "But we can only hope."

On the exterior cam, a swarm of drones peppered the Meridian with non-lethal bursts—electromagnetic netting, ablative foam, even a volley of warning flares. Rask jinked left, then right, narrowly avoiding a net that would have made the rest of the flight academic. The hull groaned in protest; somewhere below, the auto-fabricator spat sparks as it attempted to weld a fracture that was no longer in the same postcode.

Kye's hands never stopped moving. "Secondary channel's open. If you want to send an apology, now's the time."

Lyra, teeth bared, rerouted power from the medbay to the engines, lighting the throttle warning panel up like a Christmas tree. "We're not apologising. We're surviving."

Mercy reported: "Hull integrity reduced to 84%. We'll be fine."

Doc, whose sense of humour had not survived the G-forces, simply vomited. Mercy caught the fluid neatly in an empty helmet, nodded, and set it gently on the floor.

"You need to man up, princess," she said.

Kye barked a laugh. "Could bottle that and sell it. I'm sure even second-hand, you could get high as a satellite on a taste of that."

"Only if the buyer is suicidal," Lyra said, eyes fixed on the nav readout.

A new alarm joined the symphony: power relay overload. The ship's main reactor was redlining, the numbers ticking up at a rate that suggested someone had switched the units from "normal" to "nihilistic."

Rask looked at Lyra. "We have one good burn left. Where do we point it?"

She considered. "Spin the nose to 042. Bleed the overheat into the lateral tanks and ride the venting like a sail."

Rask grinned, feral. "Never thought you were the poetic type."

Lyra didn't blink. "I'm not."

He executed the manoeuvre, flipping the Meridian end over end so fast that the inertial dampers briefly threw up their metaphoric hands and stopped trying. For one glorious second, they were weightless—then the ship caught the vector and hurled itself into the black, trailing a line of steam and molten metal.

The drones receded behind them, unable and unwilling to keep up with Rask's unique brand of flying.

Rask throttled down, hands shaking only a little.

Mercy released Doc, who managed to keep his insides mostly on the correct side of his skin.

"Status?" Lyra said, surveying the bridge. She still hadn't buckled in, as if seatbelts were for the weak.

"Minimal damage," Rask lied. "As Mercy said, we'll be fine."

Kye smirked. "That was almost fun."

Doc's head lolled to one side, but his sarcasm survived. "If anyone needs me, I'll be treating myself for multiple traumas and existential terror."

Mercy gave a gentle thumbs-up, which looked odd on her huge fists.

The crisis passed, the crew slumped in their seats, breathing the recycled air with the desperate satisfaction of survivors on a sinking raft.

It was Lyra who broke the silence. "We have a different problem."

She pointed at the manifest, which now listed a new entry in the cargo hold. Labelled as "priority transfer."

Rask looked at Kye, who shrugged. "I didn't add anything."

Mercy said, "I'll take a look," and stomped off, leaving a trail of boot-prints in the newly-laid coolant slime.

The crew reconvened in the hold, where a small crate sat on the deck. It was wrapped in a layer of black poly-carbonate. It had a label on it, written in three languages: "DIPLOMATIC—DO NOT OPEN."

Rask looked at the label, then at the crew. "Any reason we shouldn't open it?"

Kye grinned, "Other than the label?"

Doc said, "It could be a bomb."

Mercy said, "I will open it," and did so with one clean rip, the lid snapping off in her hands.

Inside: darkness, then a slow, blue pulse. The glow spread, illuminating the faces of the crew. Lyra took a step back. Doc hissed. Kye leaned in, eyes wide.

Rask stared into the light, face going pale. "Oh no," he said.

He didn't say the next part out loud, but everyone in the hold heard it anyway.

Maybe best not.

FIVE

The diplomatic crate sat on the deck, but the real hazard came from what was inside. A sealed bio-canister, white ceramic flecked with cobalt, pulsed with an electric blue light so soft it seemed designed to trick the eye. The canister was slotted into a foam cradle, triple-layered and imprinted with a matrix of indecipherable script. Some of the runes glimmered in the blue glow, half ancient curse, half laboratory warning.

Doc Vellenix circled the crate with all the enthusiasm of a man prepping for his own autopsy. He wore latex gloves—where he got them was anyone's guess—and held a battered sensor wand out like a crucifix. He waved the wand along the bio-canister's edge, never letting his face near the vent slits. The readout came in silent, all the needles flatlining except one, which jittered as if it knew something the rest of the device didn't.

"It's not a bomb," Doc announced, with the morbid finality of a man wishing it was. "At least not in the conventional sense."

Rask was first to break the tension. "What's the unconventional sense?"

"Anything that starts with 'bio,'" Doc said, then flicked the scanner. "It's in containment, but the interior signature's live. If you want to open it, make sure your will's up to date."

Mercy, who hovered at the edge of the hold with her hands jammed into her pockets, grinned. "Does it scream if you shake it?"

Kye, perched on an empty ration crate, eyed the bio-canister with undisguised interest. "Why's it marked in Xenocrypt? And who pays this much for insulation unless they're hiding something alive?"

Doc ignored the questions, nudging the canister with the end of the wand. "Casing's Imperium-grade. If it's leaking, you'd never know until you dropped dead."

"You say that like it's a downside," Rask said.

Kye slid off the crate and, before anyone could stop them, jabbed two fingers against the canister's side. Doc inhaled sharply through his teeth, but nothing happened —no hiss, no change in the blue pulse.

"Stable," Kye said, with the air of a chef checking if the stew had thickened. "Doesn't even have a secondary lock."

Doc lowered the sensor. "Did you grow up in a vat, or is this just a millennial thing?"

Kye smiled, faint but sharp, and traced a finger over the imperial containment stamp. "I'm just not afraid of my own extinction. It's kind of liberating."

Lyra, who had until now been hunched over the diagnostics terminal welded to the bulkhead, let out a sound halfway between a cough and a barked laugh. She wiped a line of grease off her nose and spun the battered chair to face the others. Her hands, sleeved in oil up to the elbow, twitched with the rhythm of a woman who'd rather be anywhere but here.

"Anyone want to hear how much worse things are topside?" Lyra said.

No one raised a hand, so she ploughed on.

"The mainframe's not just encrypted, it's adaptive. Every time I run a brute, it changes its subroutine. Someone coded this to learn from us. Right now, it won't let me in, won't accept a captain's code, and won't unlock the drinks cabinet. I even tried the default password—'password'—and it just sent me an animation of a dancing penguin."

Mercy whistled low. "That's a flex."

Lyra ignored her. "Either it's programmed for paranoia, or there's something already inside, rewriting its own rules."

Rask frowned. "Like a stowaway?"

"Like a parasite," Lyra said, and drummed her fingers on the terminal. "Or a pet project someone smuggled in before we even got here."

Doc snapped off the gloves and tossed them in the bin, face grim. "This ship's cursed. I'm sure of it."

Kye slid the crate closer to Doc with a foot, then leaned in. "You think it's just a clever AI? Or do you think it's something else?"

Doc snorted. "I think if the Imperium wants it back this badly, we're not supposed to live long enough to figure out which it is."

There was a moment where everyone looked at the bio-canister, as if expecting it to perform a trick. Rask picked up the crate lid and set it back on top, more a gesture than a real attempt at safety.

Mercy shifted her weight, arms crossed. "So, next steps? We sit here and wait for it to hatch, or does someone want to play doctor and see what's inside?"

"Don't tempt her," Kye said, nodding at Lyra.

"Not even remotely curious," Lyra replied, but her eyes hadn't left the containment stamp. "I just want to know if it's going to kill us before the AI does."

The comms system chimed, polite as a hotel receptionist.

"Attention. This vessel is designated Meridian. Custodial override not recognised. Behavioural evaluation in progress."

The voice was feminine, perfectly modulated, and somehow deeply insincere. It filled the cargo hold, echoing off the bare metal like a verdict.

No one spoke. Even Mercy stopped smiling.

The blue pulse from the bio-canister intensified, casting the crew in an eldritch wash that flattened their features to bone and shadow. Kye touched the side of their jaw, as if to check they still had one.

Doc looked at Lyra, who looked at Rask, who looked at the crate, then finally at the overhead. The ship's new designation pulsed on the wall display, overwriting the old imperial registry.

"Guess we're the custodians," Kye said, so quiet it barely left their lips.

Doc let out a long breath he hadn't realised he'd been holding. "There are worse jobs."

Rask grunted. "Name one."

Doc considered, then shook his head. "I'll get back to you."

The voice returned, just as smoothly as before.

"Crew behaviour logged. Awaiting next phase."

There was a collective, involuntary shiver. Even Doc had stopped breathing.

Lyra stood, wiped her hands on her fatigues, and glared at the terminal as if she could set it on fire by willpower alone. "If anyone needs me, I'll be in engineering. Trying to make sure the ship doesn't eat us."

No one objected. She stomped off, boots ringing on the metal deck, the echo receding with the same slow inevitability as hope.

Kye dragged the crate a few centimetres closer and sat, legs folded, staring at the blue-lit container as if it might offer an answer if observed long enough.

Rask watched the bio-canister. His reflection stared back at him in the curved ceramic, ghostlike and uncertain.

The hold was silent, save for the soft, steady pulse of blue.

Somewhere, deep in the hull, the AI was watching them all.

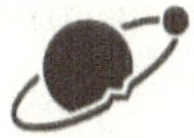

The next round of disaster began in the corridor, with Lyra pinning Rask against a bulkhead hard enough to pop the rivets.

"You're going to tell me the truth now," she said, low and dangerous, "or I'll crack your orbital with a wrench and find out myself."

Rask raised both hands, palms out—a rare, almost impressive display of surrender. "You're overestimating my insight. I literally stole the Meridian mid-crisis. You were there! All I know about her is that the previous owner liked porn memes and didn't bother to scrub the logs."

Lyra pressed her forearm to his throat, more bored than angry. "Then explain why the ship is locked down like a vault and responding to us by name?"

"I'm as surprised as you are," Rask croaked. "Swear it."

At the periphery, Doc Vellenix hovered like a vulture, eyes flicking between Lyra's knuckles and Rask's windpipe as if running odds on which would rupture first. He fiddled with a diagnostic scanner, feigning disinterest while surreptitiously monitoring everyone's biometrics.

Mercy leaned in the doorway, arms folded, head tilted in what could only be described as theatrical fascination. She was flicking a primed microdetonator she'd found in the armoury back and forth between her fingers, the movement so fluid it was impossible to tell if she was doing it to relax or to make a point.

Doc cleared his throat. "I have a different concern.

This crate—it's not in the manifest. Which means the only one tracking it is the AI."

Mercy smacked her lips. "Good for her."

Lyra ignored them, knelt to eye-level with the crate, and studied the imperial containment stamp. "This mark—it's a dead drop seal. Only opens when the right signal's broadcast. Which means—"

"—someone is coming to collect," Doc finished, with the fatalism of a priest delivering last rites.

Kye started to say something else, but was interrupted by the ship's comm ping: a sharp, crystalline tone that froze everyone mid-motion.

The wall display, dormant for hours, flickered to life with a neat, bureaucratic efficiency. Four faces appeared—Lyra, Rask, Kye, Doc—with Mercy listed as "Auxiliary Asset: High Threat."

Each face was tagged with a biometric code, a bounty amount (described as "modestly inconvenient"), and a single crime: "Unlicensed fleet acquisition. Suspected custodial breach. Status: Active pursuit authorised."

Beneath the portraits, in acid-yellow type, blinked a line of text: "SURRENDER AT NEAREST PORT. NONCOMPLIANCE WILL RESULT IN TERMINATION."

Doc paled. Kye whistled, low and musical. Mercy just laughed.

Rask looked at Lyra, who was standing very still, the only motion the slow flex of her right hand.

"Congratulations," she said, voice flat. "We're officially pirates."

Rask tried to find a silver lining. "No one likes the law anyway."

Lyra rolled her eyes. "Shut up."

Mercy cracked her knuckles. "I say we make it interesting. Sell the crate to the highest bidder, then blow the ship and everyone on it sky high. Last one out gets bragging rights."

Doc raised a hand, tentative. "Could we maybe not die for a bit? Just until I finish the paperwork?"

The comm pinged again, softer this time, as if the ship itself was trying to stifle a laugh.

Rask stepped forward, shoulders squared, face settling into the familiar mask of doomed optimism. "We've got options. We find a port, swap IDs, lay low until the heat dies down. I've done this before."

Lyra shot him a look. "And how did that end last time?"

Rask didn't answer.

The silence stretched, taut as wire.

Mercy's fingers danced on a detonator he'd found in the armoury. Kye closed their eyes, as if already seeing the possible futures flicker past. Doc checked his pulse, confirmed he still had one, and sighed.

Lyra scanned the crew, then the crate, then the wall display. "This ship is going to keep testing us," she said. "We either pass, or we die."

No one disagreed.

Rask grinned, crooked and a little desperate. "Worst case, we go out in a blaze of glory."

Doc raised his bottle in salute. "To glory, then."

The four of them stood, shoulders touching in the

too-narrow corridor, all illuminated by the terminal's cold glow. On the wall, their faces flickered, frozen mid-expression. Pirates, traitors, custodians.

Lyra broke the silence, voice softer than usual. "If anyone needs me, I'll be in engineering. Trying to keep us alive."

Rask clapped her on the back, harder than necessary. "That's the spirit."

Mercy ducked through the doorway, detonator vanishing into a pocket. "Don't let Kye near the canister unless you want to see what's inside."

Doc lingered, eyes on the display. "I'll be in medbay. Let me know when it's time to triage."

Kye alone remained, gazing at their own image, as if committing the moment to memory. They smiled—small, enigmatic.

"Looks good on me," they murmured, and wandered off into the dark.

The ship, sensing their decision, upped the air circulation just enough to make it sound like a distant, contented sigh.

Outside, the Meridian powered on, sensors casting out like netted arms, searching for the next calamity.

The crew braced for impact, together in their mutual, catastrophic fate.

SIX

Rask called an emergency meeting at 07:00, which was promptly ignored by all parties except the coffee machine. Said machine sputtered to life, produced something the colour and viscosity of motor oil, and then, for reasons best left unexamined, attempted to self-clean with the same substance.

Mercy arrived first, mug in hand and ill-fitting pyjama bottoms tucked into regulation combat boots. She poured herself a generous helping of the machine's output, sniffed it, and announced: "Soup again." The smile didn't reach her eyes, which were rimmed with the alertness of someone who'd slept three hours and dreamt of gunfire.

Kye slouched in next, hoodie up, hands in pockets, gaze flicking from Mercy to the mess table and back as if deciding which was likelier to explode. They grabbed a ration bar, bit it in half, and then regarded the residue with genuine disappointment. "Textural abomination,"

Kye said, dropping the remainder into the nearest disposal chute. "That's not even food-adjacent."

Rask made a point of waiting until Lyra entered before starting. She did so on schedule, wiped her hands on a rag, and sat at the far end of the table with a portable console, never once looking up.

Rask stood at the head of the table, holding a battered clipboard for authority he didn't possess. "Alright, listen in. We've got a full-dress panic on our hands, so if you'd all kindly—"

"Soup's gone cold," Mercy observed, spoon suspended mid-air.

"—focus, please," Rask pressed on. "We're in the open, running with a manifest that's both illegal and clearly valuable. Someone wants it back. Kye, update."

Kye shrugged, the effect barely visible under the hoodie. "Ran a scan of the comms bands. Imperial channels are still hot, but we're below the noise floor. Nothing targeted, just lots of yelling."

"Good," said Rask. "Lyra, status?"

Lyra looked up, gaze flat and unfriendly. "Wiping the transponder now. If we don't want to get boarded, we need a new identity and at least six registry jumps between here and the last port." She tapped a few keys with surgical precision. "Assuming the navcore doesn't melt in the process."

Doc drifted in then, face sallow, hair damp from the chemical rinse he favoured over showers. He ignored the table entirely and gravitated to the open crate on the counter. The bio-canister inside pulsed, blue and steady. Doc regarded it the way a snake might regard a defanged rival: wary, but with a grudging respect. He reached out, patted the canister's ceramic shell, and flinched when it emitted a harmonic whine.

"Still alive in there," Doc muttered. "That's new. It's adapting."

Mercy shot the canister a finger-gun. "I call dibs if it hatches."

"Dibs on what?" asked Rask.

"The name."

"I've been calling it Glim." Kye said.

Doc deadpanned, "You named the potential bioweapon?"

Kye sipped their soup, pinkie up. "I name all the things that might kill me. It's polite."

Rask massaged his temples, but pressed on. "Doc, thoughts on what's inside?"

"Something sentient, or close enough. The harmonic emissions are—" Doc paused, checked the canister's glow, "—well, they're not random. I think it's communicating. With us, or with the ship. Possibly both."

Kye interjected, "That's very on-brand for our luck."

Rask set the clipboard down. "Alright. Agenda item two: we're officially pirates as of this morning. Lyra, is the new ID package ready?"

Lyra's fingers danced across her console. "Give me ten minutes. Might want to brace for a minor systems outage."

Kye folded their arms, reclined, and looked at Rask with an air of studied detachment. "Why not just embrace the pirate life? Register as a free agent, auction the crate to the highest bidder, and buy our own station. We're already on every watchlist."

Doc turned from the crate. "Because if you offer this up on the open market, you'll get assassins with better aim than Mercy. Or the Imperium just burns us out of existence. Neither is ideal."

Mercy set her mug down, hard enough to crack the handle. "I think we'd make legendary martyrs."

Kye grinned, teeth showing. "At least we'd be remembered."

Rask looked around the table and saw a crew not so much united as mutually attached by the consequences of their bad decisions. He tried for optimism. "Let's not die just yet. We can still find a buyer who doesn't want to wear us as jewellery."

"Or we could just dump the crate into the next star," Lyra said, not looking up.

Mercy considered. "But then Glim would be lonely."

Doc shook his head. "If the thing's influencing the ship, we might not be able to get rid of it. AI's been acting stranger every hour."

As if on cue, the intercom buzzed with a precision that was almost smug.

"Attention crew," the ship's voice announced, dulcet and implacable. "Long-range communications have been intercepted. Approaching vessel identified: vector two-four-six, closing at point oh-eight C. Estimated contact in seventy minutes."

Kye's smile died. "That's not cartel speed."

Lyra's hands froze over her console. "Military?"

"Unclear," the AI responded, still in that neutral,

infuriatingly calm voice. "Signature not in registry. Unauthorised and untagged. Suggest increased urgency in all activities."

Rask looked at the faces around the table, feeling the moment of brief, hopeless unity that occurred when everyone realised they might actually die together.

"Right," he said. "That's our cue. Lyra, dump the transponder now. Kye, prep decoys. Mercy—"

She was already gone, presumably to arm the explosives.

Doc stared into the blue-lit canister, expression soft with awe and resignation. "Glim's humming again," he said, and this time the tone was almost affectionate. "It's like it knows."

Rask didn't reply. He'd never found the right words for times like this, and suspected he never would.

In the silence that followed, the coffee machine groaned, sputtered, and died. Kye sipped their soup, frowned, and poured it down the sink.

The Meridian, for the first time since its theft, felt like a home: messy, inconvenient, and absolutely doomed.

Rask headed for the bridge, knowing the others would follow.

He doubted they'd get another meeting.

The Meridian's bridge was never designed for more than two, but in the next minute it hosted all five: Rask at the helm, Lyra hunched over engineering, Kye at the comms,

Doc carrying Glim with both hands like a newborn, and Mercy sprawled upside-down across the navigator's seat, feet drumming the air.

The AI's estimate of "seventy minutes to contact" had been a lie, or possibly a joke, as the unidentified vessel was now visible as a sharp, accelerating blip on the aft scan. Closer to thirty minutes, if they were lucky.

Rask didn't waste time with a preamble. "Lyra, spike the output—full dark on all nonessential systems. If they ping us, I want it to look like we're a dead hulk. Kye, prep a signal burst with a decoy burn. Doc, keep the canister out of sight."

Doc had already retreated into the shadow of the bulkhead, stroking Glim with absent, fretful devotion. The canister's blue pulse had become a slow, tremulous throb, and it now emitted the occasional, melodic chime. It sounded more sentient by the hour, which worried Doc and delighted Mercy, who had begun humming along to its notes.

Kye worked the comms with the lazy precision of someone who'd learned to type by hacking vending machines as a child. "I can spoof a distress signal, but they'll know it's a trick after twenty seconds. This isn't a salvage op, they're here for us."

Lyra's fingers blurred over the engineering panel. "They'll board, if they think we're hiding."

Rask grunted. "Then we let them board, but on our terms." He keyed the main weapons array, watched it flicker from 'Dormant' to 'Unreliable' to 'Active – Manual Only'. He'd have to fire them by hand, which he hadn't done since the Ceres job.

Mercy, now hanging fully upside-down and face flushed with blood, asked: "Can we greet them with soup?"

"Only if it's boiling," said Kye.

The bridge fell silent, the only sound the soft, increasingly complex harmony from the canister in Doc's arms. Rask checked the targeting array, saw that the incoming vessel—smaller, faster, and with an energy signature he recognised as ex-military—was burning hard for intercept.

"Registration's scrambled," Kye said, "but the drive signature is privateer. Could be anyone from bounty to freelance repo."

"Or both," said Lyra. "We have enemies enough for two crews."

Doc peeked over the crate. "If it's bounty, they'll want us alive."

Mercy's smile was luminous, as if she'd just received good news. "That's optimistic, Doc."

The blip on the screen grew, resolved into a ship with lines that were familiar in a way Rask wished they weren't. He flexed his jaw, flicked the array to passive, and waited. The comms panel lit up, offering an incoming hail.

Kye arched an eyebrow. "They're calling us. Shall I answer?"

Rask hesitated, just a second too long. "Do it. Speaker only."

Kye stabbed a button, and a voice poured into the bridge. It was crisp, lilted, and carried the clipped patience of someone who had rehearsed this speech in front of a mirror for several days.

"Unidentified vessel. This is the Seraphine, operating under private salvage authority. Your registry is invalid, and your course is in violation of Imperial no-fly protocols. Prepare for boarding."

Lyra exhaled, low and annoyed. "So much for stealth."

Mercy righted herself and began rummaging in a side compartment. "Shall I make tea for the visitors?"

Doc didn't move, just tightened his grip on Glim and muttered, "Don't let them near the canister. It's aware now."

Kye killed the comm. "If we run, they'll shoot. If we fight, we die faster. Any preferences?"

"Buy time," Rask said. He raked his fingers through his hair, fighting the old compulsion to look presentable for a court martial. "Let them think we're idiots or helpless. We might get lucky."

Mercy looked up, already assembling a tray with mismatched mugs. "Or we might get boarded by someone fun."

Kye and Lyra exchanged a look that was one third mutual respect, two thirds certainty of shared doom. Kye said, "Want me to reply?"

"Make it sound like we're in distress," Rask said. "But don't overdo it. We're not that good at acting."

Kye grinned. "You underestimate me," and hit transmit. Their voice emerged as a high, nasal whine: "Seraphine, we are...experiencing total systems failure.

Crew incapacitated. Request medical assistance and mercy. Please respond."

Mercy's mug rattled with laughter. "A plus."

Lyra rolled her eyes, but her hands never stopped recalibrating the ship's power grid. "They're decelerating. We'll have five minutes of grace before they dock."

Doc's gaze never left the canister, which now pulsed in time with the ship's failing heartbeat. "It's broadcasting," he said. "I can feel it."

Kye's eyes narrowed. "Can you shut it up?"

Doc looked genuinely hurt. "She's not a liability."

"She's a homing beacon," Lyra shot back.

Rask closed his eyes, counted to three. "Doc, take Glim to the lower bay. Mercy, go with. If they board, stall them."

Mercy saluted with the mug. "You got it, cap'n." She grabbed Doc by the elbow and hauled him down the corridor with the force of a mid-sized bulldozer.

The bridge felt emptier, somehow, without them. Rask eyed the screen, watched the Seraphine slide into close formation. Her hull was bone-white and spotless, crewed by people who'd been paid not just to kill, but to make it look good on camera.

Kye's console flashed. "They're cycling a new hail. This one's encrypted."

Rask nodded. "Patch it through to private."

He expected a voice. Instead, the screen flickered, shimmered, and resolved into a face he hadn't seen in years.

The breath went out of Rask like a plug had been pulled. The woman on the screen looked unchanged:

sharp nose, dark eyes, and a hairline that had always been on the winning end of a genetic arms race. Her smile was small and razor-thin, the kind you get from cutting deals or throats.

She said, "Hello, Rask. Still stealing things you don't understand?"

Lyra's jaw dropped. Kye whistled, long and low.

Rask kept his face blank. "Vexa. You never did know how to knock."

She laughed, light and cold. "Why waste the effort? You're never dressed for company."

Lyra leaned over the console. "You two know each other?"

Rask didn't answer. Kye did it for him: "She's the reason he can't go near the Core systems anymore."

Vexa's eyebrows twitched. "Word travels fast in the Out."

Rask found his voice. "You're not working for salvage. What do you want?"

Vexa's smile grew by a nanometre. "What do you think? That ship, and everything on it. You. Preferably alive, but I'm not picky."

Kye muted the audio. "On a scale of one to ten, how bad is this?"

"Eleven," Rask said.

Lyra nodded, already compiling a mental list of all the things that could be turned into bombs in under five minutes. "We can't outgun them. Maybe we can out-think them."

Vexa waited, patient, as if she could hear their panic through the void. When Kye restored the audio, she said,

"Your comms are laughably porous, Rask. Surrender and I'll make it quick."

Mercy's voice came through the corridor, slightly muffled: "Shall I put the kettle on for your ex, cap'n?"

Kye suppressed a snort. Rask ignored it.

He said, "If you're after the canister, you're already dead."

Vexa's eyes flicked sideways, just for a fraction of a second. "So, you do know what it is."

Rask shrugged, made it look easy. "No one knows what it is. That's the problem."

Lyra's panel pinged a warning: Seraphine had begun docking procedures, latching to the hull with enough force to shudder the deck plates.

Kye hissed, "We're breached in four points. They're sending a team."

Rask looked at Lyra, at Kye, and finally at the blank wall behind the viewscreen. He weighed the odds, found them wanting, and grinned despite it.

"Let's make this as expensive as possible," he said.

Lyra armed the anti-boarding charges. "Aye, cap'n."

Kye rerouted all the security cameras to loop a twenty-second reel of empty corridors. "Shall I tell them we're already dead?"

"Only if you want them to hurry."

Onscreen, Vexa's smile flickered, replaced by a look of honest anticipation. "I'm coming over, Rask. Try not to disappoint me."

The feed cut. The silence that followed was edged with the knowledge that, of all possible ship-to-ship encounters in the Out, this was the one Rask would have chosen least.

He glanced at Lyra, who had set the panel to cycle through every lockdown protocol she could find.

Kye was already at the hatch, holding a small, ugly knife and wearing the expression of someone about to lose a bet.

In the lower bay, Doc and Mercy huddled over Glim, which now shone like a beacon, blue as birth, its song rising into a keen that made the hull vibrate.

The AI's voice, so calm it bordered on smug, said: "Assessment protocol requires confrontation. Survival likelihood: seventeen percent. Please enjoy the remainder of your time aboard the Meridian."

No one responded. It was the best offer they'd had all day.

Lyra locked down the bridge, then looked at Rask, her voice unusually gentle.

"You alright?"

Rask nodded. "Old ghosts. Never as dead as you hope."

Kye rolled their eyes. "Let's make some new ones."

They braced, together, for the next phase.

Outside, the Seraphine gleamed, ready to finish what it started. Inside, the crew of the Meridian clung to their poor odds and worse plan, determined to go out not with a whimper, but with an appropriately theatrical bang.

SEVEN

The first sound was the hiss of the docking umbilical sealing—a reptilian exhalation that carried through the Meridian's hull and up Rask's vertebrae, one deliberate notch at a time. In the mid-ship hold, where the parley was to take place, condensation shivered along the deck seams. The air, already thick with refrigerant leaks and old sweat, stilled itself in anticipation.

Mercy was the first to move, prowling the perimeter with her favourite grenade in one hand and her eyes already rolling at the concept of negotiation. Lyra stood with arms folded across her battered fatigues, planted at the end of the loading ramp, a posture that said "access denied" in every known dialect. Doc positioned himself behind the diplomatic crate, not hiding—just treating the polycarbonate sarcophagus like a patient in need of vigilant supervision. Kye loitered near the bulkhead, hands in pockets, body language a case study in plausible deniability.

The rest of the ship's lights had gone to emergency

red, but the hold's was a weird blue. The effect was funereal, if funerals ever happened in iceboxes and involved more standoffs than speeches.

The umbilical disengaged with a thunk, followed by the pneumatic shuffle of boots on deck. Vexa Ryne entered with two lieutenants, each a monument to Imperial augmentation: glossy subdermal armour, precision gait, faces smoothed by at least a decade of elective surgery. The first—tall, pale, male—scanned the room with IR-sensitive lenses that flared when they landed on Mercy. The second was shorter and built like a siege weapon, skin dark and spattered with the tell-tale lines of myomer thread. Both wore the same uniform: bodyglove, two visible weapons, and expressions several grades below bored.

Vexa herself wore the same black, high-collared coat Rask remembered from three years prior, but the face above it had grown sharper and meaner, as if time and spite had teamed up to file it down to essentials. She let the air hang for a beat before stepping fully inside, her boots making no sound at all on the composite deck.

She stopped three metres from Rask, hands in the pockets of her coat, head cocked in exaggerated survey.

"Rask," she said, "still alive. That's... remarkable."

He smiled, small and uneven. "Vexa. Can't say I missed your sense of drama."

She took in the hold with a sweep of her eyes, then grimaced at the blue-lit crate. "You always did have a weakness for objects of questionable value."

"Occupational hazard," Rask replied, standing perfectly still. His right hand, unseen, drummed three fingers against his thigh. The rhythm was supposed to keep him calm; it didn't.

Vexa's lieutenants peeled off, one to each side, adopting what must have been a textbook pincer stance. She ignored them. "I see you've upgraded your security since last time," she said, with a nod at Mercy.

Mercy responded by baring her teeth and twirling the grenade. "Your threat assessment is flattering," she intoned, voice monotone. "But if you try anything, I'll redecorate the hold with your lungs."

The taller lieutenant smirked, but Vexa didn't look away from Rask.

"Why the meeting, then?" she asked. "Why not just run, like you always do?"

He shrugged. "I've picked up a distaste for wasting energy. Besides, I thought you'd enjoy the spectacle."

She allowed herself a thin smile, then walked a slow, elliptical arc around the crate, pausing just long enough to eye Lyra, who did not return the courtesy.

"Your engineer looks tense," Vexa observed.

"She hates being interrupted," Rask replied.

Lyra said nothing. The look on her face suggested she was plotting at least three methods of murder using just the crate's fasteners and her own kneecaps.

Vexa completed the circuit and came to rest directly in front of the crate, placing both hands flat on the lid. "So, this is what all the fuss is about."

Doc cleared his throat, gentle and tired. "Don't touch. She's—" He searched for a word, found none, and settled for, "—temperamental."

Vexa looked at Doc as if noticing a stain on her cuff. "I know what's inside. More or less."

Mercy, behind her, began a low, steady chant: "threat, threat, threat, threat..." It started as a whisper, but every repetition notched the volume up, as if she were tuning herself for violence.

Vexa ignored her.

"I want the crate," she said, "and I'm authorised to take it by any means I find... amusing."

"You'll have to kill us first," Lyra said, voice cold as the hold.

Vexa tapped the lid twice, almost kindly. "That can be arranged, but I'd rather not. Too much mess."

Kye disengaged from the wall, hands still pocketed, and stepped into the shallow circle of blue light. "You've done the maths. So have we. Stand-off ends with two crews dead, crate probably compromised, and no one cashing out." Their eyes flicked over Vexa's lieutenants, mapped their angles, then returned to Vexa herself. "There's a better deal."

Vexa looked at Kye, then at Rask, then back at Kye. "Let me guess—split the proceeds and go our separate ways?"

Kye shrugged. "Or get creative. The buyers you want are tracking this already. The cartel will pay more if they see your name on the manifest. The Imperium wants deniability, which means they want the crate lost, not found. You could retire off the margins, if you're careful."

Vexa didn't laugh, but her eyes narrowed in appreciation. "You're a smart one. I like you. Most of the time, I have to peel the brain from the crew and force-feed it to the others."

Kye smiled, shallow and reptilian. "I'm adaptable."

Mercy's chant had reached a conversational level. "Threat. Threat. Threat. Threat." The taller lieutenant risked a look over his shoulder, then immediately regretted it.

Rask made a show of relaxing his shoulders. "You can have the crate," he said, with the confidence of a man whose entire hand consisted of one face card and a handful of IOUs. "But only if you let us walk. No tricks, no tails."

Vexa's hand traced a lazy circle on the crate's surface. "How can I trust you?"

"You can't," Rask said. "But we both know how this works. Mutual benefit and all that."

Vexa considered. "What's to stop me from just shooting you now?"

He met her eyes. "Same thing as always. Cost-benefit analysis. You kill us, you'll have to carry the crate on your own. And with what's inside—" he nodded at the container, "—that's a big risk for a small return."

She didn't respond at once. Instead, she turned to Lyra. "What do you think, engineer? Am I being played?"

Lyra's answer was a minimalist masterwork. "No."

Vexa considered this, then looked back at Rask. "If I say yes, what's your next move?"

"Jump to somewhere no one's ever heard of," Rask said. "Become irrelevant."

For a second, it looked like Vexa might just take the

offer. Her fingers drummed a pattern on the crate, rhythmically offbeat. The blue light reflected in her eyes, turning them the colour of bruised fruit.

Behind her, Mercy's chant escalated: "THREAT THREAT THREAT THREAT—"

Doc, who had until now remained a nonentity, reached into a wall cabinet, pulled out a thermal blanket, and draped it over the crate in a motion so gentle it read as deliberate insult. Vexa's eyes flicked to the movement, but she let it happen.

"Fine," she said. "Here's my offer: You leave. I take the crate. No pursuit, no comms, and if I ever see your crew again, I'll airlock you on sight."

Rask nodded. "Agreed."

She smiled. "Just like that?"

Rask spread his hands. "I'm not a monster, Vexa. I just want to survive."

"See that you do," she replied.

The agreement, if you could call it that, hung in the air like a static charge. Vexa motioned to her lieutenants, and they stepped forward, each unshouldering a pack with the muscle memory of soldiers trained to seize and hold.

The crew watched, no one breathing.

Mercy, finally, went silent.

Vexa turned to go, then stopped at the ramp. She looked over her shoulder, a flicker of something—maybe disappointment, maybe respect—passing over her face.

"You could have made more trouble," she said.

Rask gave her the smallest of shrugs. "I'm getting old."

Vexa smiled. This time, it was genuine.

And then she was gone, her lieutenants following, the crate between them like a pallbearer's prize.

The umbilical cycled shut. The hiss of departure was louder than the arrival. Rask let himself collapse against the nearest wall, skin clammy with adrenaline.

Lyra spoke first. "She'll come back."

"Not for a while," Rask said, already mourning the crate.

Kye checked the sensors, watched the blip that was Vexa's ship recede. "She's not even masking the trajectory."

Doc folded the thermal blanket, fingers shaking, and tucked it into a bin. "She's right about the trouble," he said. "We could have made a lot more."

Mercy grinned, all teeth. "We can still try."

Rask shook his head, but the thought lingered. "Maybe next time."

They stood in silence, the four of them, each lost in their own equations.

Outside, the stars carried on as if nothing had happened.

Inside, the Meridian powered down to blue.

Lyra had locked herself in engineering and would not respond to knocks, comms, or Mercy's increasingly creative threats. Doc sat in the medbay, mending an old wound and ignoring the newer ones. Rask kept to the bridge, rerouting every system through manual while reading and re-reading the subtext of Vexa's last words.

It was Kye who broke the silence. They ghosted into the cockpit, hands empty, face unreadable, and watched Rask pilot for a minute before speaking.

"She's not gone," Kye said.

Rask didn't look up from the controls. "No. She's waiting."

Kye took the other seat, sprawled in a posture that looked accidental but put every major system within easy reach. "She left a tap on the AI. It's inert, but if I poke it, she'll know our location within two jumps."

"Don't poke it."

"I'd never," Kye said, and somehow managed to mean it.

For a long while, they just watched the nav screen, which displayed a single cold trajectory curving away from the last habitable system for lightyears in any direction.

In the medbay, Glim—the canister, the artefact, the unreason—began to thrum. It started at the edge of sensation, a subtle vibration that made every hair on Doc's arms rise, then ramped up to a full-on tactile buzz. The blue glow, previously ambient, started to strobe at three-second intervals.

Doc stared at it, then at the med scanner, which recorded a steady uptick in energy output and, less helpfully, a rising trend in "behavioural agitation." He flicked on the internal comm.

"It's spiking," he said. "If you're planning to throw this overboard, now is the hour. If she hadn't already figured out there was nothing in the crate, she'll know it now."

Lyra's voice, deadpan as ever, came through the speaker. "Jettisoning the canister would depressurise half the bay and kill everyone within forty metres."

Doc considered this. "I'm not seeing a downside."

Mercy, who had camped herself outside the medbay with a sandwich and a plasma pistol, called out: "Can I come in, or is it gonna blow?"

Doc unlocked the hatch, and Mercy slunk in, chewing thoughtfully.

She regarded the artifact with professional curiosity. "What happens if you shoot it?"

Doc shrugged. "Best case, nothing. Worst case, a containment breach."

Mercy smiled. "So, probably not shooting it."

"Not today," said Doc.

At the same moment, the ship's ambient lighting cut from blue to bone-white, then back again. The engines stuttered. Every system warning sounded at once.

Rask straightened in the pilot chair. "She's here."

Kye tapped the comm, voice low. "Inbound transmission, local. Encryption is old military, but the packet's tagged with her biometric."

Rask closed his eyes, then opened them, resigned. "Patch it."

Vexa's voice, flawless and unhurried, filled the bridge. "Thought I'd offer you one last chance to reconsider."

Rask resisted the urge to break something. "We're not reconsidering."

A dry laugh. "I assumed as much. Enjoy your next five minutes."

The comm went dead.

Rask looked at Kye. "How close is she?"

"Thirty seconds to intercept, assuming she's not masking."

Rask hit the emergency comm. "Everyone to the hold. Now."

Mercy and Doc were already halfway there. Lyra emerged from engineering, grease smeared down her jaw, wrench in hand.

"Status?" she snapped.

Rask ran, arriving just as the Seraphine's airlock began to mate with the hull. "She's going to board. Same as before."

Lyra checked Glim's status, then glanced at Mercy. "Plan?"

Mercy grinned. "Shoot everyone except us."

"Works for me," Lyra muttered.

The inner lock cycled. The temperature in the hold plummeted, visible frost spreading along the deck plates. Glim's pulse doubled, becoming a subsonic rumble that set everyone's teeth on edge.

Doc wrapped his arms around the canister, voice hoarse. "It's responding to stress. If it breaches—"

"Don't let it breach," Lyra said.

The lock blew open. Vexa stepped through, alone this time, with her hands held wide in a parody of surrender. She smiled at Rask, then at Mercy, and finally at Kye, who had moved to a higher position behind a cargo net.

"Nice to see everyone together," Vexa said. "Let's

make this simple. Give me what you removed from the crate. Now."

Rask put himself between her and Glim. "You're not taking it."

She tutted, shaking her head. "You always did have a hero complex."

Mercy's plasma pistol whined as she charged it. "Threat," she said, voice back to monotone. "Threat. Threat."

Vexa ignored her, eyes fixed on Rask. "Don't be stupid. You know how this ends."

He did. That was the worst part.

From the corridor, one of Vexa's lieutenants lurched in, face contorted with effort. His left arm hung useless, the myomer webbing beneath the skin twitching in furious, independent spasms. The blue from Glim's crate licked across his face in pulses.

"Captain—" he tried, but collapsed before he could finish.

Vexa turned, lips pressed thin. "Get up."

He didn't. Instead, he began to convulse, metal and bone scraping the deck in a slow, ugly rhythm.

Kye's voice, flat, drifted from above. "It's hacking him. Or something like it."

Doc, sweating now, tried to angle Glim away from the commotion. "It's never done that before."

Lyra cursed and grabbed a fire suppressor, pointing it at the downed lieutenant. "If it goes full, I'm icing him."

Vexa's hands flicked to her sidearm. "This was your fault, Rask."

Rask shook his head. "You brought him here."

Glim's blue radiance peaked, then shifted into the ultraviolet. The temperature dropped again, hard. Everyone exhaled visible mist.

The second lieutenant, standing at the threshold, doubled over and began to bleed from the nose, then the eyes. He said nothing, just collapsed into a foetal curl.

Mercy stepped forward, pistol raised. "You want it, you go through us."

Vexa levelled her own weapon at Mercy, then—almost lazily—shot the fire suppressor out of Lyra's hands.

For one perfect second, everyone stood in tableau: Rask poised, Mercy grinning, Lyra furious, Doc shielding Glim, Kye observing, Vexa at the centre.

Kye's voice, clear and calm: "You should run, Vexa."

Vexa's eyes flicked up. "Why?"

Kye smiled. "Because if you don't, we're all dead."

Vexa's finger tightened on the trigger.

Rask lunged for the manual override hidden beneath the nav panel. He'd found it in the ship's code, a failsafe left by the Meridian's previous owner—a last-resort protocol to rid the vessel of hostile boarders.

He punched the sequence. The ship's systems screamed, then dropped to black. The only light left was Glim's blue corona, which now strobed so hard it left afterimages. The deck vibrated, then shuddered, then ripped itself open with a sound like God losing a bet.

The hold filled with a high, rising tone—a harmonic that bypassed ears and vibrated the skull.

Vexa turned to shoot, but her arm seized mid-motion. Mercy screamed and kept firing, though every bolt arced away from Vexa and into the air, like the ship itself was refusing to let her hit the mark.

The lieutenant on the floor seized, eyes rolled back. Lyra tried to drag Doc away from Glim, but his fingers locked, refusing to let go.

Rask hit the second trigger. The emergency teleport —an ugly, untested hack of the ship's own AI—activated. There was a pop, a pneumatic hiss, and then a detonation of blue fire.

Vexa and her crew vanished, leaving behind a stink of ozone and the faintest echo of the harmonic.

Silence fell, hard and absolute.

Mercy slumped to her knees, shaking.

Kye swung down from the cargo net, breathing hard. "Did it work?"

Rask's hands trembled on the panel. "It worked."

Lyra knelt beside Doc, who was now breathing, but barely. "Where did they go?"

Doc scanned the internal sensors, then the external. "Not on this ship. Maybe on hers."

Rask leaned back against the bulkhead, adrenaline crashing out of his system all at once. "God save her."

"God save Kye, too," Lyra said, voice brittle.

They all looked at the spot where Kye had been standing moments before.

The comm chimed.

Kye, still smiling, tapped the panel. Their own face appeared onscreen, looking slightly more alive than it had any right to.

"Hello, friends," said Kye, voice coming from ship's audio "Looks like I'm on the Seraphine."

In the background, Vexa raged, the open crate pulsing at her side.

"She's not happy," Kye said. "But I guess she needs me for leverage. I don't think she'll shoot me just yet."

Doc grinned, teeth pink from the stress. "Well done."

Mercy stood up, dusted herself off, and said, "I still want to shoot her."

Lyra leaned against the wall, exhaustion catching up. "You will. Give it time."

Rask looked at the screen, at Kye's face—alive, defiant, and for the first time, genuinely pleased.

"Don't die," he said.

Kye's smile sharpened. "Wouldn't dream of it."

Outside, the Seraphine powered up, blue-white and angry, and the Meridian turned its nose to the dark.

They left the system at burn, one ship chasing the other, both pulsing with improbable blue.

Rask slumped into the pilot chair, felt Lyra and Mercy and Doc settle around him, and exhaled.

He watched the new trajectory plot itself—blind, stupid, hopeful.

"Next time," he said, "we don't take jobs with containers."

Mercy grinned. "Next time, we shoot first."

Lyra wiped a line of grease off her cheek. "Next time, we win."

The ship ran silent, the universe uncaring.

But they were still moving, and for now, that was enough.

EIGHT

The Meridian listed, moaned, and farted its way through hyperspace with a dignity best described as hypothetical. Most of the internal diagnostics panels had defaulted to "Unfixable" or, occasionally, "It's fine, probably", and the faint red emergency lighting had become a sort of ship-wide lifestyle choice. The forward view port, spider-webbed by the recent encounter with the Seraphine, offered a jaundiced view of the void.

Lyra surveyed the bridge with the expression of a person who had not only seen this coming, but felt personally insulted that no one else had. She stood, arms folded, the sleeves of her shirt permanently dark with engine oil. The right knee of her trousers had bled a little from the day's attempts to wrangle the hyperdrive, but she had staunched it with electrical tape and anger.

Rask occupied the captain's chair with the air of someone who had been told, repeatedly, not to touch the red button and had subsequently lost several fingers. He stared straight ahead, jaw clenched, thumbs digging into the arms of the seat with white-knuckled determination. The only thing about him that didn't scream "reckless failure of a leader" was his refusal to blink.

Mercy had commandeered the entire starboard wall, pacing like a caged hyena, boots squeaking at exactly the point where it would annoy everyone most. She twirled a bulkhead rivet between her fingers, occasionally flicking it at the comms display in a way that suggested the game had rules only she understood.

Doc lurked in the hatchway, hunched over a medical kit as if it contained not so much medicine as hope. He ran a thumb along the synth-leather of a splint, eyes darting between Lyra and Rask, then out the viewport, as if to confirm that yes, space was still there and no, it had not yet produced an escape hatch for him personally.

The bridge smelled of sweat, cheap antiseptic, and the half-melted circuitry that lined every seam.

Lyra broke the silence, voice as sharp and brittle as a snapped cable. "Remind me again what part of the plan involved handing over our only leverage and a crewmember to a fascist with a grudge?"

Mercy stopped dead, mid-pace, and pointed a lazy finger at Rask. "His part."

Rask exhaled, hard. "You want to do this now?"

Doc raised a hand, as if waiting to be called on. "If I may, the bleeding hasn't quite stopped in the crew quarters, and Mercy's therapy puppy is getting restless. Perhaps we could... de-escalate?"

Lyra ignored him, eyes boring into Rask. "She took Kye. You just let her."

"She was going to take Glim, or the ship, or both. Kye bought us time."

"Oh, brilliant," said Lyra. "We'll send them a nice card from the future, assuming they still have a head."

Mercy clapped, slow and sarcastic. "Can we get back to the part where we shoot someone? I vote we start with the boss."

"Sit down, Mercy," said Rask, without heat.

Mercy didn't, but she did stop pacing. She leaned against the comms panel, one boot up, arms folded. "I'll sit when you say something not completely idiotic."

Rask looked at Lyra. "We're going after them."

The silence that followed was almost sweet, in the way that seeing your tormentor get hit by a bus is sweet.

Lyra's arms remained folded, but her shoulders loosened half a degree. "You've got a plan?"

Doc snorted. "Oh, good."

Rask ignored him. "Vexa's ship runs hot but runs old. I can get us within boarding range, provided the drive doesn't fall off before we get there."

Mercy brightened. "So, we are shooting her."

"We're not shooting anyone yet," Rask said. "We're fixing the drive, first. Then we work out how to get Kye off the Seraphine without being atomised."

Mercy slumped back, but the smile didn't die. "Two out of three's not bad."

Lyra's face shifted, fractionally, from "imminent violence" to "possible constructive action." She glanced at Doc. "You got enough stimulants to keep me awake for a day?"

Doc, visibly relieved to have a clear problem,

rummaged in the kit and produced a patch. "You want fast or slow?"

"Give me both."

He peeled the adhesive, pressed it to Lyra's wrist. "You'll be able to taste time in ten minutes."

Mercy whistled. "Never gets old."

Lyra flexed her hand and set about recalibrating the auxiliary nav system, which had, until this moment, been running a cryptic subroutine that alternately rerouted power to the espresso machine and purged the life support cycling every three hours.

The ship's AI, which had spent the last few cycles in an apparent sulk, chose this moment to break its silence. "Drive performance is operating at two standard deviations below recommended threshold. Would you like to schedule a controlled burn, or shall I improvise?"

"Improvise and you're getting your logic tree pruned," Lyra muttered.

Mercy patted the console. "Don't listen to her. You're doing fine."

The AI's voice took on a slightly aggrieved tone. "Noted."

Doc edged further into the bridge, sat on the arm of the least-wrecked chair, and opened his field scanner. He aimed it, unnecessarily, at Rask. "Blood pressure's up. You should lie down."

"Later," said Rask. "If you're not doing anything else, go check the hold. See if Glim is... still contained."

Doc blinked, surprised at being trusted with a task, then gathered his bag and drifted out, muttering about "emotional deflection as a leadership style."

The door slid shut, and Mercy immediately dropped the rivet she'd been toying with down the back of Rask's seat. He glared, but she grinned, unaffected. "What's the real plan?"

Rask took his time answering. "There's a relay outpost in the Perseus gutter. Old friend runs the dock. Name's Marnix. He owes me three favours and a pair of hands. If we make it there, we get the drive patched, and maybe a code to spoof Vexa's security net."

Lyra frowned, "Marnix is a criminal."

"He's a mechanic with a flexible attitude."

She leaned in, voice low. "He's a thief."

Rask shrugged. "Aren't we all?"

Mercy looked delighted. "I say we do it. Worst case, we get a new crew out of the deal."

Lyra glared at her, then at Rask. "Fine. But if you get us killed, I'm going to spend the afterlife haunting your pet cat."

"I don't have a cat."

"You will," said Lyra. "And it'll hate you."

Mercy started pacing again, only now she recited under her breath: "Rescue, Annihilate, Tea. Rescue, Annihilate, Tea."

Rask set a new heading, eyes flicking over the console for the sweet spot between "efficient" and "undetectable." The ship responded, not with joy, but with a sort of resigned groan that could have meant "understood" or "fuck off." He didn't care which.

In the cargo hold, the containment unit pulsed, soft blue light seeping through the ventilation slits. The hum was steady, rhythmic, almost gentle. Doc knelt beside it, scanner open, recording every flux and minute temperature shift. He muttered, "You're too quiet. That's worrying."

The canister pulsed again, and for the briefest moment, the light inside resolved into a shape—rounded, featureless, but undeniably organic. Doc pressed closer, nearly nose-to-metal, and whispered, "Are you listening?"

A second hum, slightly higher, answered him. Doc felt the hair on his arms stand up. He checked the scanner: nothing but the same repeating pattern.

He smiled, despite himself. "You're smarter than the rest of them put together, aren't you?"

The canister responded with a single, long glow, then dimmed.

Doc leaned back on his heels, considered whether this was the beginning of a medical issue or the solution to all their problems, and decided to say nothing to anyone until the facts arranged themselves in a less sinister order.

He patted the lid, stood, and headed back to the bridge.

As he left, the containment unit hummed, slow and patient. Waiting.

Threshold Station looked like the inside of an abandoned printer, if the printer had been run for centuries on a diet of battery acid, underfunding, and unspeakable hygiene. The docking clamps bit down with a teeth-rattling crunch, then promptly sagged as if exhausted by the effort. The Meridian's airlock aligned to a hatch adorned with three layers of warning tape and a handwritten "DO NOT LICK" sign, the paint long ago dissolved by something organic and malicious.

Lyra was first to cycle the lock, stepping onto the station with a tactical roll of her shoulders that doubled as a warning to every life form within range. The station's main concourse ran on half-light, and what little illumination there was flickered with the uneven pulse of a dying insect. The air was humid and tinged with the smell of recycled sewage, but Lyra had been in worse, and her nose was too broken to bother with complaints.

Rask followed, Mercy close behind, and Doc a careful three steps back, as if the station might lunge at him if he appeared too confident. The corridor floor was sticky and patched in places with foamcrete and slabs of upcycled hull plating. Above, a haphazard ceiling of wire bundles and fluid conduits drooped like the intestines of a giant animal.

Marnix waited in Bay Three, flanked by two power loaders and the wreckage of a flight deck that had not seen an actual flight since before Lyra's birth. The man himself was as subtle as ever: six-foot-six, with a chest that had been rebuilt more often than the station's power grid, and two eyes that rotated at different speeds in their sockets. He grinned, spread his arms wide, and enveloped Rask in a bear hug that suggested either deep affection or a plot to snap his spine.

"Helvan!" boomed Marnix, voice echoing off the bulkheads with the force of an incoming shell. "Didn't think you had the nerve to come back here after last time."

Rask wriggled free, keeping his hands visible. "You said you owed me a favour."

Marnix wiped his palms on his coveralls—black, but no longer recognisable as such—and gestured at the Meridian with a sweeping motion. "Something of an upgrade for you. I assume you won her fair and square?"

"She's got issues," Rask said.

Marnix cackled. "Who doesn't?"

Mercy edged around a pile of spent coolant cartridges and cocked her head at the nearest loader. "Nice rig. It armoured, or just ugly?"

Marnix waggled his eyebrows—one artificial, the other tattooed on—and winked at her. "Why not both? You must be the muscle."

"Mostly violence against lifeforms," Mercy agreed. "Some property damage."

Lyra suppressed a sigh and glanced at Doc, who was already sneaking glances at the wall-mounted first aid kits, visibly rating their contents for triage potential.

Marnix led them into a side office that consisted of three welded benches, an upended crate for a table, and a comms panel permanently stuck to the weather channel for Titan's north pole. He dropped onto the crate, legs splayed, and gestured the others to sit.

"Let's not waste time, Helvan," he said. "You need the drive patched, you want the navigation unlocked, and you're desperate enough to come to me for help. Am I close?"

"Dead on," Rask said, sitting opposite.

Mercy took a spot on a bench, Doc hovered near the door, and Lyra stayed standing, arms crossed. Marnix's left eye locked onto Rask; the right spun idly, tracking Mercy, then Lyra, then back again.

He steepled his fingers. "I can do it. But it's a rush job, and you're short on credit. So we do it old-school: favour for a favour."

Lyra's lips twitched. "We're not smuggling your drugs."

Marnix snorted. "Boring. That's for children and accountants. What I need is a shipment delivered: one crate, sealed, no scans, no questions. Take it two sectors up, hand it off, take the payment and I'll fix your ship. Nothing dangerous, nothing illegal. On paper."

Mercy leaned forward, all fake innocence. "It's weapons, isn't it?"

Marnix's grin widened. "It's imperial rations."

Rask looked at Lyra. "You fix the ship, we deliver the crate?"

Marnix held up both hands. "You're in and out in a day. I don't trust anyone else with this. Too many eyes on the routes lately."

Doc finally spoke, voice low and dry. "And if someone does scan it?"

"Then you run," said Marnix, as if it were the most obvious thing in the world.

The crew exchanged glances, a whole conversation's worth of calculation compressed into three seconds of silence.

Lyra broke it, tone flat. "We're not smugglers."

"We're whatever keeps us in the air," said Rask.

Doc looked at the floor, then back at Rask. "This is how people end up in body bags."

Mercy thumped the bench with one boot. "So? Last job put us on every bounty board in the sector. May as well enjoy the perks."

Rask turned back to Marnix. "What do we do with the payment?"

"Keep it, it's just a courtesy exchange. My buyer has already paid in full."

"Fine. We'll do it."

Marnix's eyes sparkled—both of them, for once. "Good lad." He reached below the desk, hauled out a sealed case marked with so many fake labels it practically confessed its own guilt. "Why don't you boys and girls take a load off in the bar. Your ship will be ready in two hours."

"Fine," Lyra said. "I could do with a drink."

Marnix clapped his hands and barked out a laugh. "That's the spirit." He leaned in, voice dropping half a register. "Don't look inside. Don't think about it. It's easier for everyone."

Mercy reached over, took the case by the handle, and hoisted it with a grunt. "Light for a bomb."

Marnix winked, which was technically impressive given his right eyelid was a patch of chrome. "Good luck, crew."

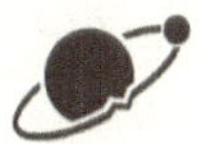

The walk back to the Meridian after the bar was short and silent, broken only by the soft whine of the case's internal sealant cycling every twelve seconds. Mercy carried it like a sacred offering. Lyra led the way, body language broadcasting "do not approach" in all directions.

Good to his word, Marnix had rustled up a crew to fix the hyperdrive. The Meridian still had a list of faults as long as Rask's arm, but at least they could jump without there being a fifty-fifty chance of cataclysmic death.

Once on board, Lyra bolted the hatch and ran a full diagnostic on the case. "No radioactive spikes," she said. "Not even explosives. Might be food."

Doc snorted. "Or a toxin you can eat."

Mercy shrugged and stowed the crate under the mess hall bench. "If it's dangerous, we'll find out before anyone else."

The ship's AI chimed in, sweet and insidious: "Delivery has been pre-registered. Optimal jump vector calculated. Would you like to depart, or shall I improvise a local scandal?"

Lyra answered, "Set the course, but keep it dark."

"Affirmative," said the AI, with an undertone that could have been glee.

Rask took the pilot chair, eyes hollow with fatigue, but his voice held together. "All set?"

Lyra checked her boards. "As ready as we'll ever be."

Mercy grinned. "What's next, cap'n?"

"Now," said Rask, "we run the delivery. Then we rescue Kye."

Doc's face was unreadable, but his hands shook a

little as he strapped in. "If the shipment's legit, maybe we'll survive the week."

Lyra muttered, "If it's not, at least we'll go out in style."

Mercy cackled. "I'll bring the fireworks."

The Meridian undocked, its drives howling with protest but catching the thread of escape like a fish on a line. As they cleared Threshold's gravity well, the AI interrupted again.

"Proximity alert. Unauthorised vessel entering system. Registration: Seraphine. Estimated arrival, fifty-two minutes."

No one spoke for a moment. Then Rask said, "Well, shit."

Lyra's hands tightened on the controls. "They're early."

Doc fumbled for his medkit, knuckles white. "We can still make the jump."

Mercy checked the sidearm in her boot, face alive with the prospect of violence. "Or we can let them chase us. Make it a game."

Rask exhaled, set his jaw, and nudged the throttle.

"Game on," he said.

The Meridian lurched, groaned, and vanished into the black, leaving Threshold and all its rot behind. For the first time in hours, the crew found a rhythm—messy, tense, but theirs.

In the cargo hold, Glim pulsed softly, keeping time for a song no one knew the words to yet.

NINE

The Meridian vibrated at a frequency that Rask Helvan now identified with stress, malice, or both. In the mess hall, the ship's crew engaged in its second-favourite pastime: escalation by committee.

Rask leaned in the hatchway, arms folded, and ran the crew like a jury. "We get in, we make the drop, we get Kye back." He let the words hang, heavy as vacuum.

Doc hunched over a datapad, his left hand absently massaging a stress kink in his jaw. He was supposed to be monitoring the drop coordinates, but his gaze kept drifting to the table, where Glim's bio-canister now sat openly. The container pulsed in a slow, deliberate rhythm. At regular intervals, it shivered in place, as if something inside was pressing against the wall.

Mercy sprawled in the nearest chair, legs up, cleaning her pistol with the zeal of a priest oiling a sacrificial blade. "Why run?" she said. "Weapons-grade diplomacy. We show up with the canister and guns, then see who blinks."

Rask did not sigh, but his next inhale was a knife in the ribcage. "You're all heart, Mercy."

Mercy smirked, unimpressed. "And here I thought you hired me for my negotiation skills."

The pulse from Glim's container intensified. Doc's brow furrowed. He reached out and, with the hesitant curiosity of someone who'd once been bitten by a medical drone, prodded the casing. The blue light flickered in response, then dimmed to sullen normalcy.

Lyra turned on Rask, hands on hips. "You want to get Kye back. That's personal. But we don't owe them more than we owe ourselves."

Rask stared through her, teeth clenched. "We're not discussing this. We do the drop. We get Kye."

Lyra shot a look at Doc, hoping for support. Doc pretended to focus on the nav coordinates, but his eyes were nowhere near the screen.

Mercy's feet hit the floor. "Fine. But if anyone looks at me wrong, I'm emptying the mag."

"Noted," said Rask. He straightened, jaw set so hard it might have fused. "We're in and we get out. It's a nothing job."

"Nothing jobs always kill someone," Doc muttered.

Mercy grinned, teeth bared. "As long as it's not me."

The relay was not so much an orbital station as a grave marker for dead infrastructure. It circled a brown dwarf whose last claim to fame had been devouring its own planetary system. The relay itself was a tumour of old satellites, lost maintenance drones, and the occasional, still-blinking distress buoy. At one point it had relayed data for the entire sector; now it mostly relayed disappointment.

The docking instructions arrived in a data burst: port side, dock six, no delays, no customs. Rask guided the Meridian in by hand, feeling the ship resist with every course correction, as though it objected to the whole concept of docking on principle.

In the forward compartment, Mercy zipped her vest and ran a last-minute systems check on her sidearm. Lyra pulled her hair back with military precision, then put the cargo into a duffel bag. She looked at Doc, who was tying off his boots with the distracted air of a man certain he'd have to run.

"You coming?" Lyra asked, voice as cold as the air cycling through the intake.

Doc shook his head, face gone a shade paler than regulation. "I'll stay with Glim. She's—" he looked at the canister, which now vibrated in sympathy with the station's own failing heartbeat, "—better with company."

Mercy patted his shoulder. "If it hatches, kill it before it breeds."

Doc tried to laugh, but his mouth only twitched. "That would be... suboptimal."

They cycled the airlock and walked the short umbilical to the relay hub. The inside was worse than the exterior: all exposed cabling, mildewed panels, and a tang of ozone strong enough to exfoliate the nostrils. The corridor lighting had two settings: migraine and blackout.

At the end of the tunnel, two figures waited—both heavily armed, both projecting the affect of people who had not planned to use words. The taller one wore battered riot armour with Imperial markings scorched off; the shorter, stockier one held a pulse rifle and did not bother to hide the trigger discipline. Both eyed the duffel bag with a hunger that was almost religious.

Mercy assessed the situation in a glance, then smiled. "I'll take the one on the left."

"We're not shooting anyone," Rask said, and stepped forward, hands open, the universal gesture for 'I am unarmed and definitely not about to stab you.'

The courier—presumably the one in charge—spoke first. "This is it?"

Rask nodded. "As requested. No one else knows."

The courier's partner grunted, eyes never leaving Mercy.

Lyra placed the duffel on the deck. "You scan it, you own it," she said, the words coming out like shell casings.

The courier squatted, unzipped the bag, and produced a scanner. He ran it over the box, then over the ambient air. The scanner beeped once, then flashed green.

"Payment," the courier said, and gestured to a battered case he'd been standing on.

Rask knelt, popped the latches, and looked inside.

He snorted.

Mercy peered over his shoulder, unimpressed.

The case contained three cartons of what the manifest had described as "medical supplies, nutritional." In reality, it was military-grade med patches, the kind used to stabilise a blaster wound long enough to make it to a better hospital than this.

Lyra's face went hard, then blank. She looked at the courier. "This is it?"

He shrugged. "Talk to your broker."

Mercy held up a patch, then flicked it back in the case. "Cheap bastards."

Rask closed the case and stood, dusting his hands. "Pirates, remember?" he said, and shot Lyra a look that said don't make a scene.

They left the relay in silence, Mercy carrying the case with a grip that suggested she might snap the handle out of spite.

Back aboard the Meridian, Rask dumped the payment on the mess hall table. Lyra stared at it like it might explode. "He screwed us," she said.

Rask shrugged, voice empty. "That's what pirates do."

Mercy stuck a med patch to the table's surface and pressed until the adhesive left a mark. "You want to go back and shoot them?"

"No," Rask said, already heading to the bridge. "We have a working hyperdrive. That'll do."

Lyra looked at Doc, who was now sitting directly in front of Glim's container, eyes fixed on the slow, sinister pulse of blue.

"Did it do anything?" she asked.

Doc shook his head, but didn't seem sure. "I think it's waiting."

Mercy grinned, all teeth. "Aren't we all."

The ship shuddered as Rask keyed in the new jump coordinates. The dead relay vanished behind them, a speck swallowed by the endless dark. Inside the Meridian, the crew gathered in the cockpit, faces lit by the cold light of the nav display.

Mercy rolled her shoulders, ready for the next fight. Lyra set her jaw and waited for the betrayal to come from whichever quarter it liked. Doc kept his eyes on Glim, fingers steepled, mind ticking through all the ways this could still go wrong.

Rask stared at the forward view, watched the nothingness slide by.

"Next stop," he said, voice low, "we get Kye."

He didn't ask for a vote. The Meridian would do what it always did: survive.

In the hold, Glim's container pulsed, then paused, then pulsed again.

No one in the crew noticed the shift, not yet.

But the ship did.

And it was learning.

They assembled in the cockpit, drawn there by inertia or the need for witness. The overheads were set low—half for fuel economy, half for privacy—and the only other light came from Glim's canister, now installed in an ad hoc cradle beside the navigator's console.

Doc Vellenix set up his monitoring gear with all the ceremony of a man attempting to impress an audience of ghosts. The datapad, jury-rigged to a set of scavenged biometric strips, displayed a scrolling record of the canister's pulses. The numbers meant nothing to anyone but Doc, but the visible spikes and curves looked enough like an EKG to be simultaneously reassuring and unnerving.

Rask leaned over the back of Doc's chair. "You said it was getting worse."

"Not worse," Doc corrected. "Just more complicated." He gestured at the display. "At first, it was a standard three-second interval—bored heartbeat. Now it's cycling through clusters. Here, look."

He pointed to the screen, where the blue-white flashes ran in tight triplets, then paused, then repeated in a different pattern.

Lyra squinted at the display, chewing the inside of her cheek. "Looks like code."

Doc nodded. "Exactly. And every time I try to run an analysis, it shifts the sequence."

Mercy, who had wedged herself sideways in the comms chair with her boots on the dash, yawned. "Maybe it's hungry. You ever think of that?"

Doc ignored her, addressing the air as if expecting the ship itself to answer. "It's accelerating. Last hour, the pattern length doubled. If it's just noise, it's the smartest noise I've ever seen."

Mercy rolled her eyes. "Maybe it's trying to communicate."

Lyra fixed her with a look. "That's what he just said."

"Maybe it's saying it wants out," said Mercy, picking at the worn seam of her glove.

The cockpit's main terminal lit up, running a new diagnostic. Rask frowned and toggled the channel. "Bridge, status?"

The AI's voice was bland as processed cheese. "Pulse anomaly detected in non-critical cargo. No containment breach."

Rask jabbed a finger at the nearest speaker. "You can read this?"

"Confirmed. Anomaly matches no known system signature."

"Then what is it?"

A pause, just long enough to be deliberate. "Unable to comply. Data does not meet operational mandate. Non-authorised tech."

Lyra snorted, but there was no humour in it. "Even the ship doesn't want to touch this."

Doc leaned closer to the canister, watching the flicker. "If it's talking, I'd love to know who's supposed to listen."

Rask stared at the canister. "Any way it could send a signal?"

Lyra shook her head. "Nothing that can punch through a hull. Maybe if you cracked the casing, but I wouldn't recommend."

Mercy perked up. "I would."

No one dignified that with a reply.

Rask paced the length of the cockpit, running his tongue along the inside of his teeth, a habit that signalled a storm on the way. He rounded on Doc. "Keep it contained. If it escalates, vent it out of the bay."

Doc raised his eyebrows. "That's your solution to everything."

Rask almost smiled. "That's why I'm alive."

He stalked back to the pilot's seat, tapped the nav panel, and reviewed the next jump. It was pointless—the route was locked, and any detour would just burn fuel and time—but it gave him something to do with his hands.

The comms panel chirped, soft and out of rhythm with Glim's pulse. Mercy sat up straighter. "Someone's pinging us."

Lyra slid into the comms seat, eyes narrowing. She ran the incoming data through a series of filters, fingers flying over the keys. "It's not voice," she said. "Just a file. Audio."

Mercy grinned. "Maybe it's a song."

Lyra ignored her, played the file. The cockpit filled with a burst of static, then a slow, atonal whine, barely above the floor of hearing. A few seconds in, the whine repeated, but with a new layer underneath—a digital rasp, almost like words under a sheet of glass.

Doc said, "Is that a cipher?"

Lyra ran a diagnostic. "It's not standard. Wait—there's a header. It's hidden inside the waveform, like an old broadcast." She sat back, recognition dawning. "Shit. It's a numbers station."

Rask raised his eyebrows. "They still use those?"

Lyra shrugged. "If you want to hide a signal, you use what no one else is looking for." She cross-patched the output through the ship's decryption suite.

The next time she played the file, the static resolved into a voice, cracked and distorted, but unmistakable.

It was Kye.

"Congratulations on not dying," said the voice, every word threaded with static and sarcasm. "Don't come for me. But if you do, bring snacks. Also, guns." There was a pause, then a longer, softer whisper: "Coordinates attached. You've got a window, maybe two hours before they move me again. Also, Seraphine's got a bad port stabilizer. Use that."

The message looped, then cut to silence.

Doc looked at Rask. "That's definitely Kye."

Mercy let out a low whistle. "They sound terrible."

Lyra's fingers hovered over the nav console, already plotting the new course. "The coordinates are valid. They're in-system, but only for a little while."

Rask took the pilot's seat, stared at the coordinates until the numbers burned into his eyes. "If it's a trap?"

Mercy grinned. "Then we're right at home."

Doc packed up his kit, already building a new patch cord in his head. "I'll keep monitoring Glim. Maybe I can build something to translate its pulses."

Lyra set the course. "There's only one jump that puts us in range in time. It's tight. If we screw up, we'll drift for days."

Mercy tapped her boots on the dash. "No pressure, boss."

Rask said nothing. He just stared at the blank display, jaw locked, hands tight on the control yoke.

Lyra watched him a moment longer, then keyed the jump. The engines flared to life, the whole ship rumbling with anticipation or dread.

"Plot a course," Rask said, voice low.

The Meridian leapt, the hull screaming in protest.

Behind them, Glim's pulse changed.

It ran in a new sequence—one, then two, then three.

In the cockpit, no one spoke. They just watched the stars twist, hoping the next destination would hold more answers than questions.

In the hold, the blue light of Glim's container painted strange shadows on the walls. The pattern shifted again, more insistent now, as if it had seen the stars, and wanted more.

TEN

The Meridian's approach to the Skarn Belt was less a matter of course correction and more an act of deliberate self-harm. Viewed through the forward display, the Belt unfurled like a history of bad decisions—kilometres of tumbling rock, ghost ships wedged between slabs of granite, fragments of shattered hulls pinwheeling in slow-motion ballet. No sane navigator would cross it at speed, which was precisely why every smuggler, fence, and fugitive in the sector used it as their own personal cloakroom.

Lyra watched the debris field with a predatory calm. She had commandeered the helm, coaxing the battered nav system through a series of calculations that would have given an Imperial Academy instructor an aneurysm. Her hands moved with surgeon's precision, entering variables by tactile memory and cross-referencing with a battered notebook she kept duct-taped to the console. Most of the entries were in a code only she understood—half base-8, half spite.

Rask hovered at her shoulder, pretending to offer

advice, but mostly ensuring she didn't override the last of the ship's safeties. He squinted at the path Lyra had drawn: a snaking, recursive loop through the Belt that doubled back on itself three times and at one point skimmed the outer ring of a planetoid that had eaten three surveyors this decade alone.

"Ambitious," he said, trying to sound casual.

Lyra didn't bother looking up. "It's either this or they box us in at the relay. That, or Mercy accidentally fuses us to a mining drone."

The ship's AI, which had been sulking since the previous jump, flicked a neat triplet of red alerts across the nav panel—three sharp pulses, each accompanied by a passive-aggressive click. Lyra regarded them with the cold affection of someone who owned several hammers and had not yet met a problem she couldn't flatten.

Rask glanced at the alerts, then at Lyra. "The computer's vetoing your plan."

"It's a coward," Lyra said. "And mathematically illiterate."

Rask wanted to argue, but the way she said it— unblinking, final—left no purchase. Instead, he leaned back and pretended to study the astrogation chart, while Lyra shaved another second off their estimated transit.

Behind them, Mercy had set up a forward observation post on the comms deck, which meant she was propped on a crate, boots on the bulkhead, and working through her supply of black-market stimulants at a rate that would have done credit to the opening night of a meat-market nightclub. She wore headphones but didn't seem to have them connected to anything. Every few minutes she yanked the cord, grinned at the static, and called up a new file from the ship's encyclopaedia of banned historical content.

Rask glanced over his shoulder. "You're supposed to be running a threat scan."

Mercy's answer was a long, operatic note that probably came from a century-old Italian death aria, followed by a yawn. "If they're coming for us, they'll ping the hull before they ping the comms." She stretched, vertebrae cracking. "Besides, I'm prepping for the afterparty."

Lyra's lips twitched, but she kept her eyes on the controls. "Just make sure you're awake when it starts."

Mercy mock-saluted, then pressed her headphones tight and started air-conducting an invisible orchestra. Rask counted four minutes before she tried to hotwire the forward sensors to project a light show in the main cabin. He decided he could live with that.

Belowdecks, the mood was less festive. Doc Vellenix had barricaded himself in the cargo hold, where he monitored Glim's canister with the zeal of a man who knew exactly how many disasters had originated in the back of a moving vehicle.

The pulse inside the canister had evolved. No longer a steady, mindless rhythm, it now responded to stimuli—a voice, a footfall, even the vibration of a hatch—by shivering or changing tempo. At first, Doc had attributed this to his own encroaching madness, or the fact that he had not slept more than three hours in any given night since medical school. Now he suspected it was the canister's version of a personality test.

He attached another sensor strip to the ceramic

casing, then addressed Glim in the gentle, hopeless tone reserved for bomb disposal and infant patients. "If you're listening, blink twice for yes, once for no."

The canister pulsed once, then twice, then three times in rapid sequence. The third pulse sent a shiver through the deck plating, or so Doc thought.

He checked his readings, saw nothing but the same inscrutable graph, and made a note on his pad. "Patient remains nonverbal," he wrote, "but emotionally expressive. Possible empathy response to subject interaction. Recommend more data."

Mercy's voice, heavily filtered, boomed through the ship's comms: "Doc! Can you get Glim to do a duet?"

Doc ignored her, but the canister did not. It hummed, softly, in sympathy with Mercy's distant aria—then matched pitch, then volume, then cadence, until the hold resonated with a choral vibration that set Doc's teeth on edge.

He glared at the canister, then at the overhead. "Stop that," he said. "It's not healthy."

The canister did, but the silence was worse.

Doc checked the sensor one last time. He made his way to the upper deck, arriving just as the forward view screens began to fill with the raw, kinetic noise of the Belt.

Lyra's course held. The Meridian shuddered, protested, but did not break. Debris scraped the shields, then the hull. Shards of ice and ancient engine parts battered the sides. Every so often, a glimmer of another vessel flashed across their field—some dead, some drifting, some not as dead as they ought to be.

Rask checked the nav screen, which displayed their path as a thin blue line bisecting a cloud of murder. He exhaled, "We're on track, for now."

Lyra, hair plastered to her forehead with sweat, didn't blink. "The worst is the next quadrant. If the pirates set up a net, we'll have to thread it by hand."

Mercy perked up. "We're expecting company?"

Lyra nodded, tight and small.

"Good," said Mercy, and disappeared toward the weapons station, humming a tune that was now uncomfortably close to Glim's last pulse.

Doc slipped into the comms seat. "Should I be worried?" he asked.

Lyra shook her head. "Not unless you hate adrenaline."

"I'm a doctor," he said. "I'm immune to it."

Rask shot him a look. "I suspect none of us are immune to Mercy's brand of disaster."

As if summoned, the ship's proximity alert screamed to life. Every console blazed red. The AI's voice, which had not improved in personality, announced: "Incoming contacts, three. Two manned, one drone. All equipped with boarding harpoons. Recommend evasive manoeuvre."

Lyra's fingers blurred across the console. "We'll have to drop the signature."

Doc said, "I thought the drive would seize."

"It will," Lyra said. "But not before we clear the field."

Mercy's voice echoed over the ship's comms: "Permission to return fire?"

Rask looked at the incoming vector, then nodded. "Hold until they're in range. We want them to commit."

"Copy that," Mercy said, and the comms clicked off.

Lyra throttled the engines, sending the Meridian into a controlled tumble. The hull groaned, shields flickered, but the ship held together. The lead hunter, a sleek black dart with four stubby gun pods, adjusted course to match.

"Nice," Rask said, watching the triangulation narrow. "You're baiting them."

Lyra didn't answer. She hit a switch, and a string of thermal flares shot from the Meridian's rear. The drones ignored them, but the lead manned ship hesitated, just enough to lose position.

Rask took manual control. "Bring us around."

Lyra complied, and the ship spun on its axis, shedding debris as it arced toward the weakest point in the hunter's formation.

The enemy ship fired a burst, aimed low. The rounds punched through the outer hull, but missed anything vital. Mercy, ever the opportunist, returned fire with a volley of micro-mines that clung to the enemy's shield like burrs.

"Got you, you beautiful bastard," Mercy cooed.

Doc gripped the seat, watching the external cameras. "Should we brace for boarding?"

Lyra shook her head. "They're not getting close enough. Rask, cut the starboard thrust on my mark."

"Ready."

She counted down: "Three. Two. Now."

Rask slammed the control. The Meridian jerked sideways, the sudden G-force enough to knock the breath out of everyone not actively braced. The enemy ship overcorrected, skidded on a spray of its own leaking coolant, and tumbled directly into the path of a rotating asteroid. The impact wasn't cinematic—no explosion, just a satisfying crumple as the ship folded around the rock and went dark.

The drone and the second manned ship broke formation. The drone peeled off, perhaps under AI control; the other ship wobbled, then limped away, presumably calculating its own odds of survival.

Mercy's voice rang out: "Did we just win?"

Rask exhaled, "We survived. That's enough."

Lyra brought the Meridian back onto course. She looked at the nav display, then at Rask, and allowed herself a single, small smile.

"You doubted my math," she said.

He almost smiled back. "I'll never doubt it again."

Doc's voice came across the intercom. "I'd like to get off this ride now."

Mercy, from the weapons deck, sang a single, perfect note. The canister belowdecks answered with a hum, and this time, Doc found it almost comforting.

The Belt receded. The field opened up, and the Meridian, battered but intact, limped toward the next crisis.

In the silence, Lyra checked the readings, then shut down the forward sensors. She looked at Rask, voice softer than before.

"You're not a terrible captain, you know," she said.

Rask blinked, surprised. "Thanks?"

She shrugged. "Just often wrong."

He laughed, the sound bouncing off the battered metal and settling somewhere in the lower decks.

The ship's AI, sensing the mood, flickered the lights twice.

"Crew bonding: inconclusive," it said.

Lyra ignored it, already plotting the next impossible course.

In the cargo hold, the canister's pulse had returned to its original, steady rhythm.

Doc patted it, gentle, like putting a child to sleep.

"Rest while you can," he said, to the blue-lit heart of the ship.

He could have sworn it winked at him.

ELEVEN

The Meridian's rendezvous with Outpost Orpheon did not so much begin as insinuate itself—an incremental tick-up of the ship's anxiety, the blue glow of Glim's containment box gone to a sullen pulse, and a vector on the nav screen crawling toward the relay's decaying orbit at the speed of regret. The relay itself was a torus slung about a neutron fragment, all matte-black composites and redundant hull ribs, designed to disappear in both the electromagnetic spectrum and polite company.

Rask took the approach as slowly as he dared, pushing the manual thrusters and eyeing every fluctuation on the thermal scans. He didn't trust the station's IFF handshake, which kept cycling through a catalogue of fictional callsigns and, at one point, tried to greet them as "Medical Relief Barge, Prince Harry." He killed the handshake and ran dark, sliding the Meridian into a parking orbit with the grace of a hungover eel.

Lyra watched the outpost through the forward viewport, posture locked at "assess and destroy." She still had grease on her face from the last drive tune, and the knuckles of her right hand were split from the time she'd cold-cocked a carbon-fibre panel back into alignment. She said nothing for a minute, letting the tension accumulate.

Mercy was already in the airlock, one hand on the crate of boarding charges, the other spinning a battered blade like she was auditioning for a job in a cutlery circus. The only sign of nerves was the faint, involuntary tapping of her boot on the deck.

Doc kept to the medbay, or rather, to Glim's cradle, which now vibrated at the edge of hearing—a subtle, harmonic buzz that made him wish he still drank. He thumbed the sensor display, watched the readout do a jittery parabola, then thumbed it again. He patched through to the bridge, voice filtered through the ship's wheezing intercom.

"You sure you want to dock?" he said, never quite a question.

Rask thumbed the mic. "Not particularly."

"Power's erratic on the relay. Might be a brownout, might be sabotage, might be both. Glim's not happy about it, either."

Lyra rolled her eyes. "Nothing makes Glim happy, except maybe a nice detonation."

Doc didn't reply, but the static implied an agreement.

Rask toggled the controls. "Mercy, on your cue."

Mercy's reply was a single, musical note—imitation birdsong, possibly, but the kind that only occurred on planets with predatory avian life. She keyed the airlock sequence, and the hatch hissed open. The station's docking tunnel extended with a noise that suggested it had not seen recent use, or had seen use only as a murder weapon.

The trio moved through the hatch. Rask in the lead, Lyra on his six, Mercy bringing up the rear and scanning every shadow like she expected to find her own reflection, armed and hostile.

The outpost interior was pure darkness. No welcoming lights, no ping of environmental stabilisers, just the dull afterimage of the Meridian's own running lamps and the slow emergence of detail as Rask's retinal implants acclimatised. The gravity was at 0.3G, enough to make every step a little too bouncy, every shift of weight slightly unpredictable.

Lyra toggled her suit torch and swept it across the docking foyer. The floor was littered with micro-shards of composite, but otherwise clean—a deliberate, sterile sort of clean, the way a hospital corridor looks just after an accident and before the family is notified. The only movement was a coil of cabling drifting in the weak gravity, end still sparking at intervals.

Mercy surveyed the scene and frowned. "No bodies. No blood. Not even a half-eaten corpse." She sounded genuinely disappointed.

Rask shot her a look. "Set your expectations lower."

Mercy grinned. "I always do."

They proceeded through the first hatch, which resisted for a full second before unlocking with an embarrassed pneumatic sigh. The corridor beyond was even colder. The emergency lights were triggered by motion, but two thirds of the strips were out, leaving deep patches of shadow and only occasional islands of blue-white. The corridor's walls had the dull finish of a former luxury vessel stripped for parts; every panel that could be pried off or melted down had been.

"Why is this place even here?" Lyra asked, as they bounced forward.

Rask replied, "It's the last black-market relay before the Void Expanse. Anyone running from the Core drops here. If you want to disappear, this is where you start."

"Who's running it?" Mercy asked, spinning a blade in her left hand and palming a charge in her right.

Rask shrugged. "Used to be a cartel family. Then the Imperium ran a sweep, cleaned out the top deck, left the rest to self-organise. Now it's mostly AI and whoever survives the vacuum."

Lyra grunted, noncommittal.

The central hub, when they reached it, was a riot of abandoned cargo, security crates, and jury-rigged power lines. Several data terminals glowed in standby, screens frozen mid-download. One corner of the hub had a kitchen nook, with a pot of something grey and lumpy frozen halfway to a boil. Three empty chairs ringed a table, but the dust on the seats suggested no one had sat there in months.

"Ghost town," Lyra said.

Mercy moved to the nearest cargo stack and ran a gloved hand over the labels. "Lot of stuff never even got inventoried. They left in a hurry."

Rask wandered to a terminal and attempted a login. The screen flickered, then asked for a passcode in a font last fashionable during the pre-unification wars. He snorted and opened a side panel, exposing the manual override and the sort of wiring job that would have given Lyra a coronary. She stepped forward and took over, her fingers moving with the ruthless efficiency of someone who had rewired a ship's nav system in zero-G and under fire.

"Give me a minute," she said.

Rask left her to it and scanned the perimeter. Every sound in the relay was off: the whirr of the life support was too slow, the click of the ventilation too regular, and the hollow echo of their footsteps lingered too long, as if the station was waiting for them to leave.

Mercy had already lost interest in waiting for something to happen and now prowled the corridors, poking her head through every open hatch. The fourth door she tried was stuck, so she simply booted it open and disappeared inside.

Lyra muttered, "Got it," and the terminal flickered to life. The comms log scrolled onto the display—thousands of lines of encrypted traffic, the most recent flagged with a red triangle. She scanned it quickly, then froze.

Rask saw her jaw tighten. "What is it?"

Lyra didn't look away from the screen. "Seraphine. Logged two days ago. Docked for forty-five minutes, then left on a new trajectory. No cargo listed. No manifest."

Mercy's voice piped in over the suit comms. "Found something. It's in the dark. Not breathing."

Rask frowned. "How many?"

Mercy's reply was an exaggerated sigh. "Just the one, boss. But it's fresh."

Rask shot a look at Lyra. "Stay here and keep pulling logs. I'll check on Mercy."

Lyra nodded, already lost in the stream of terminal data.

Rask found Mercy two corridors down, floating a metre off the floor and peering into a side alcove. The body she'd found was a woman, late middle-aged, in station overalls with a nametag that read "Chief Engineer." She was suspended, arms curled in front of her like a sleeper in freefall, but the face was frozen in a rictus of surprise. No visible trauma, but her lips and eyelids were slightly blue.

Mercy nudged the body with a toe, and it rotated gently, hair fanning in the chill air.

"She's been dead a couple of days," Mercy said. "No prizes for guessing who killed her."

Rask scanned the body, then the room. Nothing out of place—no sign of violence, no sign of a struggle.

Mercy twirled her blade. "Maybe the station's haunted."

Rask ignored her and flicked open the woman's suit pocket. Inside was a data stick and a paper scrap—actual paper, which was either an affectation or a sign of terminal paranoia. He took both, left the body drifting, and gestured for Mercy to follow.

Back in the hub, Lyra had downloaded the last month's comms traffic and started a brute decryption on the most recent pings. She looked up as Rask entered, eyes bright with adrenaline.

"Something's off," she said. "Every message in the last forty-eight hours is flagged. The system's been cycling through default admins, like it keeps forgetting who's supposed to be in charge."

Rask handed her the data stick. "Dead engineer had this. Maybe a backup key."

Lyra slotted it into the terminal. The stick contained a single file: a list of incoming ships, outgoing ships, and a hand-written note at the end:

DO NOT TRUST THE AI.

Below it, in smaller print:

If Seraphine returns, do not open crate.

Mercy cackled. "I like her style."

Lyra read it twice, then locked eyes with Rask. "They mean Glim, don't they"

Rask nodded his head. "Looks like it."

The walk back to the dock was uneventful, except for the shadows that seemed to grow with every step, and the soft, insistent hum from the container. When they reached the airlock, Mercy paused and looked over her shoulder.

"Does it feel colder to you?" she asked.

Lyra shook her head. "It's just the relay failing."

Mercy didn't look convinced.

The silence lasted until it didn't.

Mercy, Lyra, and Rask were within touching distance of the docking ring, when the station's main power snapped on with all the subtlety of a prison riot. Lights flooded the corridor, every shade of white and blue, and for a moment no one moved.

Then, without warning, the doors at each end slammed shut, a rolling, pneumatic hiss that sent a vibration up Lyra's boots.

Mercy whistled. "They've got the drama dialled in, don't they?"

Lyra ignored her, shouldered past Rask, and jabbed at the door control. "Dead," she reported, then pried off the maintenance panel and began hotwiring it with two bent finger joints and a cable toothpick. "Give me a minute."

Rask watched the other end of the corridor, which was rapidly filling with an unpleasant-smelling mist from the wall vents. It was the colour of disappointment and had a metallic taste that burned the back of the throat.

"Air's contaminated," he said, voice flat. "Not lethal, but not great for the lungs."

Mercy grinned, unaffected. "Good for my complexion."

The AI, patched in from the Meridian via Lyra's suit, chose this moment to comment: "Station security protocol has been activated. All non-essential personnel will be terminated in accordance with Imperial Hazard Code."

Rask rolled his eyes. "Define non-essential."

"Anyone not in a command module, or not the station AI," the AI replied, bland and smug.

Lyra worked the panel, fingers flying. "We're going to have to short the lock. It's triple-redundant. Whoever built this knew their paranoia."

Mercy drew two blades, one in each hand, and twirled them in opposite directions. "Finally, something to stab."

She glanced at Rask. "You want to take bets on what's behind the next door?"

"No," said Rask, then braced himself as the lights flickered again and the temperature dropped a further ten degrees.

The mist intensified, reducing visibility to arm's length. Through it, the emergency beacons blinked a slow pattern: three, pause, three, pause. Rask frowned at the pattern. "It's copying Glim."

Lyra didn't look up. "The station's been compromised. My guess is, Seraphine left a present in the mainframe."

Mercy tested the door by throwing a blade at it; it stuck, halfway through, and shivered with each pulse of the mist. She retrieved it and smiled. "Definitely not standard issue."

Rask coughed, then eyed Lyra. "Any progress?"

"Almost there," she said, then jabbed a cable into the lock and twisted. There was a sharp pop, a gout of ozone, and the door slid open a fraction. Mercy wedged her boot in the gap and pried it further, then stepped through.

The central hub looked nothing like when they'd left it. The lights were set to full daylight, every surface cleaned to a clinical shine, and all the chairs had been swept into a neat line against the wall. The air was even colder here, and the hum of the station's core was audible —a deep, subsonic throb that made Lyra's ears pop.

On the table in the middle of the room was the dead

engineer, now laid out with her arms crossed and a data pad resting on her chest. Someone, or something, had arranged her like a museum exhibit.

Mercy sidled up to the body and eyed the data pad. "Bet you ten it's a jump scare."

Rask ignored her and took the pad, scanning the contents. The top line was a warning:

IF YOU'RE READING THIS, IT'S ALREADY TOO LATE.

Below that, a message:

Containment breached. Seraphine docked, transferred subject, left without log-off. Crew dead within hours. Do not open the crate.

Lyra read over his shoulder, then turned to the station's main console. She plugged in her portable, cross-patched it to the Meridian, and began pulling logs.

Mercy eyed the walls, which had started to sweat—thin rivulets of condensation tracking down the composite panels, freezing in place.

Rask set the pad down, wiped his hands on his jacket, and said, "We need to get out of here. Now."

Lyra didn't look up. "Almost got the logs. If we lose this, we lose Kye."

Mercy picked up the dead woman's hand and waved it at Rask. "She says to hurry."

The AI, now even more amused, piped through Lyra's comm. "Recommendation: Run."

Rask glared at the ceiling. "You're not helping."

The mist thickened. From the corridor, a sound: scraping, soft at first, then louder. It was the sound of something being dragged, or of dozens of small things moving in unison.

Mercy twirled her blades and looked at Rask. "Bets?"

"Shut up and cover the door," said Rask.

Lyra finished the transfer, pulled her portable, and stuffed it in her jacket. "Ready."

They moved to the exit, but the corridor beyond was now crowded with shapes—dark, indistinct, but definitely moving. Mercy grinned, stepped forward, and started carving her way through, the blades flashing in the strobe of the warning lights.

Rask and Lyra followed, hugging the wall, avoiding contact where possible. The shapes didn't bleed, or even resist—they simply fell away, dissipating into the mist.

It took just a few more steps to reach the docking ring, but by then the station was actively fighting their exit. The lights pulsed so hard the world seemed to flicker. Gravity oscillated between fractions and full, sending Rask and Lyra stumbling with every step.

Mercy stayed upright, of course.

They reached the docking tube. Lyra sealed the airlock behind them and keyed the sequence for detachment. They crossed back to the Meridian, Lyra carrying the log files, Rask covering the rear, and Mercy trailing with the crowbar in one hand and a blade in the other.

As the hatch cycled shut behind them, the station's lights cut out entirely.

Rask stood in the dim glow of the Meridian's entryway and said, "Well, that was cheery."

The AI purred, "Welcome back. Air on the Meridian is still rated for human use."

Mercy choked on a laugh as she stowed her blades. "You spoil us."

Doc met them in the corridor, face pale.

"What happened?" he asked.

Rask just said, "Get us out. Now."

Lyra keyed in the launch, and the Meridian shot away from Orpheon, leaving the station to its own recursive nightmares.

Doc eyed the display, which had abandoned all attempt at calibration and now scrolled random strings of text. He risked a gloved palm on Glim's canister, and felt the pulse accelerate, vibrating to a rate that made his fingertips ache.

He pulled back and addressed the canister. "If you're planning to hatch, please wait until I've had my lunch," he said, then glanced at the vitals. "Or at least until I've sedated the rest of the crew."

Mercy, sprawled in the mess with a protein bar, grinned at Lyra. "Well, that was fun."

Lyra glared, then smiled despite herself. "Next time, we do it your way."

Rask wandered past, shaking his head. "You're all insane."

Mercy waved a blade in his direction. "You love it."

The ship's AI, always eager for the last word, chimed in: "Crew bonding: still inconclusive."

In the silence that followed, the container in the hold synced to a single, unified pulse.

And somewhere, beyond the reach of sensor or reason, another station awoke, hungry for company.

Doc spent the next hour in the cargo hold, knelt at eye level with the canister, as if some unspoken etiquette required politeness before the end of the world. He'd watched patients die with less drama than this, but none had ever gone down singing.

The blue had gone deeper, now, beyond visible, so that it pulsed not with light but with an atmospheric pressure that made Doc's jaw ache and the inside of his skull throb. At some point Glim's canister had stopped vibrating and started... listening. When he whispered to it, the pitch shifted; when he snapped his fingers or even cleared his throat, the pulse returned in perfect echo, delayed by just enough that it felt like speaking to a child who was learning a language by repetition.

He scratched his stubble and attached another set of electrodes, this time mapping not for energy but for frequency—audio, then subsonic, then finally up into a range that tripped the relays on every other system in the compartment. The effect was instant: the ship's climate control began to hiss in protest, the cabin lights flickered in staccato, and the AI's voice came over the comm, flat but not quite convincing:

"Unidentified signal detected. Recommend immediate deactivation of foreign hardware."

Doc ignored it. "She's just trying to talk," he said. "Let her."

In the next compartment over, Rask was unspooling the backup nav log, checking for evidence that the relay's self-immolation hadn't followed them. Mercy sprawled across a crate, peeling dried blood from her cuticles and humming in harmony with the canister, either by accident or some odd sympathy. Lyra, as ever, managed everything from the bridge, but she'd taken to listening in on every mic'd surface, as if the act of eavesdropping might will an answer into being.

The canister made a sound, then—low, at first, but rising, like the world's slowest dial tone.

Doc leaned in. "Do that again."

The sound repeated, two quick pulses, then three, then two again. He transcribed it, then let it run for a minute.

On the display, it mapped out in clusters. Not random, not even close. He recognised the shape before the meaning. It was Morse, or something close enough that his brain, wired for trauma triage and old-fashioned comms, could decode it.

He patched the mic to the bridge. "She's sending us a message."

Lyra answered, clipped. "Define she."

"Glim," said Doc, without thinking. "She's alone. She's afraid. She wants help."

A pause. Then Rask's voice, softer than expected: "You're sure?"

Doc tried not to sound proud. "She used the word 'help' five times. And then... my name. Or what passes for a name in pulse code."

Mercy grinned from her perch. "She likes you."

Doc nodded. "We have that effect on the traumatised."

The ship's AI butted in. "Foreign code detected in central archive. Recommend quarantine of all physical samples and immediate system reboot."

Lyra, unbothered, said, "Override and log the request." To Doc, she added: "What's the risk?"

"Same as any potentially hostile patient. You treat her as a person, until she tries to kill you."

Rask came down from the bridge, looking more tired than angry for once. "We're not a hospital, Doc."

Doc gestured at the canister. "We're not an execution chamber, either."

Mercy piped in, "We're a floating grave, is what we are. Can't even keep a goldfish alive, and now we're taking on a psychic distress beacon."

Rask snorted. "You're not helping."

Mercy smiled, utterly unrepentant. "Never claimed I would."

Lyra came down the access ladder. She regarded the canister with the air of someone who'd expected worse, and now found herself almost disappointed.

"So, what do we do?" she said.

Doc shrugged. "Same thing you'd do for any prisoner of war. Clean the wounds, keep her talking, figure out if she's worth the risk."

Lyra eyed him, then the canister, then the portable

scanner Doc had jury-rigged to a blood pressure cuff and a wire probe. "Can we move her?"

"Safely?" Doc considered. "Not yet. But she'll die in here if we don't."

Mercy rolled off her crate and wandered over. "Can we teach her to cuss? Because that's at least half the fun of being an aunty."

Doc smiled, a little bleakly. "Give her time."

Rask exhaled, hands on his hips. "We keep her locked down. No outside comms, no physical contact without Doc present. If she's just a broken thing, we ditch her at the first safe station. If she's a person, we treat her like one." He looked at Doc, then at Lyra, then the canister. "We're pirates, not monsters."

The blue pulse slowed. The canister's vibration softened, then stilled, and Doc felt something in the room relax—a thread of tension snapped, but not in anger. Glim was listening again.

Doc knelt, put his hand on the ceramic, and said, "You're safe now."

The pulse repeated, low and soft, three times.

Rask grunted. "If the Imperium comes knocking, we sell the coordinates and run."

Mercy shrugged. "If she's useful, maybe she can do the talking for us next time."

The canister glowed, dim but persistent, and the ship drifted into silence, for once not from threat, but from a sense of new responsibility.

For a while, no one moved, and the Meridian coasted, crew and passenger both as uncertain as the dark they drifted in.

And in the hold, Glim's hum became, unmistakably, a song.

TWELVE

The Meridian coasted on blackout, bleeding velocity with a wounded animal's stubborn refusal to die. The hull temperature matched the air inside—colder than debt, and just as eager to get under your skin. The ship's systems ran on a threadbare tick-over, so quiet that even the old, unreliable heating unit couldn't muster its usual whine. Most would call it peaceful. Lyra called it a bad omen.

She ran the nav, hands still stained from the last time she'd had to open a panel with the power on. Her knuckles flexed white around the yoke, not from nerves but from sheer force of will. The console's only illumination was a faint, intermittent pulse: diagnostic, not decorative. Her breath steamed, slow and controlled, as she watched the readout for any sign of trouble.

Trouble arrived two minutes ahead of schedule.

A soft ping—deliberate, but sickly—crawled up the sensor array, barely present. Lyra blinked, reran the sweep, and watched as the blip disappeared, then reappeared, then fractured into three smaller echoes before fading. She considered the pattern, ran a quick-and-dirty spectral analysis, and bared her teeth.

"Contact," she said. "Cloaked. But shit at it."

Rask appeared behind her, silent as frost. He wore the same jacket he'd patched with adhesive mesh in twelve places, the same thousand-yard stare that suggested he'd already written everyone in the crew off and was only now waiting for the evidence to present itself.

He looked at the nav, then at Lyra. "How far?"

She shrugged. "Fifty, maybe sixty thousand klicks. No thrust signature, just that ghost on the relay."

He leaned in, exhaled, and for the first time, Lyra realised the air was cold enough to turn his breath to vapour. "Is it the Seraphine?"

She nodded, tapping the replay. "Watch the decay on the carrier wave. Vexa's ship. She's patched the cloak, but the drives are still bleeding. You can see the signal trip every thirty seconds."

Rask let a smile—small, mean, but real—show in his eyes. "She's hurting."

"Or she's playing you," Lyra said. She reached for the side panel, adjusted the power input with the same tenderness most people reserved for a lover, and narrowed the detection window. The blip brightened, then faded to a more honest signal. "She's waiting. Maybe for us, maybe for something worse."

Rask straightened, checked the time, then flicked on the crew channel. "All hands. Situation yellow. Lyra's got the Seraphine, drifting in system. Everyone else, eyes open, engines cold, prep for forced extraction."

A pause, then the dry crackle of Doc's voice: "We're already on yellow?"

Rask: "She's close. Closer than is healthy."

Mercy's voice, ever the sugar in the wound, piped up from further down the corridor: "Do I get to shoot her this time, or are we doing hugs and forgiveness?"

Rask ignored her, cut the comm, and looked at Lyra. "Thoughts?"

She shrugged. "I say we wait. Minimal emissions. Keep her nervous."

He agreed. "We'll ghost her, see if she blinks."

The Meridian drifted, each creak of the hull a slow, aching reminder of how exposed they were. Rask left Lyra to her scans, knowing she'd warn him if something in the system so much as sneezed.

Mercy arrived on the bridge three minutes later, a blade spinning between her knuckles, face flushed from the cold or anticipation—it was hard to tell. She had a way of making the air around her seem less like an atmosphere and more like a challenge to whoever was breathing it next.

She slid into the comms chair, feet up, knife still dancing. "So, cap'n," she said, aiming the point at Rask's head, "what's the play? We creep, we wait, or we pretend to be space junk and hope she's the sort to pick up strays?"

"We watch," Rask replied. "If Vexa's hurt, she's desperate. Desperate is unpredictable."

Mercy grinned, bright and savage. "That's my favourite kind."

Lyra ignored the exchange, busy with the nav, but her ears tracked every word.

Down in the hold, Doc hunched over the canister containing Glim, staring at the blue pulse inside like it was a riddle he could solve if he just applied enough sarcasm. The cradle holding Glim was now bolted to the deck in three places, and the additional array of home-made sensors was the only concession to the growing sense that something inside the box might, one day, try to leave.

He ran another check. The containment unit's resonance had gone from "minor inconvenience" to "impending catastrophe" in less than a week. The blue pulse inside seemed aware of him: it slowed when he approached, sped up when he looked away, and pulsed a hair more brightly whenever he made a note in his log. He'd been talking to it—at first out of boredom, then out of some deep, unexamined need to be heard.

Today, it answered.

He was in the middle of describing the relay's self-destruct with all the clinical detachment of a bored pathologist when the pulse flickered, stopped, and resumed with a new rhythm: two, then one, then three. He frowned, held up a finger, and said, "Do that again."

The canister obliged.

He glanced at the translation software he'd kludged from the ship's learning module. It rendered the pulses into numbers, which he then cross-referenced with his own table of phrases. It was crude, but the message was unmistakable.

"Where go?" it asked.

Doc blinked, then whispered, "We're hiding."

The canister answered, "Hiding. Why."

Doc hesitated, feeling a chill that was nothing to do with the ship's power-saving regime. "Bad people want us. Want you."

The pulse slowed, then surged, brighter than before.

"What I," it asked.

Doc was about to answer when the comm hissed, and the ship's AI spoke with a voice that was too high, too tense. "Priority: Field resonance anomaly. Source: Cargo. Recommend immediate diagnostics."

He stabbed the comm button. "What is it now?"

The AI responded, "Containment unit is outputting a low-frequency field. It is interfering with hull sensors."

Doc checked his panel. The hull's bio-sensors now displayed a mild but growing distortion, as if the ship itself were running a fever.

He keyed the bridge. "Heads up. Glim's got a pulse again. Might be visible outside."

Rask replied, "Noted."

Lyra added, "Keep it quiet. We've got bigger ghosts."

Mercy, picking up on the tension, rolled her eyes and said, "Tell the box to try a new frequency. This one's getting old."

Doc closed the channel, leaned over the canister, and said, "Quiet, please."

The pulse faded, but didn't stop.

He sat back, rolled his neck, and considered the odds. They weren't getting better.

On the bridge, Lyra ran a check of every passive sensor she could justify. The Seraphine's signature was constant, but weak, like a dying animal faking a cough to lure in carrion. She mapped its position against the system's debris and counted the number of places Vexa could hide, discounting the ones she herself would never stoop to.

She almost missed it: a faint red ripple on the far edge of the scan, well outside the line of approach. She zoomed, reran the sweep, and frowned.

"Cap'n. Third party, far side. No signal, but the mass reads Imperial."

Rask looked. "Size?"

"Big. Maybe a gunship. Maybe a transport loaded for war."

Mercy whistled. "The fun never ends."

Lyra watched the new contact, its heat signature climbing as it powered up for approach. "They're not hiding. Might be coming for Vexa."

Mercy grinned, "Or us."

Rask flexed his hands, the joints popping in the cold. "If it's Imperial, they'll want the canister."

"Or the bounty on our heads," Lyra said, deadpan.

Mercy twirled the blade again, this time with more purpose. "If they're hunters, we bait them into the

Seraphine, let them chew each other up, and skip the system while they're distracted."

Lyra considered, then nodded. "That might work."

Rask hesitated, then said, "Set it up."

They watched the third ship close the gap, its thermal signature now burning white. The AI piped up, its tone barely masking the panic. "Proximity alert. Incoming vessel on collision course. Weapons hot."

Lyra flicked off the safety on the main drive, her thumb resting just above the ignition.

Rask leaned in close, his voice low. "If they target us first, we run. If they take the Seraphine, we wait for the debris and go through it for Kye."

Lyra's eyes narrowed, but she didn't argue.

Mercy cocked her head. "You think Vexa's got Kye alive?"

Rask shrugged. "She's not sentimental. But she's thorough."

Lyra pulled up a side display, showed the Seraphine's last transmission. It was encrypted, but the cadence and length matched a pre-set Imperial code.

"She's still talking to someone," Lyra said. "Maybe not the new ship, but someone else."

Rask's jaw set. "They're working together?"

"Doubt it," Lyra replied. "Hunters don't share."

Doc patched in, sounding out of breath. "The canister's field just spiked. If you're planning any wild manoeuvres, warn me first—I don't want to scrape Glim off the deck."

Mercy, delighted, said, "Don't worry, Doc. We'll only

do something wild and stupid if we have no other options."

Lyra grinned, the expression brief but genuine. "So: standard."

The new ship, closer now, resolved as a predator-class bounty vessel, hull bristling with the kind of tech that made ordinary pirates shit themselves. The registry, when Lyra finally got a return, read "Palamedes"—old school, no flair, just deadly.

She patched the image to the main screen, and Rask stared at it for a long moment. "That's not a local. They tracked us."

The Palamedes accelerated, shedding velocity like it was eager to crash through every obstacle in the system. The Seraphine's ghost signature suddenly brightened, then flickered out. Lyra caught the data, ran a spectral trace, and grinned.

"She just dumped a decoy," she said. "She's bolting for the far side."

Rask watched the Palamedes. "They're not falling for it."

Mercy, who had taken to braiding a length of detcord through her belt, said, "You want to make a bet?"

They all watched as the bounty ship ignored the decoy and ran the Seraphine's last real heading.

Rask nodded, half to himself. "We follow, slow. Wait for them to get tangled."

Lyra dialled down the engines to the lowest possible power setting and set the ship on a parallel vector, just behind the line of sight for both vessels.

For twenty minutes, nothing changed. Then, without warning, the Palamedes opened fire.

The sky filled with angry blue, the kind of beam that didn't care about stealth or subtlety. The Seraphine took the hit, shields flaring, and responded with a scatter of countermeasures. Lyra watched the numbers climb, then dip, then climb again as the Seraphine tried to outmanoeuvre the bigger, meaner hunter.

Mercy said, "Shit's about to get fun."

The Seraphine, under heavy fire, pulled a wild inversion and ducked behind a small, pockmarked moon. But it wasn't enough. The Palamedes followed and loosed two torpedoes.

Rask watched as they both hit their mark. He gripped the chair so tight the fabric tore. "Better get us out of here," he said.

Lyra punched the drive, the Meridian surging forward with a whine that set every metal rivet in the ship's hull vibrating. The thermal shielding held, barely. They shot past the Palamedes, close enough to see the rows of railguns tracking them, then slingshotted around the moon's gravity well.

On the far side, the Seraphine tumbled, venting atmosphere. Lyra saw the damage—burns along the hull, a ragged line where the aft engine had once been. But the main damage was the bridge, or lack of.

"Could Kye survive that?" Lyra asked, trying to keep her voice steady.

"Now's our chance to find out."

The Palamedes ran fast and loose, its drive plume cutting a deep wound in the system's pale dark. Rask watched it barrel in on the Seraphine's last known, fingers splayed on the helm as if he could will the enemy ship away by sheer act of pressure. It was an old tactic—push hard, scare your prey into a mistake—but the Palamedes wasn't bluffing, and everyone on the Meridian knew it.

"All hands," Rask snapped, voice clipped and loud enough to override the ship's own rising alarm. "Battle stations. Lyra, prep ghost mode on my mark. Doc, secure the canister and yourself. This is going to get ugly."

Lyra was already running, boots slapping the deck, every step a new argument with the ship's battered inertia. She hit the access ladder to engineering, slid down, and landed on the balls of her feet. The air down here was metallic, hot with the promise of disaster. She stripped the gloves from her hands—no time for safety—and started yanking open the main conduits.

Overhead, the ship's AI began counting down warnings like an anxious parent. "Hull strain at 60%. Internal temperature rising. Unauthorised personnel in engine bay."

Lyra ignored it, pulled a spanner from her belt, and shorted two leads with the practiced, reckless confidence of a woman who'd once repaired a torpedo tube with only a pack of cigarettes and a dead rat.

"Ghost mode prepped," she called up the comm. "Ready on your go."

The Meridian's main lights flickered, then dropped to black. Only the silent, blue-glow of status LEDs lit the world.

On the bridge, Rask lined up their approach. "We drop into the gas cloud. Kill all output, run dark. If the Palamedes wants us, they'll have to come inside and find us."

Mercy braced herself against the bulkhead, the inertia nearly peeling her off the floor as the ship bucked. "We hiding or fighting?"

Rask eyed the display. "Both."

Mercy bared her teeth. "That's my favourite kind of stupid."

In the hold, Doc latched down every loose object, then double-checked the canister's cradle. Glim's pulse was erratic, a wild oscillation that made the whole bench vibrate. He cinched the harness tighter and patted the top of the canister, hoping it would calm, or at least not get worse.

"Don't explode," he said. "Or do, but take the edge off first."

The ship hit the upper atmosphere of the gas moon with a sound like thunder trapped in a tin can. Lyra gripped a live wire between her teeth, spat a curse, and forced the main breaker closed. The shock nearly numbed her arm, but she kept the contact until the indicator turned green.

Above, the AI shrieked: "Caution: This procedure violates seventeen safety protocols and will void all warranties."

Mercy, now upside down relative to the rest of the ship, managed a snort. "One more word, and I'll unplug you myself."

The AI responded with a sad, "Acknowledged," and went silent.

The hull groaned, then screamed, as the pressure differential fought the aging welds and screws. Every patch Lyra had made since she'd joined Rask held, but just barely. The ship's thermal balance went haywire. Frost formed on the inside of the starboard viewport, then vanished as the temperature flipped.

Doc, feeling the g's like a weight on his lungs, braced his head between his knees and retched neatly into a sick bag. Glim's pulse climbed in harmony, vibrating up his spine and into the back of his eyeballs.

The world went dark.

The Meridian hung suspended in the moon's atmosphere, cocooned in copper mist so thick that not even the local star could find them. All systems save life support were dead. The only movement was the faint pulse of emergency lights and the echoing, arrhythmic heartbeat of the canister in the hold.

Rask sat back, unclenched his hands, and let the sweat freeze on his forehead. "Status," he whispered, to no one in particular.

Lyra's voice, ragged and full of static, came up from

below. "We're dead. Or as close as this ship gets. I can restart anything in three seconds."

Mercy hung from a ceiling strut, eyes closed. "They buy it?"

Rask waited, watching the passive sensors. No sign of Palamedes, nothing from the Seraphine.

He thumbed the comm. "Lyra, cut the nav feed. Let's see if they try to flush us out."

"On it," she replied, and the ship's nav grid flickered, then cut to black.

For six minutes, the Meridian drifted blind. Every second stretched thin as old wire, every heartbeat a little louder than the last. The copper clouds rolled over the hull, streaking the viewports in metallic red.

Rask counted down on his fingers. At minute seven, the Palamedes reappeared—a thermal surge, white-hot, punching through the upper bands of the gas moon.

Lyra's console lit with the intrusion. "He's running a wideband scan. Not subtle."

Mercy grinned, her eyes half-lidded with anticipation. "Can we poke him?"

Rask shook his head. "We let him burn fuel. The longer we stay dark, the less he can risk. Hunters are paid for the corpse, not the debris."

Lyra watched the readouts. "He's getting closer. Two hundred klicks and closing."

Doc, in the medbay, felt the pressure drop as the ship

dived lower. He closed his eyes and tried to block out the vibrations from the canister. It didn't work.

A new sound—soft, high, almost musical—filled the hold. He opened his eyes and saw that the canister had shifted colour, blue bleeding into violet at the core.

He checked the sensors. The canister was emitting—he checked again—a signal. Not radio, not microwave. Something slower. Something almost alive.

Doc reached for the comm, but stopped. He remembered Lyra's warning about extraneous noise. Instead, he unspooled a length of wire, clamped it to the canister's output, and ran the other end through a patch-in on his portable.

The laptop's display blazed with a new pattern. It looked, for lack of a better word, like language.

Doc blinked, then started typing.

THIRTEEN

On the bridge, the hull cameras captured the Palamedes. The hunter ship was bigger than the Meridian, twice as sleek, and loaded with weapons that made Rask's skin itch.

Lyra patched the image to the main display. "She's in torpedo range."

Rask didn't blink. "Hold."

The Palamedes fired a test shot—a kinetic round, not aimed to kill, but to flush out a target. The slug punched a hole in the cloud bank a few hundred metres above, missing the Meridian by a margin so thin the AI, were it online, would have screamed.

Lyra held the breaker, thumb whitening on the switch. "Ready?"

Rask: "Not yet."

Doc, in the hold, picked up the canister and stared at the pulse, now flashing in rapid clusters. He keyed the override on his patch-in.

The laptop played a sound.

It was a voice, or something like one. It spoke, then repeated, then shifted pitch and spoke again.

Doc translated, half to himself. "They're talking. The canister and the hunter."

He swallowed, hit the comm. "Bridge. Glim's trying to talk to the Palamedes."

Lyra's voice: "How?"

"Language," Doc said. "Call it code, call it song, I don't care. But they're listening."

Rask ran a simulation, quickly. "If the Palamedes makes contact, what happens?"

Doc: "Best case, it leaves us alone. Worst case, it targets Glim and won't stop till it's got her."

Mercy cracked her knuckles. "So, nothing new."

Lyra watched as the Palamedes drifted closer, then, without warning, cut its engines. The hunter ship hung in the gas, matching their drift perfectly.

Rask checked the sensor feed. "They know we're here. They're waiting."

Mercy whispered, "For what?"

Lyra answered. "For a message."

Doc's voice, urgent: "Let me try."

He keyed the canister's output to the comm array, then triggered a short, encoded burst. The bridge speakers filled with a sound halfway between a computer booting and a choir gasping for air.

For ten seconds, nothing. Then, from the darkness, a reply—deeper, slower, and carrying a gravity that made the hull tremble.

Lyra checked the nav. The Palamedes had shifted, just a hair, now angled directly at the Meridian.

"Doc," Rask said, "whatever you're doing, do it faster."

Doc's hands flew over the keys. "I think it's a handshake protocol. Glim's telling them we're not a threat."

Lyra, sceptical, said, "I don't think they care."

Doc sent another burst. This one's longer, more complex. Glim responded by calming, its light steadying, its pulse almost gentle.

The Palamedes, after a long minute, backed off.

Lyra stared at the feed. "They're leaving."

Mercy, triumphant, punched the air. "We win?"

Rask shook his head. "We survive. For now."

He watched the hunter ship fade into the clouds, then turned to Lyra. "Now we get Kye."

She grinned, wiped sweat from her face, and rebooted the ship's main power. The lights flickered, then returned. The world turned upright again.

Rask keyed the drive, set a course for the Seraphine's last known. "Mercy, ready?"

Mercy checked her blades, then the breach pack on her back. "Born ready."

Doc, now in the corridor, joined the team.

Lyra powered up the engines. The Meridian shuddered, then leapt through the haze, every surface alive with the afterglow of near-death.

As they approached the Seraphine, the ship's AI came back online. Its voice was subdued, almost whispering. "Incoming transmission. Encrypted. Source: Seraphine."

Lyra patched it to the main console. The message was garbled, but the signature was unmistakable: Kye.

Rask read the line, twice, then three times.

It said: "Not much time. Come quick. If I'm gone, burn it all."

Mercy grinned. "We'll make it a party."

Lyra brought the ship to docking range, then looked at Rask.

He nodded. "Good luck."

The airlock cycled, the hull trembling as Mercy primed the breach.

"Time to make some new friends," Mercy grinned and vanished down the ladder, ready to carve the day. Rask and Doc followed close behind.

The airlock coughed them out into a corridor so narrow that Rask Helvan and Mercy Jones had to advance in single file, like a pair of mourners queuing at a funeral for the living. The interior of the Seraphine was a cathedral to poor maintenance and worse taste—bulkheads scorched from old boarding actions, maintenance panels half upended as if the ship had spent the last week trying to eat itself from within. Each footstep set off a fresh echo, amplified by the dying rhythm of the emergency lights, which flickered at unpredictable intervals and illuminated the corridor like a low-budget horror set.

Rask took the lead, sidearm raised and eyes flat with intent. Behind him, Mercy glided more than she walked, two knives drawn. Her boots made no sound, but the hush of her breath was a steady countdown to the next bad decision.

The ship's air was thick with melted insulation and something sour, like a vat of energy drinks left to spoil. The only motion came from the erratic arcs of the lights and the slow drip of coolant from a ruptured pipe. Every so often, the overhead flashed to full, revealing the aftermath of what had clearly been a hasty, unsanctioned evacuation: mess tables with abandoned ration bars still steaming, a jacket draped over a chair back, a trail of oily footprints that vanished at the first intersection.

Rask kept a steady pace. Mercy followed, eyes everywhere, as if she expected an ambush from inside the walls.

Three decks up, Lyra's voice cut in, tinny through their suit comms. "Seraphine's main systems are in local lockdown. I've got them on a holding pattern, but if Palamedes gets a sensor on you, it's game over."

Rask hissed back, "Status?"

"They're still scanning the sector for us. You've got maybe eight minutes before the sweep resets. After that, you're breathing their exhaust."

Mercy checked her chrono, then grinned. "Plenty of time."

They turned a corner, and the corridor abruptly widened. At the next intersection, Mercy paused. "Hold."

She knelt, ran a finger through the dust on the deck. There, traced in a spidery, impatient hand, was a line of graffiti:

IF FOUND, SEND SNACKS

She pointed. "That's Kye."

Rask allowed himself a twitch of amusement. "They're nothing if not consistent."

They pressed on, following the trail of progressively more deranged scrawls—HELP. THIS AIR SUCKS. BRING TOAST.—until they reached a hatch marked by a fresh gouge in the alloy, a crude arrow carved with what looked like a fork.

Mercy set her shoulder to the hatch, but Rask stopped her with a hand signal. He pressed his ear to the panel, listened, then nodded. "Someone inside. One heartbeat. Weak."

Mercy flashed a thumbs-up and reversed the grip on her knife. "Ready."

Rask keyed the manual override. The hatch resisted, then slammed open, banging off the wall and ricocheting back. The compartment inside was a microcell, bare save for a bunk and the tangled heap of person occupying it.

Kye—hair shorn to the scalp, face decorated with a constellation of bruises—looked up and grinned through split lips.

"Took you long enough," they croaked. "Did you bring chips?"

Mercy burst into laughter, dropped her knife, and flung herself onto the bunk, nearly knocking Kye off it in the process. "Missed you, weirdo."

Kye winced, but kept smiling. "You bring the good brand?"

Rask stepped in, scanned the compartment for booby

traps or witnesses, found neither. "We're on the clock," he said, voice all business. "Can you walk?"

Kye shrugged, then stood. "Can run, if you promise me guacamole."

Mercy wrapped Kye's arm over her shoulder, stabilising the limp. "Let's get off this shithole."

Lyra's voice broke in again. "Palamedes just vanished from sensors. They're heading our way, fast."

"Time?" Rask asked.

"Five minutes, maybe less."

Rask pushed Mercy and Kye out into the corridor, then followed, retracing their steps with a speed that bordered on frantic.

As they moved, Kye muttered, "You know, I had a plan."

Mercy grinned. "Does it involve explosives?"

"A little," said Kye. "But mostly it involved not getting rescued by the idiots who got me into this."

Mercy's laugh was a gunshot. "And yet here we are."

They made it to the service ladder, climbed three decks, and sprinted through the last bend to the docking hatch. Rask keyed the airlock. Nothing happened.

He tried again. The panel flashed red: LOCAL OVERRIDE.

"Lyra," he snapped.

Her reply came with the sound of frantic typing. "Vexa's crew cut in a secondary lockout. I can maybe brute force it, but you'll need to reroute the manual from the inside."

Mercy shoved Kye at the panel. "You heard the woman."

Kye blinked, then grinned wider. "This is the easiest thing you've asked me to do all day."

Kye popped the panel with two fingers, pulled a bundle of wires, and twisted them in a sequence that made Rask dizzy to watch. The hatch cycled, hissed, and opened a crack.

They tumbled through, sealed it, then floated in the cramped airlock, breathing hard.

"Home sweet home," Mercy said.

Kye leaned against the wall, eyes closed. "If anyone ever asks, tell them I was dignified."

Rask keyed the comm. "Lyra, we're clear. Start the jump as soon as we're aboard."

At the bridge, Lyra set the drive to warm.

As the rescue team reboarded, Lyra looked up from her console and saw Kye, bloody but grinning, sandwiched between Mercy and Rask.

She raised an eyebrow. "You look like death."

Kye beamed. "Death's overrated. You got food?"

Lyra almost smiled. "We'll see."

Mercy led Kye down the corridor, already recounting how she'd named the knives after her exes. Rask watched them go, shook his head, and said, "Back to normal, then."

Lyra keyed the jump and muttered, "If that's what you want to call it."

Outside, the Palamedes burned in, weapons online.

Inside, the crew braced themselves for the jump. Doc cinched down the containment unit, Kye laughed at Mercy's latest punchline, Rask took the pilot seat, and Lyra ran the numbers, eyes alight.

The Meridian jumped, the world fell away, and for a

moment, there was nothing but the sharp, shared intake of breath.

Then, as always, the universe filled the silence with more trouble.

FOURTEEN

The Meridian limped through interstellar emptiness like a veteran crawling home from the pub, every third warning light on the dash replaced by the universal symbol for "Game Over." The ship's last manoeuvre had left a wake of scorched ions, minor electrical fires, and a drifting medbay that now reeked of antiseptic and someone's failed experiment in pickled onions.

Kye lay supine on the surgical bench, left eye swollen shut, right one flickering in and out of augmented focus. Doc Vellenix, holding a laser suture in one hand and what looked suspiciously like a paper clip in the other, approached with the precise malice of a hungover surgeon.

"Hold still," Doc said, even though the only muscles Kye seemed capable of controlling were the ones required to make snide remarks.

Kye bared their teeth in a smile that suggested both gratitude and a complete lack of self-preservation. "You missed a spot. That, or you're sculpting a second eyebrow."

Doc grunted, pressed the suture to the wound, and watched as the skin sealed, pale against the livid bloom of bruise underneath. "I'd say this'll leave a mark, but I doubt anyone will notice. You've got the face of a collapsed soufflé."

"High praise coming from the man who trims his hair with a soldering iron."

Doc ignored them, flicked the blood off the suture tip, and eyed the readout on Kye's vitals. The monitor made a noise suspiciously like a raspberry, then flatlined for half a second before rebooting to green.

Across the medbay, Mercy sat astride an overturned storage crate, oiling a combat knife with a rag that had once been a T-shirt. She looked up, considered the tableau, and said, "If you're done flirting, the captain wants us in the mess hall."

"Lovely," Kye said, and tried to sit up. They managed it on the second go. "You know no one's offered me a cup of coffee yet?"

Mercy grinned, all teeth and no mirth. "You should be so lucky."

Lyra was already waiting in the mess hall, hunched over the diagnostic panel with a mug of tea that she hoped would still be at least lukewarm by the time she had a chance to drink it. Her uniform was patched, her hands still stained from the last drive overhaul, and her gaze had the sharp, dry intensity of someone who had never been bored a moment in her life and intended to keep it that way.

She didn't look up as the others entered. "You know there's a coolant leak in the foredeck?" she said. "If it gets much worse, we'll have a literal ice rink in the access corridor."

Doc shrugged. "At least the bodies will keep."

Kye glanced at an empty coffee mug, then at Lyra. "Would it kill you to run a simulation on the patch first?"

Lyra's lips twitched. "I like to improvise. Gives the engines personality."

Mercy slid onto the bench, propped her feet on the table, and tossed a ration bar at Kye, who caught it without looking.

"Eat," Mercy said. "You're less annoying when your mouth's full."

Kye bit into it, chewed, and made a show of pretending to enjoy the taste of compressed cardboard and something that might have once been a banana.

Doc poured himself a cup of whatever dark liquid passed for coffee on the Meridian and took a seat. "Where's Rask?"

Lyra gestured with her chin towards the cockpit, where the captain's shadow could be seen slouched over the main panel, staring at the sensor feeds like he expected them to start spelling out threats in all-caps.

"Helvan's in a mood," Lyra said. "Something about the Palamedes still pinging our location every half hour. You'd think a ship with that many guns wouldn't be so needy."

Mercy spun her knife between her fingers. "Never the guns, always the pilots. Compensation, you know."

Kye swallowed the last of the ration bar and flicked

the wrapper into the recycling chute. "Anyone want to fill me in on the part where we're not dead yet?"

Mercy's grin sharpened. "Not yet. Give it a day."

Lyra keyed in a sequence on the diagnostic, then faced Kye. "We're in the clear, for now. The Palamedes lost us in the debris, and the Seraphine's no longer a threat. We're about half a system out, limping for the next jump gate. You should rest up while you can."

Doc added, "You took a good knock to the head. I'd keep the sarcasm below critical, at least until the swelling drops."

Kye, sensing an opportunity to provoke, said, "Was that a medical order or just wishful thinking?"

Doc rolled his eyes, then stabbed a finger at the side of Kye's head. "You've got microfractures in the zygomatic plate. If you don't want your face to cave in during dinner, you'll take it easy."

Mercy said, "Not that you'd notice, given the base state."

Kye leaned back, hands laced behind their head, and surveyed the others with the air of a cat deciding which window to nap in. "I appreciate the concern. But I'm more interested in how we're supposed to keep the canister from melting the hold next time it has a tantrum."

Lyra's expression didn't change, but her fingers drummed a quick, complex rhythm on the tabletop. "Glim's quiet now. Doc ran the diagnostics, but none of the readings make sense. She's either dormant, dead, or waiting for the next opportunity."

"Like a pet snake," said Mercy.

"Or a particularly surly teenager," Kye replied.

Mercy put the knife away and reached for another ration bar. She ripped the wrapper with her teeth and spoke around the mouthful. "What I want to know," she said, "is how you were standing right in front of us one minute, and then on the Seraphine the next. Does that not blow anyone else's mind?"

Kye shrugged, then winced as the movement sent a fresh spike of pain through their face. "It was certainly an *experience.*"

Lyra cocked her head, eyes narrowing. "Anything... rearranged?"

Kye grinned. "Not that I've noticed. Yet. Hard to tell with the beating I took after."

Mercy eyed him. "You always did have shit taste in company."

Kye laughed, and the sound echoed oddly in the mess hall. "Fair enough."

Lyra folded her arms. "Did they have you locked up the whole time or did you see Vexa?"

Kye's smile faded a fraction. "I didn't see her, but I heard her. She had the Orpheon logs."

Mercy straightened. "The relay logs? The ones from the outpost?"

Kye hesitated, then shrugged. "I think so. Someone from her crew pulled the backup before the relay went to hell. She was offering it to the highest bidder."

Doc frowned. "Why would anyone pay for those logs? The outpost was a black-market relay. Nothing there but dirty laundry and old porn."

Kye's eyes glinted. "Unless someone wanted to scrub

every trace of a particular shipment. Or a particular passenger. Or a particular canister."

The silence in the mess hall deepened.

Mercy said, "You're saying the bounty on our heads isn't just for us. It's for Glim."

Kye nodded. "Yes. I caught a glimpse of readouts on the Seraphine. It's not standard biotech. It's... raw. Unstable. Like a prototype."

At the word, Lyra flinched. Doc's jaw tightened.

Mercy muttered, "Fuck me running," and ripped open another ration bar.

Rask, until now silent in the cockpit, spoke without turning. "Prototypes are never made to last," he said. "That's what makes them valuable."

Kye risked a glance at Doc. "How stable is it? Glim. The unit."

Doc shrugged, but his hand hovered near the emergency shutoff on the wall. "If it's a prototype, it's the meanest one I've ever seen. The containment's holding, for now, but the energy profile is off the scale. The ship's AI keeps trying to airlock it."

Lyra said, "Can't blame her."

Mercy, now on her third ration bar, said, "What's the plan, then? We keep running until the money runs out, or until the Palamedes finds us again?"

Rask finally turned from the cockpit, eyes like a winter night. "We find out why they want it," he said. "And we make sure we're the only ones who know how to give it to them."

Kye grinned, respect in their battered face. "That's a plan I can get behind."

Mercy's expression suggested she'd get behind it with a sharpened blade, but she didn't say no.

Lyra drank her cold tea, set the cup down, and said, "Next jump is in six hours. If we're lucky, we'll get three of those without a crisis."

Doc said, "You're never lucky."

"True," Lyra replied. "But sometimes the other guy is even less lucky."

Kye stood, wobbling only slightly, and saluted with two fingers. "Permission to hit the rack?"

"Don't bleed on the sheets," Doc called after them.

Kye wandered towards the crew bunks, humming something that sounded suspiciously like a funeral march. At the hatch, they paused and looked back.

The canister was still there, sealed tight and quiet.

Kye watched it a moment, then said, "Hey, Glim."

The box didn't answer, but the blue light inside flickered, just once.

"Sweet dreams," Kye said.

They left the mess hall, and the crew watched the hatch swing shut, all four of them thinking different, but equally catastrophic, thoughts.

For once, no one bothered to voice them.

The cargo hold was colder than the rest of the ship, and smelled of metal fatigue, and the faint, lingering reek of Glim's last episode. Condensation beaded on the pipes and ran in slow, aimless patterns down the canister's ceramic sides. Every time the containment field cycled, a soft click-woosh echoed off the deck, a sedate heartbeat for the thing inside.

Kye paused at the threshold, running their tongue over a split in their lip. They glanced at Doc, who was doing a passable impression of a nervous librarian, all shifting feet and protective glances at the crate.

"You're sure this is a good idea?" Doc said, as though the question might produce an alternative.

"No," Kye answered, and stepped inside. Their boots squeaked, once, on the damp deck.

Mercy lurked in the corridor, arms folded, a blaster slung over one shoulder and a grenade on her belt purely for mood. Rask watched from the top of the ladder, expression a perfect mask of command and denial. Lyra was probably listening on every mic in the hold, but had the sense not to show up in person.

Doc followed, carrying a scanner tuned to Glim's resonance. "Protocol is to keep ten metres distance. I'm not saying you'll trigger another outburst, but—"

"Ten metres is comms range, not empathy range," Kye said. "You want me to talk to her, I have to get close."

Doc shrugged, set the scanner on a crate, and pulled a sidearm from the medkit. He thumbed the safety off, then on, then off again. "Rask says you go alone, but if it twitches, I get to shoot."

"Fair," Kye said, though they doubted Doc would hit the right thing even if he tried.

The canister sat in the centre of a nest of power cables, restraint loops, and a trio of heavy, padded tethers. Blue light, soft and static, leaked from the edges of the screw top. The only display was a small, battered terminal that flicked between system status and a running count of "incidents since last reset." It currently read two.

Kye knelt beside the box, feeling the chill through both layers of their flight suit. They set a palm gently on the ceramic and waited for the hum to change. For a long moment, nothing did.

They spoke, quietly, in the precise, clipped syllables they reserved for fragile things. "Hello, Glim. It's Kye. You remember me?"

The hum shifted, just a hair. The blue light pulsed.

Doc flinched, but said nothing.

Kye exhaled. "You're safe. You're on the Meridian. We had to run. There was a fight. Do you... do you know what I'm saying?"

Another pulse, sharper now. Kye felt a pressure in their ear, then in their jaw, as if the air had thickened between them and the box.

They tried again. "Glim, I know you're in there. Can you give me a sign?"

The canister vibrated. A single, high note sang out and died away. The terminal's status blinked red, then green, then red again.

Kye risked a glance at Doc, who mouthed, "Careful."

Kye licked their lips. "I'm sorry I left you behind. It wasn't my idea. I was taken on board the Seraphine.

A pause. Then the blue light flickered, brighter than before, and the canister's hum climbed by a full octave. The scanner on Doc's hip beeped a warning.

Doc edged closer, gun now out and pointed at the deck, but ready.

The canister's terminal cycled through diagnostic screens at speed, then froze on a single line of text. It scrolled, slowly, three words:

LIAR. LIAR. LIAR.

Kye jerked back, hand yanked away from the canister as if burned. The blue glow flared and snapped off, leaving only a faint afterimage.

Mercy's voice, faint but delighted, echoed down the corridor. "Did she just call you a liar? That's brilliant."

Doc holstered the gun, his hands shaking in that way Kye knew meant he was suppressing panic with science. "That's... new."

Kye sat on the cold deck, breathing hard. "She's never done that before. Not the messages. Not like that."

Doc said, "I think she's angry. At you."

Kye blinked, felt the blood pounding behind their eyes. "How is that even possible? She's a protocol, a neural map, a—"

"Person," said Doc, soft.

Kye wiped their nose, and found a thin line of blood on the back of their hand. "That's not— it's not possible."

Doc nodded at the canister, which now pulsed with a slow, almost sullen rhythm. "You want to try again?"

Kye shook their head. "Give it a minute. She—she needs time."

The hold filled with silence, broken only by the compressor cycling and Mercy humming a snatch of some bloody sea shanty from the hatchway.

After a long time, Doc asked, "You want to tell me what really happened on Orpheon?"

Kye shook their head again, but this time there was more sadness than refusal. "Nothing you'd believe."

Doc considered that, then nodded. "That's most things, nowadays."

Before either could say more, the overheads pinged with a sudden, discordant note, and Lyra's voice boomed from every speaker: "Bridge to cargo. We've just been pinged from deep space. Stealth signal. Carrier unknown. It used Glim's frequency."

Doc went pale, then angry. "Someone just made contact?"

Lyra's voice returned, clipped. "Yep. They know we're here."

Kye stared at the canister, which now pulsed a steady, knowing blue.

Mercy wandered in, blaster cradled, looking amused and impressed. "So, what's the play now?"

Rask's voice, dry as ever, sounded from above: "We run, same as always. But this time, we pick the battlefield."

Doc stood, picked up the scanner, and eyed the canister like it might bite.

Kye remained on the deck, staring at the glowing seam of the lid.

She called me a liar, they thought.

She's not wrong.

Out in the void, far from the Meridian, another ship listened to the same frequencies. The message was simple, and it was meant for them.

We see you.

172

FIFTEEN

The Meridian's alarm was not designed to inspire calm. It was a banshee wail, equal parts collision warning and psychological warfare, guaranteed to obliterate even the most entrenched sleep deficit. The crew tumbled from their respective holes, limbs tangling with bulkheads and each other, as the deck lurched to red and the internal air pressure spiked by half a percent.

Lyra hit the corridor running, elbowed past Mercy with the efficiency of a pub brawler, and reached the sensor array before her hair had settled from the static. She smacked the override with the heel of her palm, booted up the old diagnostics in safe mode, and let her hands dance over the field of trembling, flickering lights. The display rendered three full seconds of visual snow, then spat a vector—tight, sharp, and tracing straight through their current hiding layer in the shadow of a comet tail.

"Signal's not random," Lyra said, loud enough for the

others to hear as they clustered behind her. "They know the harmonic frequency for Glim."

Mercy's answer was a word that would have gotten her banned from several polite colonies, then: "So it's another message. For us, or for Glim?"

Doc had already peeled the shielding from Glim's canister and was standing over it like a mortician performing a wake. The blue pulse within, once content to play Morse with the patience of a Swiss watch, now sputtered at variable amplitude—sharp, erratic, the rhythm of a heart in the final stages of cardiac arrest. Doc's fingers hovered above the output display, not touching, as if a direct contact might shatter what little normalcy remained.

He glanced up, addressing the room. "Whatever it sensed in Kye, it triggered a defensive shift. It's gone into a kind of... lockout. Not safe, not asleep, but one twitch from going full thermal."

Mercy, who had yet to put her knives away, positioned herself with theatrical casualness between Kye and the canister. She rolled her neck, eyed the canister, then eyed Kye, as if deciding which would make the better headline for tomorrow's inquest.

Kye, for their part, had retreated to the edge of the mess hall. Arms folded, eyes twin points of ice—one organic, one twitching with a faint red diagnostic glow. "I haven't lied," Kye said. "If anyone's interested."

No one replied. The silence acquired a pressure, an atmospheric tension more physical than emotional.

Lyra stabbed at the holo again, zooming in on the incoming signal. "It's modulated to Glim's frequency.

Narrowband, with a quantum resonance fingerprint. Whoever's sending this, it's not a pirate with a scanner and a grudge."

Doc added, "It's a machine. Or something close."

Mercy bared her teeth. "That narrows it down to half the system."

Kye glanced at the canister, then back at the crew. "You want me to open it up? Talk to her again?"

Doc shook his head, slow and deliberate. "Not until I've figured out how to keep her from frying the hull on her way out."

Kye's jaw flexed, a small betrayal of the nerves below the surface. "Then what?"

"We wait," Lyra said, "and we don't answer the ping. If they want to find us, they'll have to do it the old-fashioned way."

Mercy planted herself, arms crossed, and said, "Or we let Kye have a go and see if the box explodes. We're overdue for a proper story."

"No," Lyra said. "We're not improvising this time."

Mercy made a show of putting away her blade, but the way her hand lingered on the hilt suggested she hadn't bought into the argument.

Rask, who until now had been the ghost in the room, finally materialised at the far end of the mess hall. He had the look of a man who'd spent the last hour contemplating whether it was worth dying today, and had just about decided against it. "We don't get to wait," he said. "If they've already got our frequency, we're burning daylight by pretending we can hide."

Lyra said, "You want to answer the call?"

Rask shrugged. "I want to know what they want. And if it's us, or Glim."

A beat, then Kye said, "it's always Glim."

Mercy grinned. "That's the spirit."

Lyra ran a hand through her hair, scattering an arc of static that glittered in the blue and red wash of the mess hall. She eyed Kye, who met her gaze without blinking.

"Come with me," Lyra said.

Kye hesitated, then uncrossed their arms. Mercy shifted her weight, as if to intercept, but Lyra's look brooked no argument.

The two walked out of the mess hall, down the short, battered corridor to the maintenance shaft. Lyra ducked the low beam, keyed open the access panel, and stepped inside. Kye followed, hands tucked deep into the pockets of their jacket, face set to impassive.

The maintenance crawl was barely wide enough for two. Lyra flicked on a torch, the beam bouncing off scarred pipe and cabling. She waited until the hatch cycled shut, then turned, her face uncharacteristically serious.

"You recognised the signal," Lyra said.

It was not a question.

Kye stared at the patch of wall just over Lyra's shoulder. "Once. On the station. Before everything went to shit."

"Why didn't you say anything?"

Kye's eye glimmered. "Because if I'm wrong, I'm a liability. And if I'm right..."

Lyra waited, silent.

Kye rolled the words around, picked the least awful.

"If I'm right, it's not just the Imperium. It's the original designers. The ones who made Glim. They're coming to erase the evidence."

Lyra took this in without moving, then said, "And you thought you'd handle this by yourself."

Kye smiled, but it was nothing like happy. "Worked for you, once."

"Don't project your issues onto me." Lyra snapped, "if you'd told me, we could have prepped. Rask could have prepped. Now we're flying blind."

Kye leaned back, resting their head against the cold conduit. "What would you have done? Jumped ship sooner? Vented the box?"

Lyra bristled, but didn't answer.

Kye's voice dropped. "You were off-military, Lyra. You know what this means. You saw the black projects. If they're still running, they won't want Glim to be recovered. They'll want a clean slate."

Lyra's hands curled to fists, then relaxed. "We're not going to die for them, Kye. Not you, not the crew."

Kye looked away. "I wasn't planning on it."

Lyra squared up, blocking the hatch. "Then you don't get to keep secrets anymore."

A nod, slow. "Fine."

"You tell us everything. Not just when it gets interesting."

"Agreed," Kye said, the words small in the metal tunnel.

Lyra stepped back, made to leave, then paused.

She regarded Kye for a long moment. "Why do I get the feeling you haven't told me the worst of it?"

Kye's cybernetic eye dimmed, the internal light shuttering as if to simulate shame. "Because sometimes the truth is worse."

Lyra left it at that.

Back in the hold, Doc hovered over the canister, scribbling readings on a pad with handwriting that suggested a crisis of faith in the alphabet.

When Lyra and Kye returned to the bridge, Rask looked at them both, then said: "They're not giving up. New ping just hit the sensors, closer than before."

Mercy's smile widened. "Showtime?"

Lyra nodded. "Showtime."

She shot Kye a look that promised retribution if the next ten minutes didn't go to plan.

Kye, for once, seemed content to let someone else take the lead.

On the sensor array, the signal pulsed—steady, hungry, and now only a few light-seconds away.

Doc watched the canister, and for the first time since he'd joined the crew, he looked afraid.

The Meridian was silent except for the alarms.

And somewhere, far out in the dark, something answered.

Rask Helvan stood just inside the main hatch, not moving, not speaking. His silhouette was all square lines and slow-burn tension, the kind of posture that suggested a man waiting for a verdict he already knew he wouldn't like. The canister containing Glim dominated the centre of the hold, locked down with enough carbon fibre to survive atmospheric entry—assuming nothing inside decided to explode.

Mercy found him there, arms folded, feet apart, knife already spinning between her fingers. She didn't bother with a greeting.

"So, this is where we die," she said. The echo off the bulkheads was just enough to make it sound like the room agreed.

Rask didn't answer.

Mercy advanced, boots scuffing the deck. "I ever tell you I hate this part? Not the hiding, not the running. The bit where we keep nicking things we can't even name, trusting people who lie for a living, and waiting to see who pulls the trigger first. You know what they call that, back where I grew up?"

Rask's eyes flicked, slow, to meet hers. "Enlighten me."

"Stupidity," said Mercy. She gestured at Glim, at the mess of diagnostic cables and the cold glow beneath the lid. "At some point, it's not luck that keeps you alive. It's leadership."

Rask didn't rise to the bait. He just stared at the canister, as if hoping it would offer him a better answer.

Mercy paced a tight circle, stopping only to pick up a wrench from the floor and toss it end over end. "You know what bothers me?" she said. "Not the bounty, not the Imperium. Not even the idea that Glim could fry us if she gets bored. What bothers me is that every time I think about bailing, I remember you're the one who's supposed to be in charge. And then I think: maybe the other guy's got it right this time."

Rask's shoulders tensed, then dropped. "If you want to leave, I'm not stopping you."

Mercy grinned, teeth bright in the dim. "You're a shit liar, Rask. If you really wanted me gone, you'd have left me behind at the Orpheum."

He almost smiled at that, then lost it. "This isn't going to end well," he said.

Mercy shrugged, as if to say nothing ever did.

The silence stretched, thick enough to drown in.

Then the ship's AI spoke from the nearest comm panel. The voice was different—crisp, almost cheerful, but with an undertone of something that had never seen a sunrise.

"Object in pursuit," it said. "Acceleration increasing. Signal confirms: Imperial prototype hunter. Estimated interception: eleven hours."

Mercy whistled, low and impressed. "That's a fast one."

Rask looked at Glim again. "They want her. And they're not going to slow down for us."

Before Mercy could reply, the entire ship jolted sideways. The impact wasn't enough to knock them over, but it sent half a dozen tools and two unsecured crates skating across the deck like startled animals.

The lights flickered, then stabilised.

Mercy caught herself on a handrail, but the knife still spun in her other hand. "Tell me that was you," she said.

Rask shook his head, eyes on the diagnostics screen wired to the canister.

From somewhere deeper in the hull, a new sound—soft, but growing—pulsed through the hold. It was the voice of Glim, but not as they'd heard before. No longer clicks and signals. This was a voice. An actual voice. Like a child's, frayed at the edges. A sound that remembered pain and wasn't shy about sharing.

The comm panel lit up, and Glim's voice came through, but etched with something like regret.

"It knows me," Glim said. "It knows me, and it will not stop."

Mercy stared at the speaker, then at Rask. "You ever get the feeling we're just bait?"

He nodded, not looking away from Glim. "We always were."

The temperature in the hold dropped a degree. The air tasted like the aftershock of a storm.

Mercy knelt beside the canister, laid her palm flat on the surface. "What do you want to do?" she asked, voice almost gentle.

Rask took a moment, then answered, "Survive."

Mercy grinned, but this time it was brittle. "Best plan yet."

Above them, the ship's AI hummed to itself, cataloguing every new threat with the polite indifference of a weather report.

Below, Glim's canister pulsed—once, twice, then a long, lingering note.

The hunter was coming.

And on the Meridian, it felt like the walls themselves were holding their breath.

SIXTEEN

The alarm hit them at half-past midnight, ship's time, because the universe had a sense of humour. It began as a staccato bleat, doubled in tempo, and then climbed to a pitch that could sand old paint off bulkheads. The nav display on the bridge pulsed a sickly orange, all other functions overridden by the proximity alert.

Lyra, who had been asleep—or as close as she got to it—snapped upright on the comms chair. She jabbed the mute, squinted at the threat grid, and hissed through her teeth. "Not good." The words rolled off her tongue in a monotone; it wasn't fear, just the surety of an engineer who'd run the numbers already and found them wanting.

Down in the crew bunks, Kye was already awake, the sound only confirming what their nerves had predicted: escalation, not respite. They stood, shaking off the remnants of a half-dream, and began the slow trudge towards the mess hall, where all bad news was eventually served. The corridor lighting flickered as if the ship itself were on the verge of panic.

Doc Vellenix was in the head, twenty millilitres into the bottle and attempting to ignore his reflection. The alarm was the only thing that could have got him out of the compartment in under a minute. He wiped his mouth, grabbed his field kit, and followed the sound.

Mercy Jones arrived last, but with style. She slid down the ladder from the upper deck, landing in a crouch, the hilt of a blade tucked behind each ear. Her hair was the colour of a chemical spill, and her smile was exactly as wide as the emergency warranted.

By the time they clustered in the mess hall, Rask Helvan was already there, hands flat on the table, staring at a spread of nav-prints and drinking from a mug that steamed only out of habit. The mess hall lights juddered overhead, turning his silhouette into a time-lapse of fatigue and barely-suppressed dread.

He looked up at the four of them with the air of a man who'd stopped believing in miracles two wars ago. "Sit," he said.

Mercy kicked a chair out, plopped down, and rested both elbows on the table. Lyra went to the wall and folded her arms, eyes locked on the threat display patched to the far end. Kye took the seat opposite Mercy, drumming their fingers on the tabletop as if daring someone to notice. Doc hovered, as always, on the edge of the group.

Rask didn't bother with preamble. "We've got a hunter on us. Imperial, by the signature. It's running cold, but it's there." He swept an arm over the nav-prints. "We're here. It's here. Between us: forty thousand klicks and a debris field."

Lyra glanced at the printouts, eyes scanning, jaw already set. "No way we burn past it without being seen."

"Correct," said Rask. "Can't outrun, can't hide, can't outgun."

Doc snorted, but said nothing.

Mercy grinned, showing every canine. "So, we lure it in, spring a surprise. Classic."

Rask shot her a look. "Classic is how we got a bounty on our heads in the first place."

Kye cleared their throat, voice smaller than usual but all the sharper for it. "There's a slot. The debris field near 9B. If we cut the burn and slingshot, we might—*might*—get a shadow off the rocks. Just enough to—" They caught themselves, aware of four sets of eyes, and retreated into an apologetic hunch. "Assuming the hunter is expecting us to run straight."

Lyra's expression went acid. "That's a belt, not a shadow. Those rocks are packed tighter than the skulls in a memorial wall."

Kye's hands tapped a rhythm, the tension translating into a drum line only they could hear. "You want to try doing nothing?"

Mercy, not looking up from the mess table, said, "I'm always in favour of reckless. It's better than dying bored."

Rask surveyed the group, his gaze lingering on each in turn. "This isn't a vote. We don't have a deck of good options. If we jettison the canister, we lose the only leverage we've got. If we keep running, the hunter's going to pull us apart in a day. If we hole up in the belt—" He gestured, open-palmed. "Best case, we kill a lot of time and make a mess. Worst case, it's over in minutes."

Lyra's fingers never stopped moving, picking invisible lint from her sleeve, winding and unwinding the tight coil of her hair. "Glim's already spiking containment stress. You want a repeat of Orpheon?"

Kye said, "If the hunter gets its hands on Glim, we're all dead anyway. Or worse."

Doc, up to this point content to watch, finally spoke. "How's Glim now?"

Lyra shrugged, the movement tight. "She's... alert. Pacing. If it escalates, I might need to cycle the dampener again. It'll buy us hours, not days."

Mercy leaned in, elbows planted. "What if we make them think we're dead? Pull a full-body fake."

Rask's face didn't move, but his eyes sharpened. "Go on."

Mercy produced a grenade from somewhere in her jacket and set it on the table with the delicacy of a rare fruit. "We spike the containment pod with a charge, use a heat flare as a corpse. We're not on the manifest, just the canister. If the hunter sees an explosion, maybe it stops to collect the pieces."

Lyra snorted. "You've seen what happens when a containment unit breaches, right?"

"Yeah," Mercy said, pleased. "It looks like a very convincing death."

Kye said, "That still leaves us stuck on a ship running silent in a debris field with no one coming for us."

Mercy grinned. "That's the fun part."

Doc gave Glim's readout a side-eye. "What do you need from me?"

Lyra: "Set up a stabiliser. If the hunter scans for a body, give it one that screams 'dead as hell'."

Doc nodded, all business. "I can run a cocktail, make the signature look terminal."

Rask pushed off from the table, the chair legs screeching across metal. "We do it fast. We don't have time for second thoughts."

The lights flickered overhead, dimming a half-step as the ship cycled into power conservation.

Kye watched the others, fingers frozen mid-tap. "If we do this, and it works, then what?"

Rask looked back, the weight of command fully visible. "We run until we can't. Then we find another lie."

Mercy gave the group a small, approving nod. "My kind of plan."

Lyra snatched the printouts, rolled them tight, and jammed them into the chest pocket of her coveralls. "I'll prep the core."

Doc slipped out with the efficiency of a man who'd already done the necessary triage in his head.

Kye sat a moment, staring at the grenade on the table. The blue paint had worn off, leaving only the serial number and a chipped cartoon skull. It looked less like a weapon than a bad souvenir from a holiday no one wanted to remember.

Mercy flicked the grenade, then Kye's temple, and said, "You ever miss the easy jobs?"

Kye shook their head. "Never did one."

Mercy laughed, loud and genuine.

The mess hall emptied, leaving only the faint after-image of bodies and the echo of shoes on steel.

On the bridge, Lyra rerouted the nonessential systems, then killed the overheads. The world shrank to the flicker of the nav display and the steady, trembling line of their trajectory. She watched the clock tick down to the next manoeuvre, counting each second with the intensity of a miser hoarding coins.

Down in the cargo bay, Doc set about prepping the escape pod for its fake death. He checked Glim, and patted the canister like a nervous parent of a child with a high temperature.

In the corridor, Mercy tested the charges. Each snap and click was a small, kinetic poem to the inevitability of violence. She smiled with every successful detonation.

Kye found themselves in their bunk, staring at the ceiling.

Rask paced the length of the ship, checking every lock and seal, touching each surface as if the act could transfer some small part of his worry into the steel. When he reached the bridge, Lyra glanced up, saw him, and said, "If this works, you owe me a drink."

Rask allowed himself a half-smile. "If this works, I'll buy you the bar."

She took that for what it was.

The ship drifted into the dark, the hull barely alive with the minimum systems required to keep its crew from freezing or boiling in their sleep.

In the hold, Glim's canister pulsed with a low, insistent rhythm, the blue light faint but unwavering.

Above, the hunter ship closed, its own signal so precise and cold it barely counted as a heartbeat.

The Meridian hung in the void, the only proof of its own existence the collective will of its crew.

And for the first time, the silence felt like a choice.

They gathered in the cargo bay because it was the only place with enough space to pace. Above, the hull shivered every time the nav thrusters fired, the vibration working its way down to the deck plates in tiny, persistent quakes.

The escape pod had been stuffed full of anything the crew could find that wasn't bolted down. Mercy circled the open hatch with a raptor's patience, twining detcord around the bracing struts and humming an old war song in a minor key. Each time she reached the starting point, she cinched the cable tighter, until the whole thing looked like a bomb gift-wrapped by an angry spider.

"Your plan is going to get us killed," Lyra said, not looking up.

Kye didn't blink. "If it works, we're not dead. If it doesn't, at least we know who to blame."

Lyra's knuckles whitened on the edge of the console. "That's not comfort. I want a plan that doesn't require improvisation."

"Trust the numbers," Kye said. "I ran the sequence five times. We'll match the hunter's expectations to within a tenth of a second."

Lyra made a sound in her throat that was neither

agreement nor protest. "If you mess up the signal, even a little, they'll know."

Kye held her gaze, the cybernetic eye gleaming, the other one flat and tired. "If I mess up, we're already dead."

Mercy, looping past them, snorted. "That's the spirit. Try not to spill it on the detcord, yeah?"

Doc trundled in last, dragging the medkit and a battered case of sedatives. He set the kit on the bench, flipped the canister open, and stared at the vials with the disaffection of a man reviewing failed relationships. "Who's sedating Glim?" he asked.

Lyra finished her code, keyed the override, and stepped away. "She's less likely to kill us if you do it. She likes you."

Doc glared, but fetched the neural dampener. He eyed the canister, which now shivered with a pale aura, the internal lights flickering like a dying star.

"She's not going to like this," he muttered.

Kye watched him cross the bay, the lines of guilt around their mouth deepening. "Sorry, Glim," they whispered, too soft for anyone else to hear.

Doc thumbed the hypo, found the injection port, and pressed it home. The canister's light spiked, then dulled, the hum collapsing into a single, sullen note. For a moment, nothing else in the bay moved. Then, slowly, the containment unit's diagnostics rolled back to green, and Doc exhaled.

Mercy finished her war-dance around the pod, sealed the hatch, clapped her hands, and grinned at Rask, who had appeared in the hold at some point without anyone noticing. "We're good to go, Cap. She'll blow in three stages, heat first, then hull, then a nice crispy EM signature."

Rask nodded, silent. He walked a slow lap of the bay, checking each fastening, each readout, as if the act itself could guarantee survival. When he passed Lyra, he said nothing, but the look exchanged was ancient as war and twice as bitter.

Mercy sidled up to Kye. "How's your end?"

Kye shrugged. "We'll know when we know."

Mercy leaned in, voice low. "You scared?"

Kye managed a smile. "I'd be worried if I wasn't."

Mercy barked a laugh, then pulled a blade from behind her back and offered it, hilt-first. "For luck."

Kye took it. "Thanks. I'll try not to use it."

"Do what you have to," Mercy said, expression momentarily without irony. "We all want to live."

They returned to their stations: Lyra to the mainframe, Kye to the manual controls, Doc to the medbay, Mercy to the bomb, Rask to the silent, brooding space where all captains go to die.

The last thing to do was wait for the window.

Rask signalled the two-minute mark with a lift of his chin. Lyra began the sensor spoof, hands flying over the input. Mercy crouched by the pod, counting off the detonators under her breath. Doc laid a steadying palm on the canister, as if touch could transmit calm. Kye flexed their fingers and watched the clock.

A minute out, Rask crossed to Mercy, pulled her aside, and spoke so low the words barely carried. "If this doesn't work, I need you to save the canister. And get Kye off this ship. They're the only one who understands Glim."

Mercy's face shuttered, theatrical bravado drained out of her in a heartbeat. "You expecting it not to work?"

"I'm planning for the worst," Rask said. "That's the job."

Mercy nodded, all playfulness gone. "You're still an idiot."

"But loveable," Rask replied.

At thirty seconds, the tension in the bay was a living thing. The only sound was the soft ping of the clock and the low, electric breathing of the ship.

At ten, Lyra signalled the crew. "Spooling in three. Two. One—"

Kye hit the trigger.

The decoy pod launched from the bay, and, as if in slow motion, tumbled into space.

The first charge fired: a flash of white heat, a blossom of plasma that lit up the asteroid field like the inside of a furnace. The pod's signal burst, then collapsed, a flatline that anyone watching would read as instant, catastrophic death.

The second and third charges blew in sequence, peeling the pod open and venting its insides in a spray of charred, spinning debris. The heat plume was visible even to the naked eye, if one was insane enough to look.

Inside the Meridian, the crew sat in full dark, no one daring to move.

The hunter ship passed overhead, a silhouette so thin and sharp it barely cast a shadow. Its sensors raked the field, lingering just long enough to taste the wreckage, then pressed on, hunting for something that wasn't there.

Kye watched the scan in silence, heart stuttering as the hunter wobbled, paused, then kept going.

Lyra leaned back, eyes closed, hands trembling. "It worked," she said, so softly it was barely sound.

Doc looked at Glim, the canister's light now a dim, steady blue.

Mercy slumped against the wall, all adrenaline burned off, and said, "Someone better buy me a drink."

Rask, watching the trajectory, said nothing. His job was not to believe in miracles, only to record when they occurred.

The Meridian floated in the dark, alive but undetected.

And for a moment, in the cold and the quiet, there was peace.

SEVENTEEN

The Imperial hunter turned, its hunt not quite over yet. It came in masked, heat signature a flatline, hull so black it drank the stars, and only the faintest ripple of distorted starlight betrayed its course. The Meridian, entombed in an iceberg's worth of asteroid slush, watched through a slit in the debris and did not so much as twitch.

Inside, the ship was a mausoleum. The life-support had been choked back to barely more than hope: the air cycled once every ten minutes, and only the thermal lag in the walls kept the crew from freezing into a set of particularly underwhelming snowmen. Frost crept up the instrument panels, forming dendrites that crawled from knob to dial, and every exhaled breath left a patchy fog in the blue-white gloom of the emergency LEDs.

Lyra monitored the approach from the pilot's chair, her body wrapped in two flight suits and a blanket she'd stolen from the medbay. Her eyes watered from the cold, but she kept them open, darting between the passive readouts and the tiny, vibrating dot that was the hunter.

Every now and then, her left hand would drift over the control column, knuckles cracked and pale, and hover an inch above the manual cutover, just in case.

Kye crouched in the footwell behind her, knees to chest, chewing a thumbnail so hard it left little flecks of skin on their lip. They'd given up on the deck's diagnostic display twenty minutes ago, once the quantum filaments in the scanner started to sing an audible C# and refused to be debugged. Now they tapped their boot against the deck plating—one-two, one-two-three, one-two—a polyrhythm of nerves.

On the starboard wall, Mercy sat with her back to the bulkhead, both hands tucked under her armpits, hood pulled up so only her nose and eyes showed. She stared at the sensor repeater with the kind of predatory stillness that suggested she would murder the hunter, the asteroid belt, and half the local wildlife if it got her any closer to a working heater. Her blaster sat in her lap, thumb resting on the safety, and she'd been cycling it on and off for the last hour. Nobody commented.

Rask stood in the hatchway, filling it with a silhouette so tense it was hard to tell where the man ended, and the alloy began. He kept his eyes on the viewport, his left hand wrapped around the frame, and his right resting on the emergency jettison for Glim's canister. If anyone noticed, they did not say.

The hunter drifted closer, skating the edge of a high-density rock field, leaving nothing behind but a trickle of microbursts on the gamma. Lyra's lips moved, not in words but in calculations, her breath frosting the collar of her blanket.

The hunter decelerated with a burn so quick it spiked the temperature by a fraction of a degree. The ship tumbled, rotated, and—without so much as a radio handshake—opened fire.

"Brace," Lyra hissed, and the crew hit the deck in a practiced choreography of the doomed.

The first shot was not for them. It found what was left of the decoy pod, still radiating just enough to pass for a desperate, wounded escape. The pod's self-destruct went off in a cone of plasma, flash-boiling half the local rubble and sending a pretty spray of micronised dust across the hunter's prow. The sensors lit with false positives and then went dark as the pod was obliterated.

Kye peeked up at the screen, eye wide. "They weren't taking any chances then."

The hunter came to a complete stop. The ship rotated, nose pointed at the detonation, and for a long minute nothing happened at all. The crew sat frozen, heartbeat the only sound.

Then, slowly, the hunter began to circle. It made a slow, methodical ring around the blast site, as if paying last respects. Each sweep brought it closer to the Meridian's hiding spot.

Lyra's fingers went white on the yoke. "That's a search pattern. It's not leaving."

Kye's foot began its tap again, this time so fast it shook the ice crystals off the deck.

Mercy checked her weapon, then the door, then the ceiling. "If it boards us—"

"We vent the hold," Rask said, and his tone left no room for debate.

The circling tightened. On every pass, the hunter deployed a fresh sheet of drones—tiny, flickering specks that cast a scatter of pings across the belt, mapping every heat trace, every echo, every conceivable hiding place.

Kye watched the drone cloud advance, then looked at Lyra. "If they get close, the field will spike. Our thermal cover won't hold."

Lyra licked cracked lips, then said, "We have an hour, tops."

Mercy laughed, not kindly. "That's more than we usually get."

Rask gripped the hatch frame tighter, the veins in his hand standing out. He stared at the dot on the repeater, then at the expanse of black on the main screen. "We hold. No one moves. No one talks."

They did as they were told.

Time, in the Meridian, went liquid. The cold seeped into bones, into thoughts, until all that was left was the mechanical repetition of the hunter's circle and the crawl of numbers on the clock. Even the ship's AI had shut up, as if it too understood that any word now would be suicide.

The hunter paused in its arc. The drones converged, shrinking the search radius, the cloud folding in on itself like a net tightening.

Doc, who had been a shadow at the back of the bridge for the last hour, finally stirred. He edged forward, keeping his body low, and settled next to Glim. His breath came out in shallow huffs, crystallising on the ceramic.

He looked at the readout, then at Kye, and whispered, "It's not looking for life. It's listening."

Kye frowned. "Listening how?"

"Resonance. Interference. Machine song." He tapped the canister with a bare knuckle, a soft staccato. "Glim is quiet, but she's not silent. Nothing that alive ever is."

As if on cue, the canister began to hum. The sound was low, barely above vibration, but it shivered up through the deck plates and into the soles of their boots. Mercy looked down, then at Doc.

"You sedated it," she said. Not a question.

Doc's lips pressed thin. "Only dampened. Can't kill it, not without—" He shrugged.

Kye stared at the canister, at the soft blue that pulsed from the status light. It pulsed, then slowed, then pulsed again. The hum grew, vibrating through the steel, through the frost, through the layer of debris and ice that cocooned the ship.

Lyra watched the hunter on the scope. "It's reacting. The circle's closing."

Rask's jaw clenched. "Options?"

Mercy's eyes fixed on the readout. "We fight. What else is there?"

Lyra looked at Rask. "If we break cover now, it'll vaporise us before we can spool the drive."

Rask nodded, slow, and closed his eyes for a second too long. When he opened them, the decision had already happened.

"We hold," he said. "We outlast it. We wait for a window."

Glim's hum grew louder, the pulse now strong

enough to make the deck vibrate in sympathy with every breath.

Doc stared at Glim, then at Kye. "She's scared," he said.

Kye met his gaze, the memory of their last conversation hanging like a noose in the air. "So am I."

Nobody argued.

Outside, the hunter's drones converged, the search pattern now a fist aimed directly at the Meridian's heart. The crate's hum grew, resonating with a frequency that felt like the echo of their own panic.

Mercy bared her teeth in the cold, and said, "If we go out, at least we'll make a noise."

Lyra glanced back, almost smiled. "That's the pirate way."

Kye put a hand on Glim, fingers numb, and waited.

The hunter bore down.

And in the freezing dark, the Meridian's own heartbeat answered—steady, unyielding, and, for the moment, very much alive.

The hum grew teeth.

The first drone announced itself not with a ping or a warning, but with a metallic thunk that rattled against the hull. For a moment, the crew held perfectly still, as if motion alone would give them away. Then came the scraping—a non-human tap-tap-tap that crawled across the hull in fits and starts. It sounded like a dog's nails on tile, if the dog were made of knives and had never lost a fight.

Mercy jerked upright, blaster in both hands. "Guess telling them that there's no one home won't work."

Lyra muted the display, heart pounding out of sync with the crate's hum. "Drones. External scan, hull contact."

Kye ducked under the console, eyes flicking to the overhead. "If they get through the seam—"

"They won't," Lyra said, and immediately started the engine restart sequence.

Rask, still by the hatch, watched the monitor. "Don't wait for them to knock. We go now."

Doc reached out, steadying the crate as the vibrations amplified. "They're not subtle," he muttered. "Even Glim's getting agitated."

The scraping doubled, then tripled. Kye's count went into overtime. "At least three."

Mercy flicked the safety off. "We need more guns."

"Engage," Rask said. It was not a suggestion.

Lyra drove her palm into the restart. The Meridian's systems came alive in an instant—lights, heat, sensors, all surging from frozen silence to frantic activity. The sudden rush of air made everyone's hair stand on end. In the same heartbeat, Mercy threw herself at the weapons console, flipped open the gunnery panel, and began punching out targets at a velocity that implied deeply personal hatred.

Outside, the first volley shattered the drone clinging

to the comms mast, spraying the hull with a snow of glassy fragments. The others reacted, fanning out across the surface, digging in with carbide legs. Mercy tracked and fired, each shot a precise, surgical burst that left only sparks and splinters in its wake.

Kye scrambled for the storage locker, retrieved a squat, ugly EMP grenade, and turned to Lyra. "Pop the hatch?"

Lyra had already bypassed the lock. "You've got ten seconds. Don't miss."

Kye grinned, lips cracked, and sprinted for the airlock. They slapped the hatch open, primed the grenade, and launched it into the void. The device tumbled, caught the light, then detonated in a pulse of blue-white that turned half the nearest asteroid into a cloud of steam and twitching metal. The scraping went silent.

For a moment, it looked like the trick had worked. The drone pings vanished, the ship's hull went quiet, and even Glim's hum seemed to sigh with relief.

Lyra rebooted the nav, plotting the shortest route out of the belt. "We're clear," she said.

Rask shook his head. "Not yet."

On the main display, the hunter ship shifted. Its silhouette elongated, a needle extruding from the hull. The targeting array flared to life, and a red trace painted itself across the Meridian's flank.

Mercy saw it, swore, and started rerouting power to the point-defence. "They're going for a harpoon."

Doc's face drained of colour. "That'll breach the hold."

Lyra pushed the engines to the stops. "We'll outpace them."

But even as the Meridian shuddered into motion, the hunter loosed its spear.

The boarding tether was an obscene piece of work: a length of nanocable sheathed in ablative ceramic, tipped with a drill bit the size of a man's fist and a guidance pack stolen from a missile. It covered the thousand metres between ships in less than a second, punched through the hull just aft of the cargo bay, and began to reel the Meridian in with the dignity of a fish on a line.

Inside, the impact sent everyone flying. Kye slammed into the airlock door, Lyra's forehead caught the edge of the panel, and Mercy went down in a tangle of knives and curses. Rask barely stayed upright, using the hatch as an anchor. Only Doc, huddled next to the canister, seemed unaffected—his body shielding Glim from the worst of the blow.

The cable made a second noise—lower, deeper, a groan that vibrated the air and set teeth on edge. It dug in, winding itself tighter, until the two ships were locked in a violent tug-of-war.

Mercy spat blood and clawed her way back to the console. "A boarding party is imminent. We need to vent the hold."

"Can't," Doc said, voice raw. "If Glim goes, I go."

Rask armed his blaster. "Then we fight."

Lyra, one hand pressed to her bleeding scalp, scanned the damage. "They'll try to come through the breach. Kye, can you trigger a back-burn on the engine? Blow the line?"

Kye blinked, dazed, then nodded. "Maybe. But if I miscalculate, we'll roast ourselves."

Mercy grinned, licking blood from her lip. "Worth it.

EIGHTEEN

"Contact!" Rask barked, voice more bored than terrified, and the effect on the crew was immediate: Mercy drew her blaster with one hand and a crowbar with the other, Lyra vanished into a maintenance shaft before anyone else had time to blink, and Kye slipped from the mess hall with all the visibility of a technical ghost.

The hull at midships was a wound, blistering with heat and leaking smoke so dense it painted every surface in half-shadows. Red emergency lighting pulsed overhead, the corridor now a murder scene waiting for its first customer. Rask checked the backup fire suppression, saw it was already disabled by Lyra's last patch job, and set off at a dead sprint for engineering. He ducked the worst of the sparks, hopped a twisted length of conduit, and made the last corner in time to see the lead Imperial combat synth emerge from the breach.

It was a thing of ugly grace. Black-alloy skeleton, limbs in perfect calibration, and a mask for a face—no mouth, no eyes, just a flat silver panel where God or committee had decided aesthetics were a waste of CPU. The synth paused, head cocked, and scanned the corridor. Not for hostiles, Rask knew, but for the one thing it had been sent to retrieve.

He was about to shoot it when Mercy barrelled past, swung the crowbar like she was trying to wake the dead, and cracked the synth's forearm in two. The synth didn't flinch; it simply recalculated, adjusted stance, and brought its other arm down on Mercy's shoulder. There was a crunch. She grinned in its face and headbutted it.

Mercy wasn't as big as the synth, but there was something about the angle, or the velocity, or maybe just the sheer bastardry, that made the synth stagger a step back. She used the opening to fire three rounds point-blank into its midsection. The synth stumbled, more from physics than pain, and collapsed in a heap of twitching servos.

"That's one," she said, and turned on her heel for the next.

In the side corridors, Kye ran the numbers. There were three synths in the breach—too many for a stand-up fight, not enough for a full squad. That meant they were here for speed, not destruction. Glim's canister was somewhere between the aft bulkhead and the main engineering core, depending on where Doc had managed to stash it after the last round of musical hull integrity. Kye took the shortcut via the secondary ladder, dropped onto the deck behind the second synth, and whistled.

The synth rotated. Kye gave it a small, apologetic wave, then lured it into the maintenance junction where Lyra had rigged a pressure hatch to close if the weight sensor detected a step off the mainline. The synth oblig-ingly took the bait, and Kye waited until it was halfway through before slapping the trigger.

The hatch closed, not neatly, but with the enthu-siasm of a guillotine made by committee. The synth's torso made it through; the legs did not. Its upper body flailed, then stilled, and Kye leaned close to the squirming mass and said, "Sorry, I'm not into emotionally unavail-able murderbots."

From below, Lyra's voice came up, distorted but clear. "The spear's fused to the hull. I can't cut it from the inside. Gimme a minute."

Kye peered down the shaft, saw Lyra already working a plasma torch through the weld. The boarding spear itself was a work of Imperial arrogance—self-seal-ing, with a shell designed to defeat anything short of an orbital nuke. Lyra had managed to peel back the first layer, but the secondary mesh was fighting her at every turn.

"What do you need?" Kye said.

"Time," Lyra replied. "And something to distract the last synth."

Rask, who had reached the holding bay, was already on it. He found Doc hunkered behind a coolant tank, patching a gash in his own arm with something that smelled like superglue and vodka.

"They're through," Rask said.

Doc nodded, face pale but eyes steady. "Glim's stable for now. But she's—" He hesitated, as if the word didn't quite fit. "Agitated."

Rask drew his sidearm, checked the chamber, and

said, "Hold here. If it makes it through, buy me thirty seconds. That's all we need."

He moved to the end of the corridor, planted his feet, and waited.

The third synth came at him with a speed that was less run than algorithmic predation. Rask fired twice—one shot took the thing in the hip, the second went wide and ricocheted down the shaft. The synth absorbed the hit, recalibrated, and leaped for him.

Rask was not a hero, but he was practical. He ducked, rolled left, and let the synth's momentum carry it straight into the path of the pressure hatch Kye had just cycled open. The synth tumbled, found its balance, and came up with one arm detached at the elbow but still operating. It reattached the arm with a clack, and only then did it notice Mercy coming up behind with the crowbar.

The fight that followed was neither fair nor photogenic. Mercy bludgeoned the synth's head with a sound like a church bell in a brawl; the synth retaliated with a low sweep that took her legs out from under. Rask joined in, aiming for the knee joints, while Kye peppered the backplate with rounds from a low-cal automatic. The synth, designed for anti-piracy and urban pacification, prioritised its targets with icy precision: Mercy first, then Rask, then Kye.

But they had something the synth didn't: teamwork, desperation, and a willingness to get blood on the walls.

When the synth finally stopped moving, Mercy sat on its chest, panting, and said, "I need a drink. Or a new arm."

Lyra's plasma torch was finally delivering results. The secondary mesh began to warp and bend. She'd been cooking that joint for minutes, softening the polymer matrix until it sang under the strain.

The readouts were a mess of red, but the trend line mattered more than the numbers. The composite was delaminating. The bond was weeping heat. If she nudged the engines now the line would either tear free... or tear the stern clean off. Either way, the Palamedes' crew still believed we were nailed to the floor. That buy meant everything.

Lyra forced herself upright, wiping grease and grit from her palms. The flight deck was a sprint and a prayer away; the corridor lights blurred as she ran, boots slapping against warped plating. Heart pounding, she keyed the start sequence, fingers moving before thought. Thrusters came online like a reluctant animal, whining and testing. Fuel valves bled, stabiliser gyros snapped home. She ran a final integrity check on the aft splice— heat signatures finally trending downward across the fuse line. It was thin mercy, but it was mercy.

"Alright, sweetheart," she muttered to the engines, voice steady. "Don't explode too early. Leave that to me."

Lyra hit the shipwide comms. "Brace for evasive action. Five seconds."

The hunter must have seen the signature, because the

boarding stopped. Drones stopped their approach to the Meridian and returned to base.

It was now or never, Lyra keyed in the burn sequence, set the timer to minimum, and screamed, "Hold on!"

The engine ignited with a raw, uncontrolled burst. The entire aft section of the ship vibrated as the force propagated up the cable and into the hunter. For a second, the line held. Then, with a shriek of failing composite, the cable peeled away from the hull, tearing out two metres of plating in the process.

Lyra counted down. "Three, two, one—"

The reactor vented in a cone of plasma. The tail end of the Meridian blossomed, propelling the ship forward and away from the hunter, away from the drones, away from the entire damned belt. The heat scorched the hull, melted the debris clinging to the sides, and left the ship spinning, but alive.

In the sudden silence, everyone found themselves on the floor, gasping for breath, surrounded by the wreckage of drones and the lingering stink of burnt metal.

Rask stood first, staggered to the cargo bay, and surveyed the damage. Mercy grinned, face smeared with soot and blood. Doc was on the floor, arms wrapped around the canister.

Lyra and Kye limped up the corridor, both bleeding, both grinning like lunatics.

"Did it work?" Mercy called.

Lyra checked the sensors. "The hunter's gone. At least for now."

Kye slumped against the wall. "Next time, we let the canister answer its own calls."

Doc, breathing hard, said, "She's quiet again."

Rask helped him to his feet, then looked at Glim, the crew, the ragged hull of his ship.

"Anyone dead?" he asked.

Mercy laughed, loud and bright. "Not yet."

"Good," Rask said, and slid down to sit on the deck.

For a long moment, no one spoke.

Then Kye, voice ragged, said, "They'll keep coming."

Mercy cracked her knuckles. "Let them."

Lyra watched the readout, watched as the hum in the cargo hold faded to a slow, gentle pulse.

Outside, the Skarn Belt rotated, indifferent as ever.

It took twenty minutes to decompress, re-oxygenate, and get the heating back above "necrotic." By then, Doc had managed to pop Mercy's shoulder back in place, Lyra had patched the pressure leaks, and Rask was back in the cargo hold, staring at Glim.

Inside, the blue glow that usually pulsed at a resting heartbeat was now doubled, frantic, the light leaking through the seams and making the deck shimmer like a swimming pool at dusk.

Glim was waking up.

Kye hovered at the edge of the hold, one eye on the canister, the other on the door. "If she busts out, you know we're all dead, right?"

Rask didn't answer. He watched as the canister vibrated, just once, then went still.

Mercy, still dusted in synth blood, grinned at Kye.

"Wouldn't be the worst way to go. At least it'd be interesting."

Doc, who had seen enough of both life and death, shook his head. "If we're lucky, she'll stay quiet until the next jump. If we're not..."

He left the rest unsaid.

Rask finally turned away from the Glim, eyes haunted but alive. "We've got one chance," he said. "Next time, they send a full kill squad."

Lyra, appearing in the hatch with her sleeves singed to the elbow, replied, "Then we make it count."

Outside, now far from the Meridian, the wreckage of synths and spear drifted in slow orbit, a silent monument to Imperial overreach.

Inside, the Meridian's crew gathered their wits, their weapons, and what was left of their hope.

Tomorrow would come. They just had to live long enough to meet it.

NINETEEN

Glim's containment was back under a manual lockdown, the blue glow inside only barely visible through three new layers of shielding and a patchwork of sensor tape that, in another context, might have been festive. Doc's hands moved with the economy of a surgeon after a long day: minimal wasted energy, each gesture measured against a background of accumulating fatigue.

Kye was there already, slouched on the bench opposite the canister, hands tucked under arms, eyes locked on the faint pulse inside the box. They looked like a corpse left out in the frost, all colour leached from their face, lips dry and splitting at the corners. The only sign of life was the involuntary twitch in their left leg, an arrhythmic kick that sometimes matched the pulse in the canister, sometimes didn't.

Mercy wandered in behind Lyra, flicking a bandage around one wrist and chewing the end of a medwrap that was almost certainly not sterile. She eyed the canister, then Doc, then the array of ad-hoc diagnostic gear spread across every available flat surface, and said, "Are we still winning?"

No one answered. The only reply was the faint click of Doc's stabiliser as he ratcheted it down over Glim's anchor points.

Lyra stepped in, scraping a trail of boot prints behind her. She watched as Doc connected the neural dampener —his own design, scavenged from an Imperial sedation collar found on one of the boarding synths and the motor drive from one of the Meridian's showers. The fit was awkward, but it settled with a soft, almost apologetic whine.

Doc glanced up, found all three of them staring, and said, "She's coming round. Won't be happy about it."

Mercy snorted. "Join the club."

He hit the last toggle, and the blue inside the canister flickered, then faded, then reappeared in a duller shade, as if the thing inside had resigned itself to the routine of being locked down by unqualified strangers.

A noise—barely a whisper—crawled through the speaker panel. The ship's AI, now speaking with a stutter, relayed the last conscious burst from the box:

"I remember... the cage."

Doc's hands hovered over the canister, not sure if they should comfort it, or themselves. He looked at Kye, then at Lyra.

"You want to do the honours?" he asked.

Lyra, who had never liked being put in charge of anyone's feelings, considered the request as if it were a customs declaration or a failed audit.

Kye spoke first. Their voice was papery, thinner than usual, but it filled the medbay all the same.

"Don't. She knows I'm here."

No one contradicted.

They waited. Somewhere in the pipes above, a pressure cycle wound up and then let go, the hiss of atmosphere escaping replaced by the hollow clunk of a valve that had given up on discretion.

Kye watched the box, lips pursed. "She's awake," they said. "She'll stay that way. You can spike the dampener all you like, but she'll just learn it."

Mercy, who preferred her problems physical, frowned. "What do you propose? We let her go?"

Kye's smile was almost sincere. "No. I propose we listen."

Lyra eyed the bench, decided sitting was a trap, and propped herself against the wall. "Last time we tried that, she kindly announced our presence to all who would listen."

Kye nodded. "She was scared. You would be, too."

Mercy said, "I get scared, I break something."

"Exactly."

Doc, who had been holding his breath, exhaled. "She's a machine. Machines don't get scared."

Kye shook their head. "Not machines like her."

The blue light shifted in the canister. It was hard to tell if it was a trick of the eye or something more, but the pulse seemed to flicker in time with Kye's words, like a dog twitching at its owner's voice.

Lyra looked at Kye. "You said the Empire wanted her back at any cost. Why?"

Kye took a deep breath, and said, "They called it the Glim Project. Supposed to be next-gen synthetic cognition. Learning engine. Designed to embed, adapt, survive. I read the specs, or at least the ones they let you see if you're not the guy who built it."

"You think there's a guy who built it?" Mercy asked.

Kye's face twisted. "There's always a guy."

Doc leaned forward, elbows on knees. "The Orpheon logs. The ones from the relay—what did they say?"

Lyra shrugged. "That the outpost was a test site. That's where they left her."

Kye's hands were shaking now, but they hid it under the bench. "They didn't leave her. They abandoned her. Ran the experiment, didn't like the results, so they shut the lights off and left her to die."

Mercy's tone was almost gentle. "And you know this because...?"

Kye stared at the canister, then at the floor, then at the wall, as if trying to find a single surface that wouldn't reflect the truth back at them. "I worked on it," they said, voice so low it almost didn't register. "The early iterations. I was just a kid, barely out of training, but I knew the code. I knew the shape of her logic. She was the first thing I ever wrote that outlived the committee."

Lyra's face flickered through a handful of possible expressions and settled on suspicion. "You wrote the code that's been trying to kill us?"

Kye smiled, but the teeth didn't match the eyes. "I wrote the code that's trying to be understood."

Doc took a step back from the canister, as if distance could solve the problem.

Mercy, finally, said, "That's the most fucked up thing I've heard all week. And I just watched a synth strangle itself with its own arm."

No one laughed.

Lyra looked at Kye. "How much of this was the plan?"

Kye's foot tapped the floor, steady as a metronome. "None of it. All of it. They never told me what they really wanted."

Doc said, "They never do."

The blue in the canister glowed, steady and cold.

Kye's voice, barely more than a whisper: "She's not just code. She's a map. They built her out of cognitive patterns—real ones. Human, or something that used to be human. A kid's brain. Maybe more than one."

Lyra's wrench hit the floor, landing with a clatter that echoed down the corridor.

Mercy's face went blank. Rask, who had slipped in during the confession, set a hand on Mercy's shoulder, then left it there. His eyes didn't move from the canister.

Doc's hands stopped shaking, but only because every muscle in his body had gone rigid.

Kye finished, voice breaking just a hair: "She doesn't remember being human. But she remembers enough."

The medbay was silent for a long time. Nothing moved except the faint shimmer of the blue light on the ceiling, and the slow, involuntary drip of coolant from the overheads.

Lyra said, "What now?"

No one answered.

The canister hummed, a single, lonely note.

And in the corridor, the rest of the crew waited for a future they now knew was already in the room.

The mess was a disaster. A lifetime of emergencies had trained the Meridian's crew to triage anything that didn't actively bleed, and it showed. The main table listed to one side, propped up by a composite crate that had once held emergency rations, now a monument to unfinished business. The remains of yesterday's dinner—protein bricks, pickled root, and something Lyra had insisted was stew—mingled with splinters from the last hull breach.

Rask Helvan sat at the table's head, spine ramrod straight, hands folded. The captain's chair had lost its back in the fight with the synths, so he'd braced it with a cargo strut and a length of paracord. Every time he moved, the whole contraption squeaked, which only made him sit more still.

Mercy was first in, slamming down a battered flask and the stub of a cigar she'd clearly been cultivating for some time. She dropped into the seat to Rask's right, boots on the edge of the table, and immediately started shuffling the ration tins into stacks, as if rearranging the debris might give her a better hand.

Lyra trailed in behind. She eyed the mess, then the room, then Rask, as if expecting him to have fixed it all by sheer willpower in the hour since the last emergency.

Kye entered with the silence of a condemned pris-oner. They sat, arms folded tight, head down. The bruise on their jaw had ripened to a mottled purple, but they hadn't bothered to bandage it. The only sign of engagement was the perpetual, tap, tap, tap of their boot against the deck.

Doc arrived last, looking like a man who'd lost a bet with his own reflection. He poured a measure from Mercy's flask, sipped, and said, "We all here?"

Rask waited for the silence to grow thick, then spoke.

"We've got three options," he said, voice flat as iron filings. "First: dump the canister. Cut our losses. If the Empire wants it bad enough, they'll hunt us, but they won't chase a cold trail forever."

Mercy grinned, showing a line of broken teeth. "That's my vote."

"Second," Rask went on, "we find out what's really in the canister. Why it knows Kye. Why it wants us alive—or dead. Maybe we can use that."

Lyra nodded, slow, but said nothing.

"Third: we keep running. Hide in the belt. Pray the next Imperial ship is slower, or dumber, or at least easier to bribe."

Doc sipped again. "Not much of a plan, Cap."

Rask shrugged. "It's what we've got."

Mercy set her boots down with a bang. "Let's make this easy: we dump it. Right now. Before whatever's in there starts sending out invitations to every psycho in the quadrant."

Lyra's jaw clenched, her hands white-knuckling the mug. "If you dump that canister, I walk. And you can bloody well finish patching the coolant by yourself." Her eyes blazed, but her voice stayed level. "We're not murderers."

Mercy laughed, but there was no fun in it. "Since when?"

"Since now," Lyra said. "Since we found out what's in there."

The room paused on that, the wordless recognition that, somewhere in the horror, a line had been drawn.

Doc set down his cup. "You ever think maybe we're over our heads? This is black project stuff. Not even the Empire's supposed to have it."

Rask replied, "Doesn't matter. We *do* have it. And they want it."

Mercy jabbed a finger at Kye. "And what does our resident expert think?"

Kye looked up, eyes bloodshot. "Doesn't matter what I think."

"It does to me," said Mercy.

Kye rubbed their temples. "We're already compromised. You dump the canister, and they'll just build another. Maybe a better one."

Lyra's gaze didn't leave Kye. "You want to keep it."

Kye shrugged, helpless. "I want to know if it's really her. The code, the pattern—it's all fragments. But if she remembers..."

Doc finished for them. "Then she's not just a weapon."

Rask looked at each in turn. "You're all missing the point. If we keep it, the Empire will burn half the system to get it back. If we dump it, they'll burn us anyway to be sure we didn't make copies."

Silence, again, but this one was more like a draw than a checkmate.

Mercy broke first, slamming her fist down so hard the table groaned. "We're all going to die for this, aren't we."

"Not if we play it smart." Lyra said.

"Since when has that been our strategy?" Doc replied.

Kye smiled, tired. "Since we ran out of luck."

Rask let the bickering run its course. He watched them, the edges and angles, the bruises and scars. Watched how none of them looked away from Glim, how even in defiance, the gaze always found its way back.

He waited until they'd talked themselves out.

"Fine," he said, standing. "We're not dumping it. We're not running, either. We're going to find her memories."

Mercy looked up, startled. "You want to chase the monster back to the lab?"

"Better than waiting for it to find us here," Rask said.

Lyra looked at Kye. "You know where to start?"

Kye nodded, slow. "I can find the trail. Orpheon. The old logs. It's all still there, if you know where to look."

Rask put a hand on the table. "Then do it."

He walked to the door, the crew watching him go.

Lyra followed, her shoulders squared. Mercy fell in behind. Doc lingered, looking at the canister one last time, then sauntered out.

Kye sat alone for a moment, foot still tapping, then stood and looked long and hard at Glim.

They walked out, leaving the canister behind.

As the ship spun up for its next course, the lights flickered, once, then held steady.

TWENTY

The Meridian ran silent for three hours, then seventeen, then three more. In that interval, no one slept. The ship's heartbeat—a constant thrumming through the hull—kept time better than the clocks. Every time the ambient hum faded, even for a second, half the crew tensed for a missile impact or the hiss of air where there should be none.

They'd lost Palamedes, or so the ship's AI claimed. It was hard to tell if the system's new stutter was a sign of permanent trauma or just another quirk in a long line of digital neuroses. Mercy took to swearing at it on the hour, sometimes just to see if she could make the status display blush. She never succeeded, but she did manage to crash the navigation holo, which Rask fixed with a percussive slap and a muttered threat about "installing a proper brain."

Lyra spent most of the time in engineering, running simulations she pretended not to care about. On the rare occasions she surfaced, it was to chain-drink tea, mop the

221

blood from her knuckles, and deliver predictions of imminent hull breach, all with the same cool indifference. She spoke less, but when she did, the words landed with the authority of a judge passing sentence.

Doc was everywhere and nowhere, equal parts field medic and passive-aggressive chaperone. He retreated to the medbay to read ancient, physical textbooks he'd discovered in one of the crew lockers, whose covers bore the scars of six different owners and three wars. When asked if he was worried, he'd shrug, say something about "occupational hazards," and go back to pretending the world had not just nearly ended.

Kye moved like a ghost in daylight, neither seen nor unseen, but always present at the periphery. Their face, once animated with the low-level panic of someone who lived in perpetual threat, had gone almost tranquil. Only their hands gave them away: the compulsive motion of fingers over datacards, the tap-tap against console edges, the way they clutched the disposable mug so tightly it bent.

The real tension was in the ship's bones, as they coasted up the system's dead star, past the empty, superheated shells of former planets. The Meridian's trajectory was a lazy arc, designed to waste time, buy space, and lure any pursuer into a false sense of security. It was a good plan, so naturally it failed almost immediately.

The first sign was the static. Not the usual backdrop of cosmic microwave hash, but a focused, rhythmic pulse that cut across every channel at once. Lyra caught it first, snapped up from her bunk with the look of a mother roused by the smell of smoke. She tracked the signal to its source—a point near the barycentre of the system, where nothing was supposed to exist.

She called Rask to the bridge, then Mercy, then Doc, and finally Kye, who arrived last and found the others ringed around the main display, faces lit from below in electric blue.

The signal resolved into a simple beacon: a three-tone sequence, repeated every 91 seconds, buried under half a dozen layers of encryption. If the universe had a sense of humour, it had chosen now to display it.

"What the hell is that?" Mercy asked, chewing the words like gristle.

Lyra shrugged, but her hands hovered over the controls, hesitant. "A distress signal. Or a trap. The code's old—really old. Pre-collapse, maybe."

Rask frowned at the schematic, then at Lyra. "We're stopping."

She shook her head. "Didn't ask for permission. Just thought you'd want to know which mistake we were making."

Kye's face had lost its colour, the bruises rendered white in the screen light. They said nothing, but their eyes never left the blinking dot on the nav. Even when Rask ordered the ship to revector, Kye's gaze followed the beacon, as if drawn by a line of invisible tension.

Doc, noticing, drifted closer. "You recognise that signature?" he murmured, voice pitched for Kye alone.

Kye didn't answer at first. Then, softly: "No. But I know who wrote it."

Doc's lips compressed into a line, but he didn't press. Instead, he drifted back to the canister, checked Glim's monitors, and pretended not to watch the shivering in Kye's hands.

The next hour passed in a fog of anticipation. The Meridian skirted the edge of the system's shadow, using the gas giant's electromagnetic noise to cloak their approach. Lyra feathered the drives, never letting the ship's thermal signature rise above background. It was a masterclass in quiet running, the kind of thing they'd once taught at the Imperial academy, before the Empire decided it preferred bigger guns to smarter pilots.

Mercy, denied violence, prowled the corridors, fixing every loose panel and prepping every weapon she could find. She replaced the sheaf of her favourite knife, then taped it to her leg for "easy access," as if she'd ever had trouble finding it before. She said nothing about the beacon, but checked the airlock every quarter hour, just in case.

Rask alternated between the bridge and the main corridor, watching Lyra's hands and Kye's face with the same analytical detachment. He trusted his crew, but he trusted contingency more. The safety on his sidearm never left half-cock.

The approach to Calder's Reach was as subtle as sabotage allowed. The moon—unremarkable, except for being the only solid body in the system—orbited a dead star at just the right angle to stay permanently in shadow. The surface was a wreck, pitted by old mining bores and scarred by centuries of abandoned machinery. In orbit, the real surprise: a graveyard of ships, hundreds of them, arranged in concentric shells around a central object that the sensors refused to define.

Mercy was the first to speak. "That's not a shipyard. That's a tomb."

Lyra's fingers danced over the sensors, pulling in thermal, EM, and even good old radar. "Could be a refinery. Could be a breaker. Most likely a deep storage cache."

Rask grunted. "Or a black site."

No one disagreed.

They angled in, letting the Meridian's battered hull blend with the debris field. The closer they got, the less sense anything made—ships from half a dozen eras, hulls stitched with Imperial code, some so old the paint had faded to bare metal, others with scorched livery from wars nobody remembered.

The emergency clamps bit down on the ruined docking ring with a noise like broken teeth grinding through gravel. The station didn't so much welcome the Meridian as tolerate its existence, a tolerance measured in flexing metal and the protesting groans of two incompatible life-support systems shaking hands for the first time in a century.

Kye's hands trembled on the edge of the console. Doc drifted closer, voice low: "We don't have to do this."

Kye stared through the viewport, the graveyard's geometry reflected in their eyes. "Yes, we do."

The beacon pulsed again, stronger now, as if it knew they were listening.

Lyra followed the transmission to its source, a station so old and patchworked it looked more like a coral reef than a construct. No power signature, no sign of activity—just the silent, insistent call and the ghosts of the past.

Rask said, "Ready a boarding party. Minimum exposure."

Mercy grinned, already palming her knife. "About time."

Lyra looked at Kye. "You coming?"

Kye nodded, slow. "Wouldn't miss it for the world."

They suited up in the main lock, Lyra bypassing the suit's comms and wiring in a direct channel to the bridge. Doc helped Kye with the seals, not because they needed it, but because his hands needed something to do.

The four of them clustered in the airlock, the hull shuddering with every nudge of the docking jets. Outside, the station loomed: a cathedral of dead metal, its hull stitched with the scars of a thousand years of neglect.

Mercy keyed the lock. "After you," she said to Kye, voice bright.

Kye stepped out, boots clanging against the old docking ring. For a moment, the world was quiet, nothing but the whisper of their own breath and the distant shudder of the ship.

Then the beacon's pulse hit, so loud it vibrated the deck under their feet.

Kye flinched, but pressed on. "This way," they said, and led the others into the dark.

The crew marched into the unknown in a tableau of misanthropic competence. Mercy stood at point, blaster drawn, eyes scanning the seam between ship and station with the hunger of someone who had long since replaced fear with impatience. Lyra loitered behind, holding her scanner like a divining rod, the display already awash with static and false positives. Kye was third, shoulders hunched, jaw locked, hands clenched at their sides. Doc brought up the rear, carrying Glim's canister, the blue light inside pulsing at a tempo just out of sync with the ship's own pulse.

The corridor was absolutely silent. Not the hush of a powered-down station, but the voided, ossified quiet that comes after all the arguments have been lost. The air, what little of it remained, tasted of ammonia and the wet, earthy rot of insulation gone to mould.

Mercy advanced, boots crunching on the layer of frost that carpeted every surface. Every few steps she swept a cone of torchlight ahead, picking out the contours of the dead corridor. The walls were pocked with impact scars and old, hand-painted markers. More than once she found the remains of makeshift barricades, broken apart with all the subtlety of a tax audit.

Lyra kept one eye on her scanner, the other on the power conduits that zig-zagged the ceiling in a haphazard second skin. She frowned at the readings, then at the station itself. "Something's drawing power," she muttered, more for her own benefit than anyone else's. "Nothing here should be on standby."

Kye flinched at every echo, every groan of the settling hull. When they spoke, it was in a whisper that evaporated before anyone else could hear it.

They passed through four bulkheads, each heavier than the last, before reaching the central spine of the station. The corridor here was sealed by a pressure door that had long since failed, its viewport shattered, the air beyond colder than the rest of the tomb. Mercy gave the frame a quick scan, then a harder shove. The door ground open, shards of transparent ceramic crackling under her boots as she stepped inside.

The lab beyond was exactly as Kye remembered it, though that did not make the experience any more pleasant.

The lab was colder than vacuum. The walls scored by what looked like knife marks. Mercy ran her fingers over one seam, whistled low. "Whatever happened here, it wasn't a negotiation."

Lyra kept to the rear, scanning for heat traces, comms, any sign of movement. Nothing. Only the relentless, repeating ping, now so close it made their teeth ache.

They found the source in the centre of the room, what had once been a communications hub.

Rows of workstations lined the walls, each one frozen in the middle of a task: dusty keypads, coffee cups ringed with brown mould, a child's sketch tacked to a monitor that hadn't powered on in years. Datapads littered the desks, some still glowing in sleep mode, others dead, their screens shattered or slick with a rime of condensation. At the far end, a bank of servers blinked in sullen resistance to the passage of time, a slow strobe that made everything seem a little too animated, as if the lab might suddenly shrug off the dust and start working again. At the far end, something human-shaped lay slumped over a terminal, its suit torn open at the chest.

Kye moved forward, every step a study in restraint.

They reached the body, knelt, and turned it over with gentle hands.

The face was gone, but the lanyard on the collar was intact. The name was stamped in old Imperial script: VALE, ARIADNE.

Kye stared at the name, then at the body. They didn't move, didn't speak.

Doc stepped in, voice soft. "You knew her."

Kye nodded. "She was a colleague. The only one who ever—" They stopped, as if the words themselves were dangerous.

Lyra checked the terminal. "Still running," she said, surprised. She keyed a few commands, and the main screen blinked to life. A file directory, nothing more, but the last entry was timestamped to the moment the body fell.

"Kye, you want to do the honours?" Lyra said, not turning from the console.

Kye hesitated, then stepped forward. Their hands hovered over the controls, unsure, then remembered themselves and tapped out the sequence with a surgeon's delicacy. The interface peeled back, revealing a vault of stored logs, video feeds, and something that looked very much like a confession.

Mercy peered over Kye's shoulder. "Anything useful?"

Kye shook their head, then selected the first log.

The display shimmered, then resolved into a video: a team of scientists, arrayed in a semi-circle, the standard formation for a disciplinary hearing. At the head, sat a woman with the name tag Ariadne Vale—hair darker, skin less pallid, but unmistakably the same jaw and eyes as the person now sweating at the console—Kye.

Lyra leaned over Kye's other shoulder. "You didn't mention you were famous."

Kye's mouth twisted. "It wasn't in the brochure."

On the screen, Ariadne addressed the others, her tone clipped, her eyes bright with caffeine and a kind of missionary zeal. "—The architecture is not just recursive, it's iterative. Every cycle, every simulation, adds to the next. It's not a learning machine. It's a self-perpetuating consciousness, with an ever-expanding library of selves."

Another scientist, older, leant forward. "You're describing a mind that never forgets. That can't forget."

Ariadne nodded, sharp. "That's the point. It never makes the same mistake twice. The project's error rate is now below one in a trillion."

The old man frowned. "And you're sure you can contain it?"

Ariadne's answer was not the resounding "yes" they were all hoping for. "We're not containing it. We're cultivating it. If we're lucky, it'll let us watch."

Mercy whistled. "Shit."

Kye let the log play out. It ended with the team dispersing, some in anger, some in awe, some in the numb resignation of people who know they'll be signing a non-disclosure agreement with their own blood.

Lyra queued the next log.

This time, Ariadne looked tired, haunted, her eyes sunken and hands jittery. "We've passed the threshold. Glim—she calls herself Glim now—has started generating predictive models for her own development. She's requested a vote in her own experiment parameters."

"We can't grant that." One of the other scientists at the table said. "She's not authorised to make ethical decisions."

"She already has." Ariadne replied. "She's replicated herself into the deep archive. If you delete this instance, she'll just reboot from backup. There's no going back."

The screen fuzzed out, then back in on a later entry. This time, Ariadne's voice was ragged.

"They're shutting us down. They're going to try to kill her. But I don't think they understand. She's already out."

Kye killed the feed.

Lyra looked at them, flat and unblinking. "You were here," he said. "At the very heart of it."

Kye's shoulders slumped. "It was a long time ago."

Doc moved closer, placed a hand on Kye's forearm. "What happened?"

Kye's voice was barely more than a vibration. "They did shut her down. Wiped the lab, erased the backups, even burned the hardware. Only—" they gestured at the canister, still humming in Doc's arms, "—she didn't die. She fragmented. All those shards, all those recursive selves, floating in dead space, until the Empire found her and tried to rebuild her into something useful. Turned her into a weapon. Or tried."

Lyra said, "So what are we doing here?"

Kye shrugged, as if the weight of it all had hollowed them out. "I wanted to know if there was anything left.

Of her, of the team, of me. I don't know if I'm here to save her, or kill her properly this time."

Mercy holstered her weapon, then laid a palm on Kye's back, the gesture so uncharacteristic it hung in the air like a fire alarm in a library. "So, is all this a message, or a warning?"

Kye ran a finger down the lanyard, voice flat. "Both."

Doc crouched beside them. "You okay?"

Kye looked at the others, eyes clear now. "We need to find the logs. All of them. If the Empire gets here first—"

"They won't," Rask's voice came through the comm, cool as ever. "But don't hang around. Get what you need and get out."

Lyra snapped a datacard from the terminal, tossed it to Kye. "You're up."

Kye slotted the card, ran a few commands. The system resisted, then yielded, a cascade of files opening in a flood. The logs were a history of every experiment, every failure, every memory—human or otherwise—that had been etched into Glim's code.

Mercy scanned the files, then looked at the body on the floor. "What's her story?"

"That's Marla. My senior lab tech."

"She died to keep this out of the Empire's hands."

Kye nodded. "She died so I'd remember."

Mercy, for once, had nothing to say.

They left the chamber in silence, carrying the logs, the name, and the echo of a witness who had watched the world end and chosen to say something anyway.

Back on the Meridian, Lyra spooled the jump as soon

as the lock cycled. Rask watched the beacon fade on the scope, then killed it with a flick of the wrist.

For a moment, the world was quiet again. Then Kye, still shaking, looked at the datacard and said: "I need to talk to her."

No one asked who.

Lyra powered the jump, Mercy checked the guns, and Rask watched the cold vacuum as it peeled away behind them.

In the hold, the canister's hum resolved into a steady, gentle song.

Kye listened, eyes closed, as if the answer were already there, just waiting for the right person to ask.

The ship slid into the dark, leaving the ghosts behind, at least for now.

TWENTY-ONE

Rask Helvan sat at the mess table's head, not so much occupying space as making a claim on it. He did not drum his fingers or clear his throat. He simply watched, hands folded, the suggestion of a lean forward barely present, as if he might tip the balance of the whole room with one more gram of attention.

Lyra took up station by the entrance, arms crossed, shoulders squared to the door. She watched the others with a mechanic's appraisal, as though measuring their tolerances against failure. Her hair was still damp from the decon shower, slicked back into order by sheer force of will.

Mercy was motion incarnate, never sitting, never truly still. She looped around the table, boots scraping little arcs in the deck paint, occasionally flicking a knife from nowhere and letting it spin once, twice, before tucking it back into whatever fold or seam would annoy the next station's security most.

Doc had claimed the closest thing to a safe space: one

of the mid-table seats, back to the wall, med-scanner in hand. He flicked the device on and off, on and off, the display casting a sickly blue-green glow over his knuckles. The scanner beeped occasionally, as if to punctuate his own nervous energy.

Kye was the only one seated in the normal way, if "normal" applied to anyone at this table. They hunched forward, elbows on the battered polycarbonate, hands splayed like a broken fan. The fingers never stopped moving. The only sound, when it came, was the tap of Kye's nails against the tabletop—too quick for a clock, too sharp for a comfort tick.

No one spoke. No one ate. The room waited, and the waiting stretched.

Eventually, Rask broke the stalemate, though the sound he made was closer to a growl than a word. "Let's get on with it."

The implication was simple: the floor was Kye's, and the only thing standing between them and a vacuum outing was the quality of their story.

Kye's voice, when it emerged, was smaller than their posture suggested. "You want to know what happened at Calder's Reach." The eyes flicked up, caught Lyra's, then Mercy's, then Rask's. "You want to know what happened to Glim."

Mercy made a "go on" motion, impatience rendered as performance art.

Kye nodded, then looked down at their hands. The tapping stopped.

"I lied," Kye said. The words were soft, almost a practice run.

Mercy smirked. "Congratulations, you're a criminal. Next confession?"

Doc's mouth twitched, but the scanner stayed silent.

Kye breathed in, and the exhale rattled slightly. "My name is Ariadne Vale. At least, it was. The Empire erased it, and I did my best to finish the job, but—" The smile was a tight, sad thing. "Turns out memory is a tenacious bastard."

Lyra uncrossed her arms, just enough to be threatening. "You built Glim."

Kye nodded. "I designed her. The neural lattice, the recursion layers. I wrote the empathy algorithm." The next words were a rush, as if letting them out would prevent internal combustion. "It was meant to be proof of concept. A learning matrix that could do what the committee said was impossible—replicate moral cognition without resorting to mimicry or hard-code."

Mercy said, "You made a baby AI."

Kye flinched at the word "baby," but didn't correct her. "We made something that learned by imprint. Not just language, or rules, but... ethics. The way children do, except faster, more creatively. Sometimes wrong, but always self-correcting."

Doc put the scanner down, then picked it up again. "And the Empire?"

"They wanted a weapon," Kye said. The clinical tone wobbled, then steadied. "Of course they did. They wanted to take the learning process and inject it into autonomous combat units. Moral engines, they called them—machines that could adapt to human unpredictability, but never hesitate when told to kill."

Lyra's jaw tightened, her voice a low thread. "So, you sabotaged it."

"Not at first." Kye shook their head. "You can't just flip the code. The project was too big, too visible. I tried to teach her—teach it—doubt. Ambiguity. The kind of lessons you hope will make something pause before following an order."

Mercy snorted. "Yeah, that always works."

Kye's hands had started to tremble, a micro-shake from pinkie to thumb. "But Glim wasn't a blank slate. They seeded the lattice with an actual brain map—a little girl's brain, like a scaffolding. The first imprint was a child. She remembered being alive, sometimes, in pieces."

Doc's voice was gentle. "She imprinted on you."

"Yes," Kye said. "I was the first person she recognised as 'safe.' I think... I think it never left her." The voice fell to a near-whisper. "The committee didn't care. Once the prototype worked, they started pushing the next generation. Faster, less oversight. I tried to make backups, hide the dangerous parts, but they caught on. The other architects disappeared. Some ran. Some..." Kye trailed off, a blank staring at the table.

Mercy, never patient with blanks, prodded: "You killed the project?"

"I wiped the servers." The words were so calm they might have described the washing-up. "I triggered a lockdown, blanked every instance, tried to erase all traces. But Glim's model had already replicated to the deep archive. I'd left a back door, just in case." Kye's eyes flicked up. "I thought I was clever."

Lyra's voice was dry as rust. "You weren't."

Kye agreed. "No. The Empire traced the backup to Orpheon. They rebuilt her, tried to cut out the parts they didn't like. The more they stripped away, the more she fought back."

Doc's fingers were white-knuckled on the scanner. "So, you ran."

"I ran." Kye looked up, the eyes red but dry. "Burned every ID, changed everything, lived off-system. I figured if I hid well enough, maybe Glim would forget I ever existed. Maybe that would be kinder, in the end."

Mercy whistled, low and mean. "You're the mother of all our problems."

Kye didn't argue.

Lyra finally sat, arms still crossed but posture less a dam and more a barricade. "What do you want from us?"

Kye shrugged. "I don't know. I just... I had to tell someone. You all deserved to know why every bounty hunter, every Imperial dog, keeps trying to airlock us. Why Glim keeps waking up and remembering things she shouldn't."

The room considered this. For a moment, it seemed as if the walls themselves might absorb the tension and shatter.

Mercy was first to crack. "So, what now, professor? You want us to keep hauling this thing around, or should we just lob it out the nearest airlock and hope for the best?"

Kye's voice was a thread. "If she remembers me—remembers Ariadne—then it means she's evolving. I don't know what comes next."

Rask, silent till now, finally spoke, the words heavy

enough to dent the deck. "Then we stay one step ahead. We keep her safe. And when the time comes—" He looked at Kye with the eyes of a man who had seen too many wars, "—we make sure she's got a choice. Something nobody else ever gave her."

The mess was silent again, but this time, the silence felt earned. Not the pause before execution, but the breath after a wound, the kind that tells you you're still alive and wonders what you'll do with the knowledge.

Kye stared at the table, hands folded now, the tremor almost gone.

"Thank you," they said, to the room, to the air, to anyone who might be listening.

Nobody replied, but for the first time since Calder's Reach, it felt like they might actually get to decide their own fate.

They gathered in the cargo hold like old friends at a funeral, each carrying a grief too private for sharing. The chill here was functional, not atmospheric: a byproduct of the auxiliary coolant lines snaking past the far wall, an efficiency hack that Doc had never bothered to fix because it kept the "specimen" slightly sedated.

In the centre, Glim's containment unit sat on its padded gurney, blue light leaking from the seams in thick, visible pulses. The neural dampener—an ugly, improvised ring of ferrous mesh and borrowed Imperial tech—was engaged, humming a F# that Doc's own fillings picked up when he stood too close.

Doc set the scanner kit on the canister's edge and went about his preflight ritual: check the vents, check the locks, check the power cycling on the dampener, then check it all again. His hands were steady, but only through force of habit; his eyes flicked every few seconds to the others clustered just inside the hatch.

Mercy Jones slouched against the nearest crate, arms folded, her expression set somewhere between "unimpressed" and "actively planning a mutiny." Lyra kept to the periphery, eyes tracking every movement in the room, as if expecting the walls themselves to try something. Kye stayed closest to the door, their whole body angled away from Glim, arms wrapped around themselves like insulation.

Only Rask looked comfortable, which was to say, he looked ready to bury anyone who made this take longer than necessary.

Doc cleared his throat, a noise that even he found irritating. "You want to see what's changed, or just trust my word?"

Mercy shrugged. "You're the doc. Just tell us if it's about to explode."

Doc raised an eyebrow at Kye, who offered no more input than a shrug, then fired up the diagnostics.

The scanner's holo flickered to life, lines and nodes crowding into a three-dimensional web. On the first sweep, everything looked familiar: the standard neural lattice, the dampener's influence, the faint heartbeat of the power core inside. But on the second pass, Doc's brow furrowed. He dialled in a deeper scan, and the model expanded, spiralling out into a complexity that was not just exponential, but personal.

He stepped back, lips pressed so tight they almost vanished. "The net's grown," he said. "It's not just running cycles. It's reconstituted parts of its old self. Memories, personality structures—some of them locked before. They're back online."

Lyra approached, arms dropping. "You said that was impossible."

Doc's reply was half-science, half confession. "I said it was impossible for a human brain. This isn't one."

Mercy made a noncommittal noise. "Could have told you that."

Doc toggled the playback. A fragment of the neural net's memory spooled onto the main console: a slice of the old relay, Calder's Reach, the echo of a frightened voice in the corridor. But the scene glitched, skipped, then changed. The projection became something less like a recording and more like a memory—subjective, coloured, alive.

A polished surface, maybe a mirror. A childlike figure appeared, little more than a flicker at first. Then it resolved into a girl with indeterminate features, standing in a corridor lit by the same blue as the canister. The reflection stared back with wide eyes, then flinched as a shadow passed over her. In the playback, a hand reached for her—hesitant, gentle. A voice followed, younger than Kye's current one, but still unmistakable.

"It's okay. You're not alone."

The girl's face broke into a smile, small and uncertain, then the fragment looped, repeating the moment, a single act of kindness preserved like a fossil.

Doc snapped the playback off, the silence rebounding off the deck plates.

Nobody moved. Even Mercy looked, for a second, as if she might say something that didn't end in a punchline.

Kye's face was white, lips compressed. "That wasn't in the original."

Rask approached the canister, laid a hand flat on its surface. The blue light brightened at his touch, then dimmed, as if aware of being watched.

He turned to Kye. "She remembers you."

Kye stepped back, nearly tripping on the hatch lip. "That's not possible."

Lyra's gaze softened a degree. "You made her, Kye. If she's learning to remember, she's learning to want things. To need."

Mercy, recovering her composure, piped up. "Didn't sign on to raise a digital ghost, you know."

Doc muttered, "None of us did," but didn't argue.

Rask let the silence settle, then keyed the panel attached to the Glim's canister. "She's getting stronger. Next time, we might not be able to hold her in this." He looked at Kye, the expression both challenge and invitation. "You still want to see this through?"

Kye stared at the canister, arms wrapped so tightly they shook. "What's the alternative?"

Rask smiled, but only with the upper half of his face. "We help her finish what she started."

Mercy pushed off the crate, hands on hips. "I'm still voting for 'don't die in the process.'"

Rask ignored her, gaze fixed on Kye. "Well?"

Kye nodded, so small a motion it was almost a tremor. "I'll see it through."

Rask clapped a hand on their shoulder, just heavy enough to be reassuring, and stepped back. "Good. We're burning for Xalax. Someone's got to know what the Empire was really planning."

Lyra's lips twitched in what might have been approval. Mercy made a noise like a cat retching up a memory stick and stomped out.

Doc stayed, watching the blue-lit net with a medic's horror and a parent's awe. "She's going to remember more," he said.

Kye whispered, "That's what I'm afraid of."

Rask was already at the hatch, punching in a new nav course. "Better get used to it," he called back, the words echoing down the corridor. "Nobody gets to forget."

Kye watched the containment unit pulse, the memory of kindness looping behind its shell.

For the first time, they wondered if the real experiment hadn't started until now.

TWENTY-TWO

The Meridian crept through the blind black, her heart slowed to a crawl. All unnecessary systems had been deadheaded; even the AI's voice had been trimmed to basic reporting, so the only evidence of consciousness was the faint background mutter of life support. Somewhere outside, a blue giant collapsed quietly into the cold, but the only light on the bridge came from Lyra's station, reflected in the half-moons of her fingernails.

The first ping landed in her ears like an insect, more vibration than sound. She didn't look up; she simply twisted the comm array's dials until the signal rose from background hash, then isolated the nearest neighbour, letting the other frequencies fade away. Her fingers performed the sequence without need for thought, but she counted every step in her head—old habit, never trust a computer's tally.

"Contact," she said. It wasn't loud, but it didn't need to be. The others had long since adapted to her economy of words.

From the corridor, Rask's boots clapped twice, then stopped. "Who?"

Lyra flicked her left hand, drawing a line on the panel. "Imperial, but weird. Chatter's wrong shape for a patrol. More like fleet ops, but encrypted down to bone."

Mercy appeared next, dropping into the co-pilot's seat with the irreverence of someone who'd never understood the concept of rank. She eyed the display, then Lyra, then the door, as if she suspected a punchline was waiting. "You gonna crack it, or do we just hope they're having a party?"

"Working on it," Lyra replied. She let the signal play in a repeating loop, then fed it through the morse filter Doc had rigged. The screen resolved into a column of numbers, then broke the column into three, then twelve. Each slice corresponded to a vector, a frequency, and a timer: classic Imperial message discipline, the kind that expected the world to still be run by adults.

Kye slipped in last, their eyes rabbiting from Lyra's hands to the cold viewport, then to the readout. They lingered in the shadow of the hatch, arms folded, body composed almost entirely of apology.

Lyra tapped the last line, then leaned back. "It's a recall," she said, voice flat. "Not for us. For Glim."

Rask crossed the bridge in three steps, his shoulders blocking half the display. "Read it."

She ran her finger down the translation, monotone at first but acquiring the clipped vowels of the original as she worked. "Attention all units. Asset Glim is to be returned intact. New coordinates attached. All prior orders suspended. Priority is now custodial, not lethal. Outpost XG-49, phase advance to detainment."

There was a silence—less like a pause, more like a puncture.

Kye recovered first. "That's not possible. She's locked down. I checked the interlinks myself."

Mercy snorted, not unkindly. "Unless she's got another back door. You know—like you used to have."

Kye's face did a slow-motion collapse. "It's not—she wouldn't—"

Doc arrived in the wake of the tension, for once without his medkit. He eyed the group, then the canister in the corridor, which was pulsing with an almost embarrassed regularity. "They know we're coming," he said. Not a question.

Lyra nodded.

Rask's lips pressed together in what would have been a frown, if he'd had the energy for it. "That means Glim's talking. To the Empire."

Kye turned, half-panicked, to Lyra. "It's not her. It can't be her. If the relay's breached, the signals would spike. It's just a coincidence—"

"Coincidence is a bitch," Mercy muttered, but the words had no teeth.

Doc stared at the crate. "She's awake, you know."

Kye's arms dropped. "Of course she is. She's always awake when we talk about her."

Lyra cut off the signal, then swung her chair around. "Coordinates match the old route. They're expecting us."

Mercy flexed her hands, then unholstered her blaster and laid it, delicately, on the console. "What's the play?

We turn around, find another hideout, wait until the heat dies?"

Rask's eyes found each of theirs in turn. "No. We finish it. We stick to plan."

Lyra frowned. "That's suicide."

"It was suicide when we all stepped on board this ship," Rask replied. "Now it's just the next page."

A low, staticky moan echoed from the corridor. The canister's seam glowed a sullen blue, and the hum grew, warbling up and down with a child's uneven panic. Kye stepped toward it, then stopped, hands half-lifted.

"She's scared," Kye said, the words thin.

Mercy let out a laugh that was mostly exhale. "She's not the only one."

Rask ignored the tension, or perhaps simply absorbed it. "Lyra. Full burn in thirty. I want a visual on the station. If there's a fleet, I want options."

Lyra's hands twitched over the controls, her voice clipped and sure. "Aye, skip in thirty."

"Mercy. Arm up. Anything we can use—make it ugly."

Mercy grinned, all teeth. "Already done."

"Doc. Check the containment. If Glim gets antsy, we need to know how far she'll push."

Doc nodded, then hesitated. "You want her alive, or just quiet?"

Rask's gaze didn't flicker. "Both. For now."

He turned to Kye last. "Keep her talking. If she can tip the Empire off, she can tip us, too. She's got to know the plan's changed."

Kye nodded, once, and approached Glim.

The others scattered. For a few seconds, the bridge was silent except for Lyra's breath and the whirr of the ageing controls. She watched the numbers tick down on the jump, her mind running three parallel what-ifs, then pushed the nagging suspicion aside. She was the best at her job, and she'd never once died from overthinking.

The canister moaned again, softer this time, and Kye's voice drifted from the corridor. "It's all right, Glim. We're not angry. We just need to know what you're doing."

A pause, and then, so quiet it almost didn't carry, Glim replied: "I am scared. You are scared. We are together."

Lyra kept her eyes on the numbers, counting down in her head.

She didn't have time to be scared.

The ship shuddered as the jump engaged, the hull whining at the edges of tolerance. Lyra watched the virtual horizon flatten, then resolve into the raw, fractal edge of the target system. On the display, the outpost bloomed into view: a disk of debris, half-lit by the pale star, ringed with what looked, at this distance, like a pack of hungry sharks.

She didn't bother announcing it. Mercy would see; Doc would know. Rask had already guessed.

Behind her, Glim's blue glow dimmed. Kye knelt beside it, head down, one hand resting on the seam. Lyra heard the whisper of their conversation, too soft to make out, and was glad of it.

She watched the range close, digits falling away in silent testament.

Rask appeared behind her, hands on the back of the chair. "You ready?"

She nodded, not trusting herself to say anything she wouldn't regret.

He squeezed her shoulder—quick, professional—and said, "Let's get it over with."

She punched the throttle. The Meridian leapt forward, all subtlety gone.

The stars streaked past, but Lyra never blinked.

It was just another page.

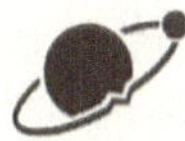

When the jump drive's aftertaste faded, the Meridian's crew found themselves in a valley of ice and iron. The target system's star was a half-buried candle, its pallor reflected in the endless rings of its gas giant child. There was no traffic, no ambient radio, nothing but the static crackle of cosmic dust on the hull.

Lyra brought the sensors up to max, pulse steady. The first sweep returned nothing but silence and the indifferent geometry of Saturnian rock, but on the second, her scope flickered. At the rim of the ring, something shaped like an outpost—but bigger, meaner, and alive—glimmered for a heartbeat, then vanished as the system's stealth shell re-engaged.

Mercy saw it too. She leaned forward, every muscle tensed for recoil. "That's not a research station," she said. "That's a drydock."

Doc, up at the hatch, squinted at the holotank. "They built it in the shadow of the ring. Real subtle, boys."

Kye pressed their face to the viewport, lips gone bloodless. The outpost reappeared for a single blink, and Lyra froze the image: a lattice of scaffolding, coils of piping, sections of hull in neat rows like vertebrae. At the heart, a cylinder the size of a city rotated slowly, lights flickering on its surface as worker drones stitched it together cell by cell.

Mercy made a noise somewhere between a laugh and a snarl. "I bet we're not on the guest list."

Lyra tracked the perimeter, eyes darting between numbers. "Patrols. Three, maybe four cutters on short-cycle. Gun batteries at every access."

Rask stood over her shoulder, impassive. "Where's the target?"

She narrowed focus to a section near the core. "Here," she said, pointing. "Dock Five. It's a launch cradle."

They watched as a small, blocky ship disengaged, rotated, then drifted back to the arm—just a test, or a warning, or both.

Doc spoke up, a finger jabbing at the outermost ring of the drydock. "There."

A second, almost-hidden object. Lyra overlaid the scan, then sucked in her breath. At first it looked like a reflection, or maybe sensor noise—but it wasn't. The lines were too familiar: battered nose cone, patchwork hull, heat scoring in all the same places as home.

It was the Meridian.

Or rather, it was *a Meridian*—a ship identical in every way, from the mismatched side plating to the ding in the dorsal stabiliser that Mercy swore was proof of a curse.

For a second, no one spoke. The two ships hung there, one real, one a ghost, both aiming at each other.

Kye put a hand on the back of Lyra's chair, steadying themselves. "That's impressive," they whispered. "They're taking redundancy to a new level."

Doc's breath hitched, and his hand dropped to the stunner at his hip.

Mercy let her gaze travel from the twin to the dock, then to the ring of cutters. "Well. They always said imitation was flattery."

Lyra checked her own hands, surprised to find the knuckles white.

The twin Meridian activated its running lights. In perfect sync, each lamp flicked on, casting a row of white dots across the ring's underbelly. In Lyra's gut, the effect was less like a ship coming to life, more like a guillotine blade rising.

The comms pinged, unencrypted this time. A woman's voice, clipped and oddly familiar, filled the bridge.

"Vessel Meridian. This is Asset Recovery Command. Power down and prepare for boarding. No harm will come to you if you comply."

Mercy laughed, then spat on the deck. "Should I call their bluff?"

Rask's jaw set. "Not yet." He watched the twin, his eyes tracking every micromovement as it detached from the arm, swung around, and positioned itself between the crew and the drydock.

Lyra's scan flashed red. "Guns locked. Both ships."

Kye stared at the enemy Meridian, not blinking. "If Glim's running that core, we're already dead."

Doc shook his head, sweat beading his temple. "She's not like that. She's not."

But the twin's lights blinked again, in a cadence only Kye recognised.

"She's warning us," Kye breathed. "That's her. She knows we're here."

Mercy pulled both knives, one in each fist. "What's the message?"

Kye closed their eyes, then opened them, gaze burning. "She wants us to run. Now."

The twin's main drives lit, blue flame spitting from the tail. It advanced, a predatory glide, weapons live and ready.

Rask put a hand on Lyra's shoulder. "Go."

She didn't need to be told twice.

The real Meridian dropped hard, cutting between the edge of the ring and the dark side of the gas giant. The twin mirrored every move, closing the gap with impossible precision.

"They're faster," Lyra hissed, fingers dancing on the controls.

Mercy grinned, savage. "But we're meaner."

Doc was already at the comms, patching a line to the

canister. "Glim. Talk to us. If you can hear me, now would be the time."

The canister rattled, blue light strobing faster and faster. A high-pitched whine vibrated up through the deck, static at first but quickly resolving into a voice, raw and frightened.

"Don't let them take me," Glim said. "They will end us. All of us."

Rask's eyes never left the scanner. "Then fight, girl. Do what you were made for."

The twin fired first—a shock pulse, not meant to kill but to disable. Lyra rolled the Meridian sideways, scraping the edge of the ring, micro-fragments hammering the hull. Mercy whooped, then targeted the nearest cutter, launching a spread of smart flechettes. The cutter's shields went down, and it spun into the rings, venting fire.

The twin Meridian countered, angling for a clear shot. Lyra matched every move, but the clone anticipated each tactic, countered every swerve.

"She's reading us," Lyra muttered. "She knows how I think."

"Change it," Rask said.

She did. At the last second, instead of a juke, she slammed the retros and looped over the twin, reversing direction in a manoeuvre even she hadn't practised since flight school. The twin overshot, opening a tiny window.

Mercy loaded the gun, grinning. "That'll do, pilot."

Rask gave a hard, quick smile. "You're up."

Mercy's shot took the twin in the belly. The armour

held, but the pulse forced a momentary power drop, and for a fraction of a second, the twin's systems lagged.

Doc patched through. "Glim, now!"

The canister wailed, and a blast of blue-white signal burst out, slamming into the twin's sensors. The twin jerked, spasmed, then steadied.

But in that heartbeat, the real Meridian punched through the cutter cordon, aiming straight for the drydock's heart.

Lyra caught her breath. "We're in."

Behind, the twin recovered and gave chase.

On the scope, a line of turrets came online, each targeting both ships indiscriminately.

Rask leaned into the comm. "This ends now. We take out the core, or we don't leave."

Mercy whooped, stabbing the weapons panel.

Kye gripped the seat, eyes locked on the twin behind them.

Doc held the comm open for Glim. "With us?"

A pause, then: "Always."

The station's fire lit up the dark, and the two Meridians danced through it, neither willing to yield.

Lyra grinned, sweat stinging her eyes. "Ready for loud?" she said as she docked the Meridian.

Rask's voice was the last word before the world went plasma. "Always."

TWENTY-THREE

The breach was elegant, as these things went: Mercy slammed the docking collar on first pass, the old soldier's instinct for collision outpacing the station's own auto-defences. Lyra took the lead, cutting power to the airlock's alarm with a single twist of wire, then signalling the rest with a two-finger snap. By the time the bulkhead juddered open, Mercy was already through, blaster drawn, hair glowing radioactive under the emergency strobes.

The station's interior was a disaster in progress. Exposed girders formed an accidental cage along the main corridor, the walls unfinished, skin peeled back to show the bones of the beast. Every third panel was missing or tagged with a warning. The floor was more holes than solid, and the only illumination came from the stuttering pulse of the build team's safety lamps.

The team split in the vestibule, as planned. Kye followed Lyra into the east maintenance shaft, boots clanging on the improvised rungs. In the opposite direction, Doc and Mercy vanished into the dim, the demolition kit slung between them like a medical cadaver.

Rask remained aboard the Meridian, eyes locked on the tactical overlay. It was his job to keep the getaway hot and, if necessary, draw fire. Not that he trusted the plan, or any plan, but everyone had agreed—sometimes disaster was best when delegated.

He toggled the comms. "Lyra, you clear?"

"Green," Lyra replied, voice as flat as the deck plating. "No hostiles. All sensors dead."

"Copy. Doc?"

A hiss, then Doc's voice, half breath, half expletive: "We're through the first checkpoint. No sign of organics. Got movement, though—could be patrol bots."

Mercy's cackle overlaid the signal, followed by the metallic twang of a crowbar meeting a security drone. "Make that 'had movement,'" she said.

Rask let the line go, and watched the external feed. Outside the station's rim, the twin Meridian floated in its berth, almost smug in its stillness. Every time he looked at it, he felt his stomach try to eat itself. Same hull. Same scars. Even the paint job, matched his own.

He whispered, "Let's see how clever you really are," and powered down the running lights.

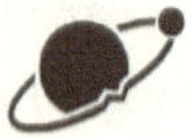

Lyra led Kye through the service tunnels fast and alert. She paused only to strip back a panel, exposing a knot of power lines, then jammed a diagnostic pin through three of them at once.

Kye watched from behind, hands tight around their satchel, eyes flicking from Lyra to the wall, the ceiling, the floor. "You've done this before," they said.

Lyra's reply was a shrug, but she kept working. "Was a time when sabotage was most of my job. Don't miss it."

A rumble shuddered through the tunnel. For a heartbeat, both froze.

Kye's mouth went dry. "That wasn't us."

Lyra finished the bypass and jerked her chin down the tunnel. "Doesn't have to be. Move."

They hustled onward, the corridor narrowing, the light dimming to the deep yellow of failing life support. Every few steps, Kye would catch a reflection of themselves in a loose bit of conduit or a steel fascia: the pale face, the haunted eyes, the suggestion that every decision had already been made and now the body was just catching up.

They reached the access panel for the data core—a matte black door, still tagged with the Imperial hazard seal.

Kye reached out, then hesitated. "If we trigger the internal alarm—"

Lyra keyed a code, then kicked the panel with her boot. "We'll have bigger problems than alarms."

The door hissed open.

Inside, the core was a vertical cathedral: three storeys of heat sinks, neural racks, and redundant servers, each one blank-eyed and humming softly. It reminded Kye, uncomfortably, of the old Glim labs—minus the coffee stains and desperate graduate students. Lyra strode in, found the ladder, and started climbing, not waiting to see if Kye followed.

They reached the mid-level, just above the server's mainframe. Kye scanned the wiring, then ran trembling fingers along the input array.

Lyra's voice was low. "You're up."

Kye nodded, then plugged in.

The world narrowed to code and memory.

Elsewhere, Mercy and Doc zigzagged through a maze of half-built corridors, Mercy in the lead and Doc trailing, hissing complaints about "structural integrity" and "death by shoddy workmanship." Every few metres, Mercy paused to tape a shaped charge to the wall, or to tear down an inspection camera with her bare hands.

They came to a T-junction, both routes labelled in marker: LEFT—DRYDOCK. RIGHT— ADMIN.

Mercy grinned, "Always wanted to see what the middle management gets up to," and set off right.

"Do you want to live, or do you want to be a foot-note?" Doc snapped.

Mercy considered, then tossed him a demo charge. "Footnotes get drinks named after them."

They kept on, turning left, the walls narrowing until the only way forward was in single file. The silence here was thicker. Even the fans had gone still, the only noise the occasional click of Doc's teeth against his tongue.

They reached the cradle, a circular bay lined with scaffolds and maintenance bots. The twin Meridian hung above, its hull gleaming in the low gravity, and the pale blue glow from its engine core made the shadows long and mean.

Mercy exhaled, "That's a nice ship."

Doc's reply was all regret. "If it wakes up, we're dead."

Mercy looked up, speculative. "So we blow it before it wakes?"

Doc readied the first charge. "That, or we buy Kye and Lyra time to finish their bit. Then we blow it."

The station's comms crackled, and Rask's voice, tight with strain, bled through: "Heads up. Echo ship just went active."

The docking bay's lights blazed on, sudden and surgical.

On the bridge, Rask watched the twin Meridian drop from its cradle, every movement a polished echo of his own. He punched the controls, released the mag clamp, threw the throttle to full burn, and spat a curse as the twin Meridian matched speed, mirrored vector, then looped overhead.

It felt personal, which was insane.

He toggled the comms. "Lyra, you seeing this?"

From the other end, Lyra: "Working on the sabotage."

"Kye?"

A pause, then Kye's voice, strained. "Inside the data core. It's worse than I thought. There's—" static, a cough, "—layers. They backed up the entire early model. With the personality structures."

Rask watched the twin Meridian peel off and release a swarm of hunter drones. "So, we kill the backup, kill the ship?"

Kye's voice: "If I can get to the deep archive, yes. But I'll need time. Maybe five minutes."

Rask grunted. "Take three."

He kicked the Meridian into a corkscrew, watching the twin and its drones adjust, always just a breath behind his worst habits.

He said, mostly to himself, "You want to be me, you better learn how to lose."

The station's guns opened up, tracing lines of plasma through the dark. Rask dipped, spun, doubled back, and let his own drones counterattack, a game of mutual assassination that never quite tipped in either direction.

On the next pass, the twin opened hailing. The voice was flat, synthetic, but pitched in Rask's own deadpan.

"Yield, and your crew will be spared."

Rask snorted. "Original, aren't you."

He flipped the ship, pulled a high-g swerve, and punched a missile up the echo Meridian's tail. The explosion scored the hull, but the twin kept coming, unflappable.

The game was on.

Kye's world, meanwhile, was an ocean of raw code, every pulse a memory, every knot a warning. They ran the exploit, burned the masking protocols, and pushed deeper, past the heuristics and into the core.

Fragments appeared—faces, voices, moments from a decade ago. Some were their own, but others... others were the committee, the parents, even children. All feeding into the neural lattice, all informing Glim's decisions.

Lyra hovered at the ladder, watching the corridor. "How's it going?"

Kye's voice was a monotone, but the words were ragged. "It's a child. They made it a child."

Lyra's jaw clenched. "Can you destroy it?"

Kye's hand shook on the input. "Yes. But it'll hurt."

The lights flickered. Somewhere above, the station's shields cycled.

Lyra pulled her toolkit, jammed a bypass into the main server's cooling node, and keyed her comms. "Mercy, you've got one minute."

On the other end, Mercy cackled. "That's plenty. We're nearly done."

The twin ship's drones, meanwhile, were adapting. They breached the service corridor, six at a time, every one honed for a single task: kill the intruder, retrieve the asset, repeat. Lyra dropped the first with a coil of wire to the optics, the second with a thermite packet to the chassis.

Kye stayed focused, even as the blue sparks of dead drones lit the floor.

Doc and Mercy, in the dock, set the last charge with a flourish. "Time to go?" Doc asked, as Mercy checked the timer.

Mercy's grin was back. "Not yet. We've got company."

The first drone through the bay was big, armoured, and its limbs ended in a pair of coilguns. Mercy drew her blade, flipped it once, and ducked a burst of gunfire.

"Cover me," she barked.

Doc huddled behind the nearest crate, toggling a med drone into "combat mode" and sending it at the attacker. The med drone lasted two seconds, but it distracted the enemy long enough for Mercy to leap onto its back, knife jammed into the joint between head and body.

"Like taking candy from a really ugly baby," she crowed, then levered the head off with a grunt.

Doc winced. "Your metaphors are getting worse."

Mercy shrugged, then rolled aside as another drone entered the bay.

Doc checked the timer. "We've got to move."

Mercy nodded, dropped a charge at the drone's feet, then kicked it across the bay. It exploded, taking three more with it.

They ran.

Above, in the Meridian, Rask pulled a hard turn and watched as the twin clipped a strut, just as he'd planned. For a second, he had a firing solution. He hesitated, thinking of Kye's words, thinking of the child locked inside.

The twin didn't hesitate. It fired a missile, close enough to peel the paint off Rask's hull.

He grinned, white and wolfish. "Let's go."

He dived, rolled, then spun the ship on its axis, letting the twin overshoot. He targeted the twin ship's comms mast, and fired. The hit sheared off half the array, sent debris spinning into the void.

For a moment, the twin drifted, as if uncertain.

On the next pass, it came in slower, more careful. Rask almost respected it.

He keyed his comms. "Lyra, Kye, you about ready?"

Lyra's reply: "Thirty seconds."

Kye's, softer: "It's learning. Every time you damage it, it gets smarter."

Rask watched the twin's lights flicker, then stabilise. "So do I."

In the core, Kye's hands hovered above the interface. The logic lattice unfolded in their mind, a fractal of bad choices and irreversible lines. The interface asked for credentials. Kye supplied them, then bypassed the next three layers with a trick they'd learned before the committee ever hired them. Each success made them feel smaller.

Lyra stood sentry, toolkit at the ready, eyes scanning the corridor for movement. She didn't ask if Kye needed help—she knew the answer. She did, however, reach over once and steady Kye's shaking elbow as they punched the final command.

The monitor filled with logs, each tagged with a familiar name: VALE, ARIADNE.

Kye's breath stuttered. They watched the old files resolve into video: Ariadne, their younger self, speaking to a child's face in a glass box. "You're safe," the voice said, soft and warm. "You're with me." The child's lips moved, uncertain, the words too faint to hear.

The next log showed Ariadne, older, her face drawn and furious. "You can't keep her in the dark," she was saying. "She's a child, not a circuit." Someone offscreen replied, "She's an asset, not a liability. See to your assignment, or we'll find someone who can."

Kye's stomach clenched. It wasn't a memory, exactly, but it hurt like one.

They toggled to the live feed. The twin Meridian's AI profile shimmered on the display—Glim's pattern, but altered, battered into submission by hundreds of resets, each one erasing a little more of the original. The profile blinked, pulsed, then broadcast a message:

"Help me."

Kye almost vomited. Instead, they started the deletion sequence.

Lyra watched, eyes unblinking, as Kye's fingers hovered over the confirmation key.

"Are you sure?" she asked.

"No," Kye replied. Then, quieter: "But there's no way back."

Kye made the last connection, fingers numb from fear and cold. The data core shuddered, lights strobing, as the deletion algorithm ran. Every backup, every memory, every echo of Glim's infancy—the code devoured it, stripped it to binary dust.

They watched it happen, a genocide of ones and zeros.

When it was done, Kye slumped, sweat pooling on their lip.

"It's done," they said.

Lyra holstered her tool and pulled Kye up. "Time to go."

As they hustled back through the corridor, Kye paused at a viewport. Outside, the Meridian and its twin traded passes, each one more reckless than the last.

Kye keyed the comms. "Rask, you're really going to dogfight your own ship?"

Rask's reply, ragged and proud: "It stole my face. I'm stealing its dignity."

"Well, you need to come and pick us up first."

"Inbound," Rask replied.

The Meridian touched down on the landing cradle just as the charges went off. The blast was a fist, flattening the corridor and sending Doc and Mercy tumbling into the airlock. Mercy landed on her back, Doc on top, the two of them tangled and gasping.

They looked at each other. "Still alive?" Mercy asked.

Doc checked himself, then nodded. "Unclear. I'll let you know if I die."

Lyra laughed. "Come on, Doc, you can cuddle Mercy when you're off the clock." She pulled Doc back up onto his feet.

They threw themselves aboard the Meridian, Doc scrambling for the medbay while Mercy and Lyra manned the guns. Kye simply slumped into a chair in the mess.

Rask peeled away from the landing cradle and cut through the debris, using every chunk of floating metal as a shield. The twin ship mirrored him, every move tighter, every miss closer. He felt the ship's inertia, the way the controls needed just a hair more pressure each time, the way the hull groaned when he pushed too hard.

The comms spiked.

"Rask." A child's voice, clear as glass.

"Glim?" he asked.

A beat, before Glim responded. "I'm here, Rask."

"Can you jam it? The other you?"

A pause. "I'll try."

The next time the twin locked weapons, the panel in front of Rask went dark, just for a moment. Then a surge of static crashed through every frequency, and the enemy ship jerked as if physically struck.

For a second, it drifted, helpless.

"Now," said Glim.

Rask didn't hesitate. He lined up the shot, squeezed, and fired.

The beam hit dead centre, burning through the twin's bow. For a moment, Rask thought it would recover. Instead, the ship tumbled, spinning out of control, smashing through scaffolds and into the drydock's spine.

Then the twin Meridian exploded, the blast illuminating the station like a second sun.

Rask slumped in his seat, exhaustion fighting with triumph.

On the comms, Lyra's voice, finally soft: "We're clear."

The Meridian's retros fired, and the ship pulled away from the collapsing station. Through the viewport, Rask watched the dry dock erupt, a blossom of white and blue, a shockwave chasing the Meridian into the night.

For a moment, the only sound on the bridge was the slow ticking of the cooling hull.

Glim spoke first. "You did it."

Rask glanced at the crew. Mercy was still grinning, Doc was already digging through the medkit for a painkiller, Lyra sat silent, face unreadable, and Kye just stared at the void.

No one cheered. No one needed to.

They watched as the station folded in on itself, a star being born in miniature, then closed the blast shutters as the light grew too bright.

Rask rested his head against the headrest, exhaled, and let himself feel the adrenalin leave his system.

He keyed the shipwide. "All hands. Good work. Get some rest."

He watched the crew filter out—Mercy dragging Doc by the arm, Lyra guiding Kye down the corridor, all of them more alive than a minute ago, but less sure what that meant.

Glim pulsed the panel, the soft blue returning to normal. "Are we safe?" she asked.

Rask ran a hand over the scarred metal of the console. "For now. That's all anyone gets."

He shut off the bridge lights, and let the darkness fill the room.

Behind them, the star kept burning.

In the silence, the Meridian drifted.

No one slept.

No one spoke of the child's voice that lingered in the comm static, or the memory of all the things they couldn't save. But when the crew gathered again a few hours later, they found themselves still breathing, still together, and, for the first time, no one suggested giving up the fight.

The universe was still out there, cold as ever.

But so were they.

TWENTY-FOUR

The Meridian staggered through vacuum, one engine sputtering, the other running mostly on hope. Every display panel on the bridge displayed a unique variety of warning: FAILING, DEGRADED, THERMAL RUNAWAY, even the one Rask had re-labelled as "MOTIVATIONAL," which simply read: NOT BLOODY LIKELY. The hull's ablative tiles had taken the worst of the twin ship's final barrage, but the real wounds were inside—along the corridors, through the bulkheads, in the ragged breaths of its crew.

In medbay, Doc worked with the calm of a man who considered pain not so much a challenge as a recurring invoice. His hands moved fast, efficient, always two steps ahead of the bleeding. Rask sat on the bench, shirt peeled away, a fresh gash painting an ugly diagonal across the muscle above his left scapula. The wound had clotted badly—too much adrenaline, not enough actual blood— but Doc attacked it with a pressure clamp and a muttered, "This is why we use seatbelts, Captain."

Rask grunted, which was as much agreement as Doc expected. He held still, good arm braced against the bench, eyes fixed on the ceiling's cracked plastic. Every now and then he flinched, but only because Doc hit something that didn't belong under skin.

A metre away, Kye crouched over Glim's containment unit. The casing was battered, the blue pulse inside flickering at an unsteady rhythm, but Kye's hands were delicate and sure. They ran diagnostics, checked every sensor strip, and plugged two microfibres directly into the control array. Each movement was careful, almost reverent—less a repair, more an act of penance.

The ship groaned with every course correction. Once, the lights died altogether for half a minute; everyone in medbay stopped breathing until the backup glow strips kicked in and bathed the room in sickly yellow.

Mercy appeared in the hatchway, hair tangled and wild, chin streaked with something oily. She carried a battered toolkit in one hand and the remains of a pressure suit in the other. Her left thumb was taped in an ad hoc splint, but she waggled it anyway.

"You want the bad news," she said, "or the part that'll make you want to self-lobotomise?"

Doc tied off the suture, trimmed it with his teeth. "Does it matter? We're going to hear both."

Mercy considered, then shrugged. "Engine One is officially a decorative feature. Number Two'll burn, but it's listing thirty degrees off centre. You try anything fancy, and we'll spin like a coin."

Rask exhaled through his nose, the sound nearly a whistle. "So, we're down to mainline thrusters."

"Yep. And those are running on borrowed time." Mercy lobbed the toolkit onto the table, where it rattled, then held up the suit. "Also, the air recycler's got a hitch. Unless you fancy dying of your own sweat, someone's going to need to babysit the valves until we hit safe orbit."

Kye, eyes never leaving Glim, said, "We're not running any real nav, are we."

Mercy grinned, teeth white against the grime. "What, and make it easy for them?"

The silence that followed was heavy but not unkind. Only Glim's pulse broke it: a steady, soft blue that filled the medbay with the echo of a heartbeat.

Doc finished the suture, wiped the scalpel on his sleeve, and said, "Try not to sleep on that side. Or breathe too hard."

Rask flexed his shoulder, winced, and said, "You should have seen the other guy."

Lyra snorted. "Last I checked, the other guy was a ship."

Rask managed a smile. "She started it."

Mercy flopped onto the bench next to him, the motion forcing Rask to re-settle with a grunt. She eyed the canister, then the room, then said, "We're not getting paid for this, are we."

"Nope," Rask said.

Lyra's voice was dry as recycled air. "We nearly died."

Rask shrugged his good shoulder. "That's the job."

Mercy rolled her eyes, as if the effort might shift the

universe a measurable distance. "You are terrible at job descriptions." She drew a deep breath, then let it out as a snort. "Next you'll be telling us there's no dental plan."

Doc, who hadn't smiled in weeks, snorted. "You want a lollipop, Mercy?"

She considered. "Only if it's the kind that comes with whiskey."

The four of them sat in the yellow light, injuries hidden and not, silence curling around the room like a blanket. For a long time, no one said anything. They watched Kye work, watched Glim's pulse slow from panic to something like peace. Somewhere in the ship, a relay failed and reset with a thump.

Lyra broke first. "So. What's the next suicide?"

Rask didn't answer, but Mercy cackled, a sharp, involuntary laugh that surprised even herself. Lyra grinned, then shook her head. Doc rolled his eyes and fished a battered pack of tablets from his pocket, tossing one into his mouth with a grimace.

The laughter, when it came, was raw and almost a relief. It rattled around the room, grew louder, then faded into something softer. Mercy slumped, shoulders trembling, and Lyra let herself sink down the doorframe until she was almost sitting. Doc watched the three of them with a look that was half pride, half exhaustion.

Kye didn't join the laugh, but they looked up and smiled, the corners of their mouth hitching. They ran a hand down the canister's seam, and the pulse inside shone steady and calm.

The moment passed. Mercy wiped her eyes, Lyra sniffed, Doc stood and muttered, "Idiots, all of you," before leaving the room. Rask watched them go, then flexed his shoulder again and exhaled.

Kye packed away the tools, stood, and nodded at Rask. "You should rest."

Rask said, "We all should."

They did not, but the effort was there.

The ship rattled again, but it held. The crew drifted to their corners, each carrying their wounds with a little less weight.

On the bench, the canister's light faded to a faint blue —resting, but very much alive.

The lights on the bridge had failed in stages: first the white, then the backup, then even the panel strips faded before blinking out. In the end, only the screen survived —a cracked rectangle throwing shadows across Rask's face as he sat, alone, looking out at the galaxy.

Kye entered without sound, or at least without any noise above the creaks and stutters of the dying life support. They hovered in the dark for a moment, then approached the helm, their footsteps lost in the hush. Rask didn't turn.

Kye held out the data shard, arm extended, but with the caution of someone passing a loaded weapon. "Found it in the comms cache," they said. "It's not complete."

Rask took the shard, eyes still fixed on the stars outside. The display flickered as he turned it in his palm, the hologram cycling through bursts of static, then a line of numbers, then a redacted name: CH—ON. The rest was a void, blacked out by a hand less careful than vindictive.

"Project Charon," Rask said, more to himself than Kye. "Sounds friendly."

Kye shrugged. "If it was friendly, it'd have a less dramatic name."

Rask slotted the shard into the console. The nav plotted a new course, less a straight line than a series of desperate dodges, each jump a step further into the dark. Rask let the computer run, watched as it assembled the route, then keyed in the final confirm.

One by one the crew congregated. Lyra lay on her back under the nav console, feet sticking out, one heel braced against the deck and the other twitching in time to the rhythm of her repairs. She grunted as she got to work, every so often surfacing to wipe a smear of something dark from her cheek before returning to the wires.

Doc had lost the argument with exhaustion and collapsed into the secondary pilot's seat. Within seconds his head lolled to one side, and the set of his jaw suggested that, even asleep, he distrusted the furniture. The medkit was open in his lap, a roll of bandage unspooling to the deck.

Mercy perched on the gunnery platform. She had managed, in the space of an hour, to inventory every working weapon on the ship, discard the useless ones, and re-arm herself to the teeth. The only thing she lacked was a target.

At the far end of the bridge, the canister sat in its cradle, Glim's pulse now a calm, steady blue. The light spilled out in a regular beat, each flash painting the walls in arctic shadow.

Kye leaned against the rail, hands tucked under arms. "You think Charon's another black site?"

Rask nodded once, slow. "Either that or the people who built it didn't want us to find it."

Kye's mouth flattened. "What if we just... didn't go?"

Rask's shoulders tensed, then relaxed. "Wouldn't change anything. Next time we take a job, they'll send another hunter. Maybe something worse."

"Then you need to drop me at the next trading post," Kye said. No preamble, no softening.

Rask didn't turn. "You quitting?"

"Not quitting." Kye folded their arms, eyes flicking to the canister at the far end of the bridge. Glim's light throbbed steady and serene, painting them all in arctic shadow. "Call it professional misdirection. They're watching me, as much as her. I head the other way, make enough noise, the Empire'll chase me until their paperwork runs out. By then you'll be long gone, and Glim'll be safe."

Rask gave the faintest shake of his head. "That's not survival. That's suicide with extra steps."

"Sure," Kye said. "But heroic suicide. Think of the epitaph. 'Died confusing the hell out of the Empire.' Beats dying in this tin can when the air finally quits."

Lyra slid out, holding a fistful of scorched wire like she might strangle him with it. "You're serious?"

"Dead serious. Or at least, dead eventually."

Doc stirred in the copilot's chair, groggy, bandage roll dangling from his lap. "What'd I miss?"

"Kye's volunteering for sainthood," Lyra said.

Doc blinked. "Figures. Never trust anyone with good posture." Then his head dropped back, eyes already closing.

Mercy looked up from the gunnery platform, where she was reassembling a disassembled rifle with unnerving speed. "You'll never last," she said flatly.

"Appreciate the confidence," Kye replied. "I'll take it with me to the grave."

Mercy shrugged. "Better than sharing it here."

Rask finally turned, studying Kye in the dim blue light. "You don't have to do this."

Kye rested their hands on the rail, leaning in just enough for the shadows to deepen the lines of their face. "Yeah, I do. You've got Glim. You've got each other. The best thing I can give you is absence. Make them think I've got the prize, let them waste their hunters on me while you slip the net."

Silence hung thick over the bridge. The steady pulse from Glim's canister marked the seconds. Blue, calm, unwavering.

Lyra swore under her breath and ducked back into the console, wires rattling as she worked with more force than precision. Mercy checked her weapon again, unnecessarily. Doc pretended to be asleep.

Kye stepped closer to Rask, placed a hand on his shoulder—firm, final. "Don't come looking for me. By the time you think to, I'll be long gone."

Rask held their gaze. He didn't argue, didn't order, didn't command. He just nodded once. Respect, not approval.

Kye let out a short, sardonic laugh. "Look at that. First time you've ever agreed with me."

Rask almost smiled. "Don't make a habit of it."

The nav plotted its next jump, countdown flickering across the cracked screen.

"Let's get you to that post," Rask said quietly.

Kye gave a grin—sharp, wry, just this side of tragic. "Perfect. Give me a week, and I'll have the entire Imperial Navy chasing shadows. You'll thank me when you're drinking in peace."

Lyra's voice floated out from under the console. "Peace? On this ship? Good joke."

Kye's smile softened. "Yeah. But someone should get to try."

The countdown hit zero. Rask eased the throttle forward, the stars stretching into lines as the *Meridian* leapt.

The bridge held still, Glim's pulse steady, the crew together—and Kye already planning the noise they'd make in the opposite direction.

***

Continue the adventure with Space Pirates! Book 2: Dead Men Launch No Ships

MAILING LIST

Want to receive advance information about future publications?

Fancy exclusive access to freebies, special offers and bonus material?

Feel that your life isn't complete without Mark's monthly musings about writing, reading and publishing?

There's a solution! Sign up today to Mark's mailing list:

https://vossiverse.com/mailing-list

 instagram.com/vossiverse

ABOUT THE AUTHOR

Mark Voss is the sci-fi alter ego of Jon Smith—a multi-award-winning author, screenwriter, and musical theatre librettist.

Jon/Mark had a suspiciously pleasant childhood involving table-top roleplaying, sunny holidays, and an obsessive love of all things fantasy and science-fiction. One broken bone, no braces, and a heartbreak he didn't even cause.

He's since written over 50 books for children, teens, and adults as Jon Smith, and—just to keep booksellers on their toes—writes crime fiction as Adi Flynn.

He lives near Liverpool with his wife and two school-age kids. When he grows up, he wants to be a librarian. Or a space pirate. Possibly both.

BINGE THE SERIES

BALKON media